W9-CYD-204

BORN AGAIN

I was so sick with horror that many of the details of that scene escaped me. But I knew that Neil was prying off the lids of the caskets in quick succession, and that the stench of natron had become almost unbearable.

Then, last of all, Neil lifted the lids from the mummy of the princess. Sick though I was, acutely, physically sick, I moved forward to see, impelled by curiosity that could not be suppressed.

Amen-Ra's eyes were wide open!

From *The Curse of Amen-Ra*
by Victor Rousseau

Also by Martin H. Greenberg
Published by Ballantine Books:

MR. PRESIDENT, PRIVATE EYE
(with Francis M. Nevins, Jr.)

MUMMY STORIES

Edited by
Martin H. Greenberg

BALLANTINE BOOKS • NEW YORK

Copyright © 1990 by Martin H. Greenberg

All rights reserved under International and Pan-American Copyright Conventions. Published in the United States of America by Ballantine Books, a division of Random House, Inc., New York, and simultaneously in Canada by Random House of Canada Limited, Toronto.

Library of Congress Catalog Card Number: 89-91553

ISBN 0-345-36354-X

Manufactured in the United States of America

First Edition: April 1990

MUMMY STORIES

Acknowledgments

"Masque" by Ed Gorman Copyright © 1990 by Ed Gorman. Used by permission of the author.

"Bones" by Donald A. Wollheim. Copyright © 1940 by Albing Publications. Reprinted by permission of the author.

"Asleep on the Job" by Scott Parson. Copyright © 1990 by Scott Parson. Used by permission of the author.

"Remains To Be Seen" by Sharyn McCrumb. Copyright ©1990 by Sharyn McCrumb. Used by permission of the author.

"The Man in Crescent Terrace" by Seabury Quinn. Copyright © 1946 by *Weird Tales*. Reprinted by permission of the agents for the author's estate, the Scott Meredith Literary Agency, Inc., 845 Third Avenue, New York, New York 10022.

"Beetles" by Tarleton Fiske. Copyright © 1938 by *Weird Tales*; renewed © 1966. Reprinted by permission of the Scott Meredith Literary Agency,, Inc., 845 Third Avenue, New York, New York 10022.

"The Weekend Magus" by Edward D. Hoch. Copyright © 1980 by Edward D. Hoch. Reprinted by permission of the author.

"The Curse of Amen-Ra" by Victor Rousseau. Reprinted by permission of Forrest J. Ackerman, 2495 Glendower Avenue, Hollywood, California 90027.

"Mummy No. 50" by D. R. Meredith. Copyright © 1990 by D. R. Meredith. Used by permission of the author.

"The Eyes of the Mummy" by Robert Bloch. Copyright © 1938 by *Weird Tales*; renewed © 1966 by Robert Bloch. Reprinted by permission of the Scott Meredith Literary Agency, Inc., 845 Third Avenue, New York, New York 10022

"Uncle Jack Eats a Mummy" by Alan Robbins. Copyright © 1990 by Alan Robbins. Used by permission of the author.

MUMMY STORIES

INTRODUCTION

When the archaeological team headed by Howard Carter and Lord Carnarvon discovered the tomb of Tutankhamen in November of 1922, they came upon an ordinary clay tablet containing a hieroglyphic inscription. Deciphered, the inscription read: *Death will slay with his wings whoever disturbs the peace of the pharaoh.* A second version of the curse was later found on the back of a statue: *It is I who drive back the robbers of the tomb with the flames of the desert. I am the protector of Tutankhamen's grave.*

Few members of the Carter-Carnarvon team took these warnings seriously. How could an antiquated Egyptian curse possibly affect them? It was ridiculous to believe that the desecration of the tomb of a minor young king of the Eighteenth Dynasty (1358–1349 B.C.) could call forth the wrath of ancient gods.

And yet, consider what happened. . . .

Two months after the main chamber of the tomb was opened, Lord Carnarvon succumbed in Egypt to a strange, undiagnosed illness. (At almost the same time, thousands of miles away in England, Carnarvon's fox terrier suddenly began to howl, sat up on her hind legs, and then toppled over dead.) Other men involved with the excavations also died of unexplained illnesses characterized by high fevers and attacks of debilitating feebleness. By 1929 twenty-two people who were directly or indirectly connected with the opening of the grave had come to premature ends.

Their mysterious deaths have been explained variously as being caused by radiation from rare chemical elements or metals found by Egyptian scientists; by forgotten poisons or disease-producing organisms that somehow managed to retain their potency over the centuries; as a massive coincidence with elements of subconscious death wish and superstitious fear—the same sort of phenomenon that causes victims of voodoo curses to take sick, wither, and die. But none of these speculative answers has ever been proven. The simple fact is no one knows for certain why all those people died, nor are we ever likely to.

It *could* just as well have been the curse, then, couldn't it? That explanation is no more farfetched than the others. Many things are possible, after all, where ancient religions, ancient evils, are concerned. Many terrible and wonderful things. . . .

Even before the King Tut mystery, such phenomena as curses and mummies fascinated writers of fantasy and horror fiction. The first to explore them was the French writer Théophile Gautier, in an obscure 1856 novel, *Romance of a Mummy*. A much more well-known early book is *The Jewel of the Seven Stars* (1903), by the creator of Dracula, Bram Stoker. A strange mummified cat, a magic jewel, and a fearful curse are three of the elements of this macabre classic.

Numerous other novels about mummies and Egyptian magic have appeared during this century. Noteworthy among them are a pair by Sax Rohmer, *The Green Eyes of Bast* (1920) and *Brood of the Witch Queen* (1924); and Robin Cook's lavish contemporary bestseller, *Sphinx* (1979), which effectively mixes murder, intrigue, an archaeological quest, and an ancient King Tut–type curse.

The first film to make use of the theme was a silent entitled *The Mummy of the King of Ramsee*, made in 1909. Other silents followed, including *The Eyes of the Mummy* (1918), which starred Pola Negri and Emil Jannings. The first sound-era mummy movie is one of the two best to date—Karl Freund's classic *The Mummy* (1932), in which Boris Karloff has the dual role of Imhotep, an ancient Egyptian priest, and Ardath Bey, a modern scholar connected with the Cairo museum. Almost as good is *The Mummy's Hand* (1940), starring Dick Foran and George Zucco, with a minor cowboy actor, Tom Tyler, surprisingly effective as the mummy. This film, in which a high priest (Zucco) uses tana leaves to keep the mummy Karis alive, and which makes disguised use of the Carter-Carnarvon expedition and the King Tut curse, is the first to depict the monster trailing his wrappings on missions of murder and mayhem.

Almost all of the short fiction devoted to mummies and their curses is of the Egyptian variety. The best of these stories explore the theme in unusual ways, sometimes as straightforward suspense, sometimes as exercises in unadulterated horror, and sometimes with satirical humor. They include such memorable tales as "Lot No. 249" by Sir Arthur Conan Doyle and "The Eyes of the Mummy" by Robert Bloch, both of which appear in this anthology. Stories involving mummies of other cultures and other lands are much less common but no less memorable when masterfully written; the best of these likewise appear in these pages.

All of the stories here are pure entertainment—and, of course, pure fantasy. Still, as you read them you might keep in mind the fate of the twenty-two members of the Carter-Carnarvon expedition, and the fact that no one has ever proven ancient curses—and ancient evils—*can't* harm the living.

Pleasant reading . . .

Pleasant dreams . . .

—Martin H. Greenberg

ED GORMAN's acclaimed novels of suspense include Rough Cut, Murder Straight Up, The Autumn Dead, *and* Murder on the Aisle. *He is the copublisher and editor of* Mystery Scene *magazine. Mr. Gorman has also published criticism and short fiction. "Masque" is a recent (and chilling) example of the latter—the first of five brand-new, never-before-published mummy stories in this volume.*

MASQUE

by Ed Gorman

From a police report:

I found the nude body of Janice Hollister in a deep ravine. Some children who'd been playing in the neighborhood told me that they'd seen a dog with what appeared to be blood on his coat. The dog led me back to her. The first thing I noticed about the Hollister woman was the incredible way her body had been cut up. Her entire right breast had been ripped away.

"I've listed it as a car accident," Dr. Temple says.

They are in a room of white tiles and green walls and white cabinets and stainless steel sinks. The room smells of antiseptic and the white tile floor sparkles with hot September sunlight.

Dr. Temple is in his mid-fifties, balding, a lean jogger in a white medical smock. He has very blue eyes and very pink skin. He is an old family friend.

"You've taken care of the records, then?" Mrs. Garth asks. She is sixty-eight and regal in a cold way, given to Dior suits and facelifts.

"Yes."

4

"There'll be no problem?"

"None. The record will show that he was transferred here two weeks ago following a car accident."

"A car accident?"

"That will account for the bandages. So many lacerations and contusions we had to cover his entire body." He makes a grim line of his mouth. "Very dramatic and very convincing to the eye. Almost theatrical."

"I see. Very good. I appreciate it."

"And we appreciate all you've done for the hospital, Ruth. Without your generosity, there'd be no cancer clinic."

She stands up and offers her delicate hand in such a way that the doctor fears for a terrified moment she actually expects him to kiss it.

From a police report:

> I thought the dog might have attacked her after the killer fled. But then I saw that her anus and vagina had been torn up just the way the rest of her had and then I knew that it had to be him. The perpetrator, I mean. I checked the immediate vicinity for footprints and anything that might have fallen from his pockets. I found nothing that looked useful.

A new elevator, one more necessity her money has bought this hospital, takes her to the ninth floor.

She walks down a sunny corridor being polished by a dumpy, middle-aged black woman who has permitted her hose to bag about her knees. The woman, Mrs. Garth thinks, should have more respect for herself.

Mrs. Garth finds 909 and enters.

She takes no more than ten steps inside, around the edge of the bathroom, when she stops and looks in horror at him.

All she can think of are those silly movies about Egyptian mummies brought back to life.

Here sits Steve, his entire head and both arms swathed entirely in white bandages. All she can see of him are his face, his eyes, and his mouth.

"My Lord," she moans.

She edges closer to his hospital bed. The room is white and clean and lazy in the sunlight. Above, the TV set mounted to the wall plays a game show with two fat contestants jumping up and down on either side of the handsome host who cannot quite rid his eyes of boredom.

"Aren't you awfully hot inside there?" she asks.

He says nothing, but then at such times he never does.

She pulls up a chair and sits down.

"I am Zoser, founder of the third Dynasty," he says.

"Oh, you," she says. "Now's no time to joke. Anyway, I can barely understand you with all those bandages over your face."

"I am Senferu, the Warrior King."

"Oh, you," she says.

From a police report:

> Her neck appears to have been broken. At least that was my first impression. The killer's strength must be incredible. To say nothing of how much he must hate women.

An hour after she arrives in the hospital room, she says, "An old man saw you."

Inside the mummy head, the blue eyes show panic.

"Don't worry," she continues. "He has vision trouble, so he's not a very credible witness. But he did describe you pretty accurately to the press. Fortunately, I told Dr. Temple that some drug dealers were looking for you. He seemed to accept my story."

She pats him on the arm. "Didn't that medication Dr. Gilroy gave you help? I had such high hopes for it. He said you wouldn't any longer want to . . . You know what I'm trying to say."

But now that he knows he's going to be safe, the panic dies in his blue eyes and he says, "I am King Tut."

"Oh, pooh. Can't you be serious?"

"I'm not serious. I'm King Tut."

She clucks.

They sit back and watch the Bugs Bunny cartoon he has on. He says, through his bandages, "I wish they'd show Porky."

"Porky?"

"Porky Pig."

"Oh, I see." My God, he's forty-six years old. She says, "In case there's any trouble, Dr. Temple is going to tell the police that you've been here two weeks and that the old man couldn't possibly identify you because even if you were out and about, you'd have been wearing bandages."

"They won't arrest Senferu the Warrior King, mother. They'd be afraid to."

"I thought after that trouble in Chicago you told me about—"

"There's Sylvester!" he exclaims.

And so there is: Sylvester the cat.

She lets him watch a long minute, the exasperated cat lisping and spitting and spraying. "You were very savage with this one," she says. "Very savage."

"I've seen this one before. This is where Tweety really gives it to Sylvester. Watch!"

She watches, and when she can endure it no more, she says, "Perhaps I made some mistakes with you."

"Oh, God, Sylvester—watch out for Tweety!"

"Perhaps, after your father died, I took certain liberties with you I shouldn't have." Pause. "Letting you sleep in my bed . . . Things happened and I don't suppose either one of us is to blame but nonetheless—"

"Great! Porky's coming on! Look, Mother, it's Porky!"

From a police report:

> Down near the creek bed we found her breast. At first I wasn't sure what it was, but as I stared at it I started getting sick. By this time the first backup was arriving. They had to take over for me a few minutes. I wasn't feeling very well.

In the hospital room, sitting there in his mummy bandages, his mother at his side, Steve stares up at the TV set. There's a commercial on now. He hates commercials.

"Maybe Daffy Duck will be on next, Mother. God, wouldn't that be great?"

Now it's her turn for silence. She thinks of the girls in Chicago and Kansas City and Akron. So savage with them; so savage. She will never again believe him that everything's fine and that his medication has gotten him calmed down once and for all and that she should let him take a trip.

But of course this time he didn't even go anywhere. Most dangerous of all, he did it here at home.

Right here at home.

"Wouldn't it be great, Mother?" he asks, wanting her to share his enthusiasm. He loves those occasions when they share things.

She says, "I'm sorry, darling, my mind just wandered. Wouldn't what be great, dear?"

"If it was Daffy on next."

"Daffy?"

"Daffy Duck," he says from inside his mummy head. And then he does a Daffy Duck imitation right on the spot.

Not even the bandages can spoil it, she thinks. He's so clever. "Oh, yes, dear. That would be great if Daffy came on next."

He reaches over and touches her with his bandaged hand and for a horrible moment she almost believes he's been injured.

But then she sees the laughter in his blue blue eyes inside the mummy head.

She pats his bandaged hand. "You'll get a nice rest here for a few weeks and then we'll go home again, dear, and everything will be fine."

He lays his head back and sighs. "Fine." He repeats the word almost as if he doesn't know what it means. "Fiiiine." He seems to be staring at the ceiling. She hopes it's not another depression. They emerge so quickly and last so long.

But then abruptly he's sitting up again and clapping his bandaged hands together and staring up at the TV screen.

"It *is* Daffy, Mother. It *is* Daffy!"

"Yes, dear," she says. "It is Daffy, isn't it?"

*SIR ARTHUR CONAN DOYLE (1859–1930) is principally re-
nowned, of course, as the creator of Sherlock Holmes. But he
also penned short works of fantasy, science fiction, and the supernatural. "Lot No. 249" falls solidly in the latter category.*

LOT NO. 249

by Sir Arthur Conan Doyle

Of the dealings of Edward Bellingham with William Monkhouse Lee, and of the cause of the great terror of Abercrombie
Smith, it may be that no absolute and final judgment will ever
be delivered. It is true that we have the full and clear narrative
of Smith himself, and such corroboration as he could look for
from Thomas Styles the servant, from the Reverend Plumptree
Peterson, Fellow of Old's, and from such other people as
chanced to gain some passing glance at this or that incident in
a singular chain of events. Yet, in the main, the story must rest
upon Smith alone, and most will think that it is more likely that
one brain, however outwardly sane, has some subtle warp in its
texture, some strange flaw in its workings, than that the path of
nature has been overstepped in open day in so famed a center
of learning and light as the University of Oxford. Yet when we
think how narrow and how devious this path of nature is, how
dimly we can trace it, for all our lamps of science, and how
from the darkness which girds it round great and terrible possibilities loom ever shadowly upwards, it is a bold and confident
man who will put a limit to the strange bypaths into which the
human spirit may wander.

In a certain wing of what we will call Old College in Oxford
there is a corner turret of an exceeding great age. The heavy
arch which spans the open door has bent downward in the center

under the weight of its years, and the gray, lichen-blotched blocks of stone are bound and knitted together with withes and strands of ivy, as though the old mother had set herself to brace them up against wind and weather. From the door a stone stair curves upward spirally, passing two landings, and terminating in a third one, its steps all shapeless and hollowed by the tread of so many generations of the seekers after knowledge. Life has flowed like water down this winding stair, and, waterlike, has left these smooth-worn grooves behind it. From the long-gowned, pedantic scholars of Plantagenet days down to the young bloods of a later age, how full and strong had been that tide of young, English life. And what was left now of all those hopes, those strivings, those fiery energies, save here and there in some old-world churchyard a few scratches upon a stone, and perchance a handful of dust in a moldering coffin? Yet here were the silent stair and the gray, old wall, with bend and saltire and many another heraldic device still to be read upon its surface, like grotesque shadows thrown back from the days that had passed.

In the month of May, in the year 1884, three young men occupied the sets of rooms which opened onto the separate land-ings of the old stair. Each set consisted simply of a sitting room and of a bedroom, while the two corresponding rooms upon the ground floor were used, the one as a coal cellar, and the other as the living room of the servant, or scout, Thomas Styles, whose duty it was to wait upon the three men above him. To right and to left was a line of lecture rooms and of offices, so that the dwellers in the old turret enjoyed a certain seclusion, which made the chambers popular among the more studious under-graduates. Such were the three who occupied them now—Abercrombie Smith above, Edward Bellingham beneath him, and William Monkhouse Lee upon the lowest story.

It was ten o'clock on a bright, spring night, and Abercrombie Smith lay back in his armchair, his feet upon the fender, and his briar-root pipe between his lips. In a similar chair, and equally at his ease, there lounged on the other side of the fire-place his old school friend Jephro Hastie. Both men were in flannels, for they had spent their evening upon the river, but apart from their dress no one could look at their hard-cut, alert faces without seeing that they were open-air men—men whose minds and tastes turned naturally to all that was manly and robust. Hastie, indeed, was stroke of his college boat, and Smith was an even better oar, but a coming examination had already cast its shadow over him and held him to his work, save for the few hours a week which health demanded. A litter of medical books upon the table, with scattered bones, models, and anatomical plates, pointed to the extent as well as the nature of his studies, while a couple of single-sticks and a set of boxing gloves above the mantelpiece hinted at the means by which, with Hastie's help, he might take his exercise in its most compressed and least-distant form. They knew each other very well—so well that they could sit now in that soothing silence which is the very highest development of companionship.

"Have some whiskey," said Abercrombie Smith at last between two cloudbursts. "Scotch in the jug and Irish in the bottle."

"No, thanks. I'm in for the sculls. I don't liquor when I'm training. How about you?"

"I'm reading hard. I think it best to leave it alone."

Hastie nodded, and they relapsed into a contented silence.

"By the way, Smith," asked Hastie, presently, "have you made the acquaintance of either of the fellows on your stair yet?"

"Just a nod when we pass. Nothing more."

"Hum! I should be inclined to let it stand at that. I know something of them both. Not much, but as much as I want. I don't think I should take them to my bosom if I were you. Not that there's much amiss with Monkhouse Lee."

"Meaning the thin one?"

"Precisely. He is a gentlemanly little fellow. I don't think there is any vice in him. But then you can't know him without knowing Bellingham."

"Meaning the fat one?"

"Yes, the fat one. And he's a man whom I, for one, would rather not know."

Abercrombie Smith raised his eyebrows and glanced across at his companion.

"What's up, then?" he asked. "Drink? Cards? Cad? You used not to be censorious."

"Ah! you evidently don't know the man, or you wouldn't ask. There's something damnable about him—something reptilian. My gorge always rises at him. I should put him down as a man with secret vices—an evil liver. He's no fool, though. They say that he is one of the best men in his line that they have ever had in college."

"Medicine or classics?"

"Eastern languages. He's a demon at them. Chillingworth met him somewhere above the second cataract last long, and he told me that he just prattled to the Arabs as if he had been born and nursed and weaned among them. He talked Coptic to the Copts, and Hebrew to the Jews, and Arabic to the Bedouins, and they were all ready to kiss the hem of his frock coat. There are some old hermit Johnnies up in those parts who sit on rocks and scowl and spit at the casual stranger. Well, when they saw this chap Bellingham, before he had said five words they just lay down on their bellies and wriggled. Chillingworth said that he never saw anything like it. Bellingham seemed to take it as his right, too, and strutted about among them and talked down to them like a Dutch uncle. Pretty good for an undergrad of Old's, wasn't it?"

"Why do you say you can't know Lee without knowing Bellingham?"

"Because Bellingham is engaged to his sister Eveline. Such a bright little girl, Smith! I know the whole family well. It's disgusting to see that brute with her. A toad and a dove, that's what they always remind me of."

Abercrombie Smith grinned and knocked his ashes out against the side of the grate.

"You show every card in your hand, old chap," said he. "What a prejudiced, green-eyed, evil-thinking old man he is! You have really nothing against the fellow except that."

"Well, I've know her ever since she was as long as that cherrywood pipe, and I don't like to see her taking risks. And it is a risk. He looks beastly. And he has a beastly temper, a venomous temper. You remember his row with Long Norton?"

"No; you always forget that I am a freshman."

"Ah, it was last winter. Of course. Well, you know the towpath along by the river. There were several fellows going along it, Bellingham in front, when they came on an old market woman coming the other way. It had been raining—you know what those fields are like when it has rained—and the path ran between the river and a great puddle that was nearly as broad. Well, what does this swine do but keep the path and push the old girl into the mud, where she and her marketings came to terrible grief. It was a blackguard thing to do, and Long Norton, who is as gentle a fellow as ever stepped, told him what he thought of it. One word led to another, and it ended in Norton laying his stick across the fellow's shoulders. There was the deuce of a fuss about it, and it's a treat to see the way in which

Bellingham looks at Norton when they meet now. By Jove, Smith, it's nearly eleven o'clock!''

"No hurry. Light your pipe again."

"Not I. I'm supposed to be in training. Here I've been sitting gossiping when I ought to have been safely tucked up. I'll borrow your skull, if you can share it. Williams has had mine for a month. I'll take the little bones of your ear, too, if you are sure you won't need them. Thanks very much. Never mind a bag, I can carry them very well under my arm. Good night, my son, and take my tip as to your neighbor.''

When Hastie, bearing his anatomical plunder, had clattered off down the winding stair, Abercrombie Smith hurled his pipe into the wastepaper basket, and drawing his chair nearer to the lamp, plunged into a formidable, green-covered volume, adorned with great, colored maps of that strange, internal kingdom of which we are the hapless and helpless monarchs. Though a freshman at Oxford, the student was not so in medicine, for he had worked for four years at Glasgow and at Berlin, and this coming examination would place him finally as a member of his profession. With his firm mouth, broad forehead, and clear-cut, somewhat hard-featured face, he was a man who, if he had no brilliant talent, was yet so dogged, so patient, and so strong that he might in the end overtop a more showy genius. A man who can hold his own among Scotchmen and North Germans is not a man to be easily set back. Smith had left a name at Glasgow and at Berlin, and he was bent now upon doing as much at Oxford, if hard work and devotion could accomplish it.

He had sat reading for about an hour, and the hands of the noisy carriage clock upon the side table were rapidly closing together upon the twelve, when a sudden sound fell upon the student's ear—a sharp, rather shrill sound, like the hissing intake of a man's breath who gasps under some strong emotion. Smith laid down his book and slanted his ear to listen. There was no one on either side or above him, so that the interruption came certainly from the neighbor beneath—the same neighbor of whom Hastie had given so unsavory an account. Smith knew him only as a flabby, pale-faced man of silent and studious habits, a man whose lamp threw a golden bar from the old turret even after he had extinguished his own. This community in lateness had formed a certain silent bond between them. It was soothing to Smith when the hours stole on toward dawning to feel that there was another so close who set as small a value upon his sleep as he did. Even now, as his thoughts turned toward him, Smith's feelings were kindly. Hastie was a good fellow, but he was rough, strong-fibered, with no imagination or sympathy. He could not tolerate departures from what he looked upon as the model type of manliness. If a man could not be measured by a public-school standard, then he was beyond the pale with Hastie. Like so many who are themselves robust, he was apt to confuse the constitution with the character, to ascribe to want of principle what was really a want of circulation. Smith, with his stronger mind, knew his friend's habit and made allowance for it now as his thoughts turned toward the man beneath him.

There was no return of the singular sound, and Smith was about to turn to his work once more when suddenly there broke out in the silence of the night a hoarse cry, a positive scream— the call of a man who is moved and shaken beyond all control. Smith sprang out of his chair and dropped his book. He was a man of fairly firm fiber, but there was something in this sudden, uncontrollable shriek of horror which chilled his blood and pringled in his skin. Coming in such place and at such an hour, it brought a thousand fantastic possibilities into his head. Should he rush down, or was it better to wait? He had all the national hatred of making a scene, and he knew so little of his neighbor that he would not lightly intrude upon his affairs. For a moment he stood in doubt and even as he balanced the matter there was a quick rattle of footsteps upon the stairs, and young Monkhouse Lee, half-dressed and as white as ashes, burst into his room.

"Come down!" he gasped. "Bellingham's ill."

Abercrombie Smith followed him closely downstairs into the sitting room which was beneath his own, and intent as he was upon the matter in hand, he could not but take an amazed glance around him as he crossed the threshold. It was such a chamber as he had never seen before—a museum rather than a study. Walls and ceiling were thickly covered with a thousand strange relics from Egypt and the East. Tall, angular figures bearing burdens or weapons stalked in an uncouth frieze round the apartment. Above were bull-headed, stork-headed, cat-headed, owl-headed statues, with viper-crowned, almond-eyed monarchs, and strange, beetlelike deities cut out of the blue Egyptian lapis lazuli. Horus and Isis and Osiris peeped down from every niche and shelf, while across the ceiling a true son of Old Nile, a great, hanging-jawed crocodile, was slung in a double noose.

In the center of this singular chamber was a large, square table, littered with papers, bottles, and the dried leaves of some graceful, palmlike plant. These varied objects had all been heaped together in order to make room for a mummy case, which had been conveyed from the wall, as was evident from the gap there, and laid across the front of the table. The mummy itself, a horrid, black, withered thing, like a charred head on a gnarled bush, was lying half out of the case, with its clawlike hand and bony forearm resting upon the table. Propped up against the sarcophagus was an old, yellow scroll of papyrus, and in front of it, in a wooden armchair, sat the owner of the room, his head thrown back, his widely opened eyes directed in a horrified stare to the crocodile above him, and his blue, thick lips puffing loudly with every expiration.

"My God, he's dying!" cried Monkhouse Lee distractedly.

He was a slim, handsome young fellow, olive-skinned and dark-eyed, of a Spanish rather than of an English type, with a Celtic intensity of manner which contrasted with the Saxon phlegm of Abercrombie Smith.

"Only a faint, I think," said the medical student. "Just give me a hand with him. You take his feet. Now onto the sofa. Can you kick all those little wooden devils off? What a litter it is! Now he will be all right if we undo his collar and give him some water. What has he been up to at all?"

"I don't know. I heard him cry out. I ran up. I know him pretty well, you know. It is very good of you to come down."

"His heart is going like a pair of castanets," said Smith, laying his hand on the breast of the unconscious man. "He seems to me to be frightened all to pieces. Chuck the water over him! What a face he has got on him!"

It was indeed a strange and most repellent face, for color and outline were equally unnatural. It was white, not with the ordinary pallor of fear, but with an absolutely bloodless white, like the underside of a sole. He was very fat, but gave the impression of having at some time been considerably fatter, for his skin hung loosely in creases and folds and was shot with a meshwork of wrinkles. Short, stubbly brown hair bristled up from his scalp, with a pair of thick, wrinkled ears protruding at the sides. His light gray eyes were still open, the pupils dilated and the gray balls projecting in a fixed and horrid stare. It seemed to Smith as he looked down upon him that he had never seen nature's danger signals flying so plainly upon a man's countenance, and his thoughts turned more seriously to the warning which Hastie had given him an hour before.

"What the deuce can have frightened him so?" he asked.

"It's the mummy."

"The mummy? How, then?"

"I don't know. It's beastly and morbid. I wish he would drop it. It's the second fright he has given me. It was the same last winter. I found him just like this, with that horrid thing in front of him."

"What does he want with the mummy, then?"

"Oh, he's a crank, you know. It's his hobby. He knows more about these things than any man in England. But I wish he wouldn't! Ah, he's beginning to come to."

A faint tinge of color had begun to steal back into Bellingham's ghastly cheeks, and his eyelids shivered like a sail after a clam. He clasped and unclasped his hands, drew a long, thin breath between his teeth, and suddenly jerking up his head, threw a glance of recognition around him. As his eyes fell upon the mummy, he sprang off the sofa, seized the roll of papyrus, thrust it into a drawer, turned the key, and then staggered back on to the sofa.

"What's up?" he asked. "What do you chaps want?"

"You've been shrieking out and making no end of a fuss," said Monkhouse Lee. "If our neighbor here from above hadn't come down, I'm sure I don't know what I should have done with you."

"Ah, it's Abercrombie Smith," said Bellingham, glancing up at him. "How very good of you to come in! What a fool I am! Oh, my God, what a fool I am!"

He sank his head on to his hands, and bursts into peal after peal of hysterical laughter.

"Look here! Drop it!" cried Smith, shaking him roughly by the shoulder.

"Your nerves are all in a jangle. You must drop these little midnight games with mummies, or you'll be going off your chump. You're all on wires now."

"I wonder," said Bellingham, "whether you would be as cool as I am if you had seen—"

"What then?"

"Oh, nothing. I meant that I wonder if you could sit up at night with a mummy without trying your nerves. I have no doubt that you are quite right. I daresay that I have been taking it out of myself too much lately. But I am all right now. Please don't go, though. Just wait for a few minutes until I am quite myself."

"The room is very close," remarked Lee, throwing open the window and letting in the cool night air.

"It's balsamic resin," said Bellingham. He lifted up one of the dried palmate leaves from the table and frizzled it over the chimney of the lamp. It broke away into heavy smoke wreaths, and a pungent, biting odor filled the chamber. "It's the sacred plant—the plant of the priests," he remarked. "Do you know anything of Eastern languages, Smith?"

"Nothing at all. Not a word."

The answer seemed to lift a weight from the Egyptologist's mind.

"By the way," he continued, "how long was it from the time that you ran down, until I came to my senses?"

"Not long. Some four or five minutes."

"I thought it could not be very long," said he, drawing a long breath. "But what a strange thing unconsciousness is! There is no measurement to it. I could not tell from my own sensations if it were seconds or weeks. Now that gentleman on the table was packed up in the days of the Eleventh Dynasty, some forty centuries ago, and yet if he could find his tongue, he would tell us that this lapse of time has been but a closing of the eyes and a reopening of them. He is a singularly fine mummy, Smith."

Smith stepped over to the table and looked down with a professional eye at the black and twisted form in front of him. The features, though horribly discolored, were perfect, and two little nutlike eyes still lurked in the depths of the black, hollow sockets. The blotched skin was drawn tightly from bone to bone, and a tangled wrap of black, coarse hair fell over the ears. Two thin teeth, like those of a rat, overlay the shriveled lower lip. In its crouching position, with bent joints and craned head, there was a suggestion of energy about the horrid thing which made Smith's gorge rise. The gaunt ribs, with their parchmentlike covering, were exposed, and the sunken, leaden-hued abdomen, with the long slit where the embalmer had left his mark; but the lower limbs were wrapped round with coarse, yellow bandages. A number of little clovelike pieces of myrrh and of cassia were sprinkled over the body and lay scattered on the inside of the case.

"I don't know his name," said Bellingham, passing his hand over the shriveled head. "You see the outer sarcophagus with the inscriptions is missing. Lot 249 is all the title he has now. You see it printed on his case. That was his number in the auction at which I picked him up."

"He has been a very pretty sort of fellow in his day," remarked Abercrombie Smith.

"He has been a giant. His mummy is six feet seven in length, and that would be a giant over there, for they were never a very robust race. Feel these great, knotted bones, too. He would be a nasty fellow to tackle."

"Perhaps these very hands helped to build the stones into the pyramids," suggested Monkhouse Lee, looking down with disgust in his eyes at the crooked, unclean talons.

"No fear. This fellow has been pickled in natron, and looked after in the most approved style. They did not serve hodmen in that fashion. Salt or bitumen was enough for them. It has been calculated that this sort of thing cost about seven hundred and thirty pounds in our money. Our friend was a noble at the least. What do you make of that small inscription near his feet, Smith?"

"I told you that I know no Eastern tongue."

"Ah, so you did. It is the name of the embalmer, I take it. A very conscientious worker he must have been. I wonder how many modern works will survive four thousand years?"

He kept on speaking lightly and rapidly, but it was evident to Abercrombie Smith that he was still palpitating with fear. His hands shook, his lower lip trembled, and look where he would, his eye always came sliding round to his gruesome companion. Through all his fear, however, there was a suspicion of triumph in his tone and manner. His eyes shone, and his footstep, as he paced the room, was brisk and jaunty. He gave the impression of a man who has gone through an ordeal, the marks of which he still bears upon him, but which has helped him to his end.

"You're not going yet?" he cried as Smith rose from the sofa.

At the prospect of solitude, his fears seemed to crowd back upon him, and he stretched out a hand to detain him.

"Yes, I must go. I have my work to do. You are all right now. I think that with your nervous system you should take up some less morbid study."

"Oh, I am not nervous as a rule; and I have unwrapped mummies before."

"You fainted last time," observed Monkhouse Lee.

"Ah, yes, so I did. Well, I must have a nerve tonic or a course of electricity. You are not going, Lee?"

"I'll do whatever you wish, Ned."

"Then I'll come down with you and have a shakedown on your sofa. Good night, Smith. I am so sorry to have disturbed you with my foolishness."

They shook hands, and as the medical student stumbled up

the spiral and irregular stair he heard a key turn in a door, and the steps of his two new acquaintances as they descended to the lower floor.

In this strange way began the acquaintance between Edward Bellingham and Abercrombie Smith, an acquaintance which the latter, at least, had no desire to push further. Bellingham, however, appeared to have taken a fancy to his rough-spoken neighbor and made his advances in such a way that he could hardly be repulsed without absolute brutality. Twice he called to thank Smith for his assistance, and many times afterward he looked in with books, papers, and such other civilities as two bachelor neighbors can offer each other. He was, as Smith soon found, a man of wide reading, with catholic tastes and an extraordinary memory. His manner, too, was so pleasing and suave that one came, after a time, to overlook his repellent appearance. For a jaded and wearied man he was no unpleasant companion, and Smith found himself, after a time, looking forward to his visits, and even returning them.

Clever as he undoubtedly was, however, the medical student seemed to detect a dash of insanity in the man. He broke out at times into a high, inflated style of talk which was in contrast with the simplicity of his life.

"It is a wonderful thing," he cried, "to feel that one can command powers of good and of evil—a ministering angel or a demon of vengeance." And again, of Monkhouse Lee, he said—"Lee is a good fellow, an honest fellow, but he is without strength or ambition. He would not make a fit partner for a man with a great enterprise. He would not make a fit partner for me."

At such hints and innuendos stolid Smith, puffing solemnly at his pipe, would simply raise his eyebrows and shake his head, with little interjections of medical wisdom as to earlier hours and fresher air.

One habit Bellingham had developed of late which Smith knew to be a frequent herald of a weakening mind. He appeared to be forever talking to himself. At late hours of the night, when there could be no visitor with him, Smith could still hear his voice beneath him in a low, muffled monologue, sunk almost to a whisper, and yet very audible in the silence. This solitary babbling annoyed and distracted the student, so that he spoke more than once to his neighbor about it. Bellingham, however, flushed up at the charge and denied curtly that he had uttered a sound;

indeed, he showed more annoyance over the matter than the occasion seemed to demand.

Had Abercrombie Smith had any doubt as to his own ears he had not to go far to find corroboration. Tom Styles, the little wrinkled manservant who had attended to the wants of the lodgers in the turret for a longer time than any man's memory could carry him, was sorely put to it over the same matter.

"If you please, sir," said he, as he tidied down the top chamber one morning, "do you think Mr. Bellingham is all right, sir?"

"All right, Styles?"

"Yes, sir. Right in his head, sir."

"Why should he not be, then?"

"Well, I don't know, sir. His habits has changed of late. He's not the same man he used to be, though I make free to say that he was never quite one of my gentlemen, like Mr. Hastie or yourself, sir. He's took to talkin' to himself something awful. I wonder it don't disturb you. I don't know what to make of him, sir."

"I don't know what business it is of yours, Styles."

"Well, I takes an interest, Mr. Smith. It may be forward of me, but I can't help it. I feel sometimes as if I was mother and father to my young gentlemen. It all falls on me when things go wrong and the relations come. But Mr. Bellingham, sir. I want to know what it is that walks about his room sometimes when he's out and when the door's locked on the outside."

"Eh? You're talking nonsense, Styles."

"Maybe so, sir; but I heard it more'n once with my own ears."

"Rubbish, Styles."

"Very good, sir. You'll ring the bell if you want me."

Abercrombie Smith gave little heed to the gossip of the old manservant, but a small incident occurred a few days later which left an unpleasant effect upon his mind, and brought the words of Styles forcibly to his memory.

Bellingham had come up to see him late one night and was entertaining him with an interesting account of the rock tombs of Beni Hassan in Upper Egypt, when Smith, whose hearing was remarkably acute, distinctly heard the sound of a door opening on the landing below.

"There's some fellow gone in or out of your room," he remarked.

Bellingham sprang up and stood helpless for a moment, with the expression of a man who is half-incredulous and half-afraid.

"I surely locked it. I am almost positive that I locked it," he stammered. "No one could have opened it."

"Why, I hear someone coming up the steps now," said Smith.

Bellingham rushed out through the door, slammed it loudly behind him, and hurried down the stairs. About halfway down Smith heard him stop and thought he caught the sound of whispering. A moment later the door beneath him shut, a key creaked in a lock, and Bellingham, with beads of moisture upon his pale face, ascended the stairs once more and reentered the room.

"It's all right," he said, throwing himself down in a chair. "It was that fool of a dog. He had pushed the door open. I don't know how I came to forget to lock it."

"I didn't know you kept a dog," said Smith, looking very thoughtfully at the disturbed face of his companion.

"Yes, I haven't had him long. I must get rid of him. He's a great nuisance."

"He must be, if you find it so hard to shut him up. I should have thought that shutting the door would have been enough, without locking it."

"I want to prevent old Styles from letting him out. He's of some value, you know, and it would be awkward to lose him."

"I am a bit of a dog fancier myself," said Smith, still gazing hard at his companion from the corner of his eyes. "Perhaps you'll let me have a look at it."

"Certainly. But I am afraid it cannot be tonight; I have an appointment. Is that clock right? Then I am a quarter of an hour late already. You'll excuse me, I am sure."

He picked up his cap and hurried from the room. In spite of his appointment, Smith heard him reenter his own chamber and lock his door upon the inside.

This interview left a disagreeable impression upon the medical student's mind. Bellingham had lied to him, and lied so clumsily that it looked as if he had desperate reasons for concealing the truth. Smith knew that his neighbor had no dog. He knew, also, that the step which he had heard upon the stairs was not the step of an animal. But if it were not, then what could it be? There was old Styles's statement about the something which used to pace the room at times when the owner was absent. Could it be a woman? Smith rather inclined to the view. If so, it would mean disgrace and expulsion to Bellingham if it were discovered by the authorities, so that his anxiety and falsehoods might be accounted for. And yet it was inconceivable that an undergraduate could keep a woman in his rooms without being instantly detected. Be the explanation what it might, there was something ugly about it, and Smith determined, as he turned to his books, to discourage all further attempts at intimacy on the part of his soft-spoken and ill-favored neighbor.

But his work was destined to interruption that night. He had hardly caught up the broken threads when a firm, heavy footfall came three steps at a time from below, and Hastie, in blazer and flannels, burst into the room.

"Still at it!" said he, plumping down into his wonted arm-chair. "What a chap you are to stew! I believe an earthquake might come and knock Oxford into a cocked hat, and you would sit perfectly placid with your books among the ruins. However, I won't bore you long. Three whiffs of 'baccy, and I am off."

"What's the news, then?" asked Smith, cramming a plug of bird's-eye into his briar with his forefinger.

"Nothing very much. Wilson made seventy for the freshmen against the eleven. They say that they will play him instead of Buddicomb, for Buddicomb is clean off color. He used to be able to bowl a little, but it's nothing but half volleys and long hops now."

"Medium right," suggested Smith, with the intense gravity which comes upon a varsity man when he speaks of athletics.

"Inclining to fast, with a work from leg. Comes with the arm about three inches or so. He used to be nasty on a wet wicket. Oh, by the way, have you heard about Long Norton?"

"What's that?"

"He's been attacked."

"Attacked?"

"Yes, just as he was turning out of the High Street, and within a hundred yards of the gate of Old's."

"But who—"

"Ah, that's the rub! If you said 'what,' you would be more grammatical. Norton swears that it was not human, and, indeed, from the scratches on his throat, I should be inclined to agree with him."

"What, then? Have we come down to spooks?"

Abercrombie Smith puffed his scientific contempt.

"Well, no; I don't think that is quite the idea, either. I am inclined to think that if any showman has lost a great ape lately, and the brute is in these parts, a jury would find a true bill against it. Norton passes that way every night, you know, about the same hour. There's a tree that hangs low over the path—the big elm from Rainy's garden. Norton thinks the thing dropped on him out of the tree. Anyhow, he was nearly strangled by two arms, which, he says, were as strong and as thin as steel bands. He saw nothing; only those beastly arms that tightened and tightened on him. He yelled his head nearly off, and a couple of chaps came running, and the thing went over the wall like a cat. He never got a fair sight of it the whole time. It gave Norton a shake-up, I can tell you. I tell him it has been as good as a change at the seaside for him.''

"A garroter, most likely," said Smith.

"Very possibly. Norton says not; but we don't mind what he says. The garroter had long nails, and was pretty smart at swinging himself over walls. By the way, your beautiful neighbor would be pleased if he heard about it. He had a grudge against Norton, and he's not a man, from what I know of him, to forget his little debts. But hallo, old chap, what have you got in your noddle?''

"Nothing," Smith answered curtly.

He had started in his chair, and the look had flashed over his face which comes upon a man who is struck suddenly by some unpleasant idea.

"You looked as if something I had said had taken you on the raw. By the way, you have made the acquaintance of Master B. since I looked in last, have you not? Young Monkhouse Lee told me something to that effect.''

"Yes; I know him slightly. He has been up here once or twice.''

"Well, you're big enough and ugly enough to take care of yourself. He's not what I should call exactly a healthy sort of Johnny, though, no doubt, he's very clever, and all that. But you'll soon find out for yourself. Lee is all right; he's a very decent little fellow. Well, so long, old chap! I row Mullins for the vice-chancellor's pot on Wednesday week, so mind you come down, in case I don't see you before.''

Bovine Smith laid down his pipe and turned stolidly to his books once more. But with all the will in the world, he found it very hard to keep his mind upon his work. It would slip away to brood upon the man beneath him, and upon the little mystery which hung round his chambers. Then his thoughts turned to this singular attack of which Hastie had spoken, and to the grudge which Bellingham was said to owe the object of it. The two ideas would persist in rising together in his mind, as though there were some close and intimate connection between them. And yet the suspicion was so dim and vague that it could not be put down in words.

"Confound the chap!" cried Smith as he shied his book on pathology across the room. "He has spoiled my night's reading, and that's reason enough, if there were no other, why I should steer clear of him in the future."

For ten days the medical student confined himself so closely to his studies that he neither saw nor heard anything of either of the men beneath him. At the hours when Bellingham had been accustomed to visit him, he took care to sport his oak, and though he more than once heard a knocking at his outer door, he resolutely refused to answer it. One afternoon, however, he was descending the stairs when, just as he was passing it, Bellingham's door flew open, and young Monkhouse Lee came out with his eyes sparkling and a dark flush of anger upon his olive cheeks. Close at his heels followed Bellingham, his fat, unhealthy face all quivering with malignant passion.

"You fool!" he hissed. "You'll be sorry."

"Very likely," cried the other. "Mind what I say. It's off! I won't hear of it!"

"You've promised, anyhow."

"Oh, I'll keep that! I won't speak. But I'd rather little Eva was in her grave. Once for all, it's off. She'll do what I say. We don't want to see you again."

So much Smith could not avoid hearing, but he hurried on, for he had no wish to be involved in their dispute. There had been a serious breach between them, that was clear enough, and Lee was going to cause the engagement with his sister to be broken off. Smith thought of Hastie's comparison of the toad and the dove, and was glad to think that the matter was at an end. Bellingham's face when he was in a passion was not pleasant to look upon. He was not a man to whom an innocent girl could be trusted for life. As he walked, Smith wondered languidly what could have caused the quarrel, and what the promise might be which Bellingham had been so anxious that Monkhouse Lee should keep.

It was the day of the sculling match between Hastie and Mullins, and a stream of men were making their way down to the banks of the Isis. A May sun was shining brightly, and the yellow path was barred with the black shadows of the tall elm trees. On either side the gray colleges lay back from the road, the hoary old mothers of minds looking out from their high,

mullioned windows at the tide of young life which swept so
merrily past them. Black-clad tutors, prim officials, pale, reading men, brown-faced, straw-hatted young athletes in white
sweaters or many-colored blazers, all were hurrying toward the
blue, winding river which curves through the Oxford meadows.

Abercrombie Smith, with the intuition of an old oarsman, chose
his position at the point where he knew that the struggle, if there
were a struggle, would come. Far off he heard the hum which
announced the start, the gathering roar of the approach, the
thunder of running feet, and the shouts of the men in the boats
beneath him. A spray of half-clad, deep-breathing runners shot
past him, and craning over their shoulders, he saw Hastie pulling
a steady thirty-six, while his opponent, with a jerky forty, was
a good boat's length behind him. Smith gave a cheer for his
friend, and pulling out his watch, was starting off again for
his chambers, when he felt a touch upon his shoulder and found
that young Monkhouse Lee was beside him.

"I saw you there," he said, in a timid, deprecating way. "I
wanted to speak to you, if you could spare me a half hour. This
cottage is mine. I share it with Harrington of King's. Come in
and have a cup of tea."

"I must be back presently," said Smith. "I am hard on the
grind at present. But I'll come in for a few minutes with pleasure. I wouldn't have come out only Hastie is a friend of mine."

"So he is of mine. Hasn't he a beautiful style? Mullins wasn't
in it. But come into the cottage. It's a little den of a place, but
it is pleasant to work in during the summer months."

It was a small, square, white building, with green doors and
shutters, and a rustic trelliswork porch, standing back some fifty
yards from the river's bank. Inside, the main room was roughly
fitted up as a study—deal table, unpainted shelves with books,
and a few cheap oleographs upon the wall. A kettle sang upon
a spirit stove, and there were tea things upon a tray on the table.

"Try that chair and have a cigarette," said Lee. "Let me
pour you out a cup of tea. It's so good of you to come in, for I
know that your time is a good deal taken up. I wanted to say to
you that, if I were you, I should change my rooms at once."

"Eh?"

Smith sat staring with a lighted match in one hand and his
unlit cigarette in the other.

"Yes; it must seem very extraordinary, and the worst of it is
that I cannot give my reasons, for I am under a solemn promise—a very solemn promise. But I may go so far as to say that I

don't think Bellingham is a very safe man to live near. I intend
to camp out here as much as I can for a time."

"Not safe! What do you mean?"

"Ah, that's what I mustn't say. But do take my advice and
move your rooms. We had a grand row today. You must have
heard us, for you came down the stairs."

"I saw that you had fallen out."

"He's a horrible chap, Smith. That is the only word for him.
I have had doubts abut him ever since that night when he
fainted—you remember, when you came down. I taxed him today, and he told me things that made my hair rise, and wanted
me to stand in with him. I'm not straightlaced, but I am a cler-
gyman's son, you know, and I think there are some things which
are quite beyond the pale. I only thank God that I found him out
before it was too late, for he was to have married into my family."

"This is all very fine, Lee," said Abercrombie Smith curtly.
"But either you are saying a great deal too much or a great deal
too little."

"I give you a warning."

"If there is real reason for warning, no promise can bind you.
If I see a rascal about to blow a place up with dynamite no pledge
will stand in my way of preventing him."

"Ah, but I cannot prevent him, and I can do nothing but warn
you."

"Without saying what you warn me against."

"Against Bellingham."

"But that is childish. Why should I fear him, or any man?"

"I can't tell you. I can only entreat you to change your rooms.
You are in danger where you are. I don't even say that Bellingham would wish to injure you. But it might happen, for he is a
dangerous neighbor just now."

"Perhaps I know more than you think," said Smith, looking
keenly at the young man's boyish, earnest face. "Suppose I tell
you that someone else shares Bellingham's rooms."

Monkhouse Lee sprang from his chair in uncontrollable excitement.

"You know, then?" he gasped.

"A woman.'

Lee dropped back again with a groan.

"My lips are sealed," he said. "I must not speak."

"Well, anyhow," said Smith, rising, "it is not likely that I
should allow myself to be frightened out of rooms which suit

me very nicely. It would be a little too feeble for me to move out all my goods and chattels because you say that Bellingham might in some unexplained way do me an injury. I think that I'll just take my chance and stay where I am, and as I see that it's nearly five o'clock, I must ask you to excuse me.''

He bade the young student adieu in a few curt words and made his way homeward through the sweet spring evening, feeling half-ruffled, half-amused, as any other strong, unimaginative man might who has been menaced by a vague and shadowy danger.

There was one little indulgence which Abercrombie Smith always allowed himself, however closely his work might press upon him. Twice a week, on the Tuesday and the Friday, it was his invariable custom to walk over to Farlingford, the residence of Dr. Plumptree Peterson, situated about a mile and a half out of Oxford. Peterson had been a close friend of Smith's elder brother, Francis, and as he was a bachelor, fairly well-to-do, with a good cellar and a better library, his house was a pleasant goal for a man who was in need of a brisk walk. Twice a week, then, the medical student would swing out there along the dark country roads and spend a pleasant hour in Peterson's comfortable study, discussing, over a glass of old port, the gossip of the varsity or the latest devlopments of medicine or of surgery.

On the day which followed his interview with Monkhouse Lee, Smith shut up his books at a quarter past eight, the hour when he usually started for his friend's house. As he was leaving his room, however, his eyes chanced to fall upon one of the books which Bellingham had lent him, and his conscience pricked him for not having returned it. However repellent the man might be, he should not be treated with discourtesy. Taking the book, he walked downstairs and knocked at his neighbor's door. There was no answer; but on turning the handle, he found that it was unlocked. Pleased at the thought of avoiding an interview, he stepped inside and placed the book with his card upon the table.

The lamp was turned half down, but Smith could see the details of the room plainly enough. It was all much as he had seen it before—the frieze, the animal-headed gods, the hanging crocodile, and the table littered over with papers and dried leaves. The mummy case stood upright against the wall, but the mummy itself was missing. There was no sign of any second occupant of the room, and he felt as he withdrew that he had probably done Bellingham an injustice. Had he a guilty secret to preserve, he would hardly leave his door open so that all the world might enter.

The spiral stair was as black as pitch, and Smith was slowly making his way down its irregular steps when he was suddenly conscious that something had passed him in the darkness. There was a final sound, a whiff of air, a light brushing past his elbow, but so slight that he could scarcely be certain of it. He stopped and listened, but the wind was rustling among the ivy outside, and he could hear nothing else.

"Is that you, Styles?" he shouted.

There was no answer, and all was still behind him. It must have been a sudden gust of air, for there were crannies and cracks in the old turret. And yet he could almost have sworn that he heard a footfall by his very side. He had emerged into the quadrangle, still turning the matter over in his head, when a man came running swiftly across the smooth-cropped lawn.

"Is that you Smith?"

"Hullo, Hastie!"

"For God's sake come at once! Young Lee is drowned! Here's Harrington of King's with the news. The doctor is out. You'll do, but come along at once. There may be life in him."

"Have you brandy?"

"No."

"I'll bring some. There's a flask on my table."

Smith bounded up the stairs, taking three at a time, seized the flask, and was rushing down with it, when, as he passed Bellingham's room, his eyes fell upon something which left him gasping and staring upon the landing.

The door, which he had closed behind him, was now open, and right in front of him, with the lamplight shining upon it, was the mummy case. Three minutes ago it had been empty. He could swear to that. Now it framed the lank body of its horrible occupant, who stood, grim and stark, with his black, shriveled face toward the door. The form was lifeless and inert, but it seemed to Smith as he gazed that there still lingered a lurid spark of vitality, some faint sign of consciousness in the little eyes which lurked in the depths of the hollow sockets. So astounded and shaken was he that he had forgotten his errand and was still staring at the lean, sunken figure when the voice of his friend below recalled him to himself.

"Come on, Smith!" he shouted. "It's life and death, you know. Hurry up! Now, then," he added as the medical student reappeared, "let us do a sprint. It is well under a mile, and we should do it in five minutes. A human life is better worth running for than a pot."

Neck and neck they dashed through the darkness and did not pull up until panting and spent, they had reached the little cottage by the river. Young Lee, limp and dripping like a broken water plant, was stretched upon the sofa, the green scum of the river upon his black hair and a fringe of white foam upon his leaden-hued lips. Beside him knelt his fellow student, Harrington, endeavoring to chafe some warmth back into his rigid limbs.

"I think there's life in him," said Smith, with his hand to the lad's side. "Put your watch glass to his lips. Yes, there's dimming on it. You take one arm, Hastie. Now work it as I do, and we'll soon pull him round."

For ten minutes they worked in silence, inflating and depressing the chest of the unconscious man. At the end of that time a shiver ran through his body, his lips trembled, and he opened his eyes. The three students burst out into an irrepressible cheer.

"Wake up, old chap. You've frightened us quite enough."

"Have some brandy. Take a sip from the flask."

"He's all right now," said his companion Harrington. "Heavens, what a fright I got! I was reading here, and he had gone out for a stroll as far as the river, when I heard a scream and a splash. Out I ran, and by the time I could find him and fish him out, all life seemed to have gone. Then Simpson couldn't get a doctor, for he has a game leg, and I had to run, and I don't know what I'd have done without you fellows. That's right, old chap. Sit up."

Monkhouse Lee had raised himself on his hands and looked wildly about him.

"What's up?" he asked. "I've been in the water. Ah, yes; I remember."

A look of fear came into his eyes, and he sank his face into his hands.

"How did you fall in?"

"I didn't fall in."

"How then?"

"I was thrown in. I was standing by the bank, and something from behind picked me up like a feather and hurled me in. I heard nothing, and I saw nothing. But I know what it was, for all that."

"And so do I," whispered Smith.

Lee looked up with a quick glance of surprise.

"You've learned, then?" he said. "You remember the advice I gave you?"

"Yes, and I begin to think that I shall take it."

"I don't know what the deuce you fellows are talking about," said Hastie, "but I think, if I were you, Harrington, I should get Lee to bed at once. It will be time enough to discuss the why and the wherefore when he is a little stronger. I think, Smith, you and I can leave him alone now. I am walking back to college; if you are coming in that direction, we can have a chat."

But it was little chat that they had upon their homeward path. Smith's mind was too full of the incidents of the evening, the absence of the mummy from his neighbor's rooms, the step that passed him on the stair, the reappearance—the extraordinary, inexplicable reappearance of the grisly thing—and then this attack upon Lee, corresponding so closely to the previous outrage upon another man against whom Bellingham bore a grudge. All this settled in his thoughts, together with the many little incidents which had previously turned him against his neighbor, and the singular circumstances under which he was first called in to him. What had been a dim suspicion, a vague, fantastic conjecture, had suddenly taken form, and stood out in his mind as a grim fact, a thing not to be denied. And yet, how monstrous it was, how unheard of, how entirely beyond all bounds of human experience. An impartial judge, or even the friend who walked by his side, would simply tell him that his eyes had deceived him, that the mummy had been there all the time, that young Lee had tumbled into the river as any other man tumbles into a river, and the blue pill was the best thing for a disordered liver. He felt that he would have said as much if the positions had been reversed. And yet he could swear that Bellingham was a murderer at heart, and that he wielded a weapon such as no man had ever used in all the grim history of crime.

Hastie had branched off to his rooms with a few crisp and emphatic comments upon his friend's unsociablility, and Abercrombie Smith had crossed the quadrangle to his corner turret with a strong feeling of repulsion for his chambers and their associations. He would take Lee's advice and move his quarters as soon as possible, for how could a man study when his ear was ever straining for every murmur or footstep in the room below? He observed, as he crossed over the lawn, that the light was still shining in Bellingham's window, and as he passed up the staircase the door opened, and the man himself looked out at him. With his fat, evil face he was like some bloated spider fresh from the weaving of his poisonous web.

"Good evening," said he. "Won't you come in?"

"No," cried Smith fiercely.

"No? You are as busy as ever? I wanted to ask you about Lee. I was sorry to hear that there was a rumor that something was amiss with him."

His features were grave, but there was the gleam of a hidden laugh in his eyes as he spoke. Smith saw it, and he could have knocked him down for it.

"You'll be sorrier still to hear that Monkhouse Lee is doing very well and is out of all danger," he answered. "Your hellish tricks have not come off this time. Oh, you needn't try to brazen it out. I know all about it."

Bellingham took a step back from the angry student and half closed the door as if to protect himself.

"You are mad," he said. "What do you mean? Do you assert that I had anything to do with Lee's accident?"

"Yes," thundered Smith. "You and that bag of bones behind you; you worked it between you. I tell you what it is, Master B., they have given up burning folk like you, but we still keep a hangman, and, by George, if any man in this college meets his death while you are here, I'll have you up, and if you don't swing for it, it won't be my fault. You'll find that your filthy Egyptian tricks won't answer in England."

"You're a raving lunatic," said Bellingham.

"All right. You just remember what I say, for you'll find that I'll be better than my word."

The door slammed, and Smith went fuming up to his chamber where he locked the door upon the inside, and spent half the night in smoking his old briar and brooding over the strange events of the evening.

Next morning Abercrombie Smith heard nothing of his neighbor, but Harrington called upon him in the afternoon to say that Lee was almost himself again. All day Smith stuck fast to his work, but in the evening he determined to pay the visit to his friend Dr. Peterson upon which he had started the night before. A good walk and a friendly chat would be welcome to his jangled nerves.

Bellingham's door was shut as he passed, but glancing back when he was some distance from the turret, he saw his neighbor's head at the window outlined against the lamplight, his face pressed apparently against the glass as he gazed out into the darkness. It was a blessing to be away from all contact with him, if but for a few hours, and Smith stepped out briskly and breathed the soft spring air into his lungs. The half-moon lay in the west between two Gothic pinnacles and threw upon the silvered street a dark tracery from the stonework above. There was a brisk breeze, and light, fleecy clouds drifted swiftly across the sky. Old's was on the very border of the town, and in five minutes Smith found himself beyond the houses and between the hedges of a May-scented, Oxfordshire lane.

It was a lonely and little-frequented road which led to his friend's house. Early as it was, Smith did not meet a single soul upon his way. He walked briskly along until he came to the avenue gate, which opened into the long, gravel drive leading up to Farlingford. In front of him he could see the cozy, red light of the windows glimmering through the foliage. He stood with his hand upon the iron latch of the swinging gate, and he glanced back at the road along which he had come. Something was coming swiftly down it.

It moved in the shadow of the hedge, silently and furtively, a dark, crouching figure, dimly visible against the black background. Even as he gazed back at it, it had lessened its distance by twenty paces and was fast closing upon him. Out of the darkness he had a glimpse of a scraggy neck, and of two eyes that will ever haunt him in his dreams. He turned, and with a cry of terror he ran for his life up the avenue. There were the red lights, the signals of safety, almost within a stone's throw of him. He was a famous runner, but never had he run as he ran that night.

The heavy gate had swung into place behind him but he heard it dash open again before his pursuer. As he rushed madly and wildly through the night, he could hear a swift, dry patter behind him and could see, as he threw back a glance, that this horror was bounding like a tiger at his heels, with blazing eyes and one stringy arm outthrown. Thank God, the door was ajar. He could see the thin bar of light which shot from the lamp in the hall. Nearer yet sounded the clatter from behind. He heard a hoarse gurgling at his very shoulder. With a shriek he flung himself against the door, slammed and bolted it behind him, and sank half-fainting onto the hall chair.

"My goodness, Smith, what's the matter?" asked Peterson, appearing at the door of his study.

"Give me some brandy."

Peterson disappeared and came rushing out again with a glass and a decanter.

"You need it," he said as his visitor drank off what he poured out for him. "Why, man, you are as white as a cheese."

Smith laid down his glass, rose up, and took a deep breath.

"I am my own man again now," said he. "I was never so unmanned before. But, with your leave, Peterson, I will sleep here tonight, for I don't think I could face that road again except by daylight. It's weak, I know, but I can't help it."

Peterson looked at his visitor with a very questioning eye.

"Of course you shall sleep here if you wish. I'll tell Mrs. Burney to make up the spare bed. Where are you off to now?"

"Come up with me to the window that overlooks the door. I want you to see what I have seen."

They went up to the window of the upper hall whence they could look down upon the approach to the house. The drive and the fields on either side lay quiet and still, bathed in the peaceful moonlight.

"Well, really, Smith," remarked Peterson, "it is well that I know you to be an abstemious man. What in the world can have frightened you?"

"I'll tell you presently. But where can it have gone? Ah, now, look, look! See the curve of the road just beyond your gate."

"Yes, I see; you needn't pinch my arm off. I saw someone pass. I should say a man, rather thin, apparently, and tall, very tall. But what of him? And what of yourself? You are still shaking like an aspen leaf."

"I have been within handgrip of the devil, that's all. But come down to your study, and I shall tell you the whole story."

He did so. Under the cheery lamplight with a glass of wine on the table beside him, and the portly form and florid face of his friend in front, he narrated, in their order, all the events, great and small, which had formed so singular a chain, from the night on which he had found Bellingham fainting in front of the mummy case until this horrid experience of an hour ago.

"There now," he said as he concluded, "that's the whole, black business. It is monstrous and incredible, but it is true."

Dr. Plumptree Peterson sat for some time in silence with a very puzzled expression upon his face.

"I never heard of such a thing in my life, never!" he said at last. "You have told me the facts. Now tell me your inferences."

"You can draw your own."

"But I should like to hear yours. You have thought over the matter, and I have not."

"Well, it must be a little vague in detail, but the main points seem to me to be clear enough. This fellow Bellingham, in his Eastern studies, has got hold of some infernal secret by which a mummy—or possibly only this particular mummy—can be temporarily brought to life. He was trying this disgusting business on the night when he fainted. No doubt the sight of the creature moving had shaken his nerve, even though he had expected it. You remember that almost the first words he said were to call out upon himself as a fool. Well, he got more hardened afterward and carried the matter through without fainting. The vitality which he could put into it was evidently only a passing thing, for I have seen it continually in its case as dead as this table. He has some elaborate process, I fancy, by which he brings the thing to pass. Having done it, he naturally bethought him that he might use the creature as an agent. It has intelligence and it has strength. For some purpose he took Lee into his confidence; but Lee, like a decent Christian, would have nothing to do with such a business. Then they had a row, and Lee vowed that he would tell his sister of Bellingham's true character. Bellingham's game was to prevent him, and he nearly managed it, by setting this creature of his on his track. He had already tried its powers upon another man—Norton—toward whom he had a grudge. It is the merest chance that he has not two murders upon his soul. Then, when I taxed him with the matter, he had the strongest reasons for wishing to get me out of the way before I could convey my knowledge to anyone else. He got his chance when I went out, for he knew my habits and where I was bound for. I have had a narrow shave, Peterson, and it is mere luck you didn't find me on your doorstep in the morning. I'm not a nervous man as a rule, and I never thought to have the fear of death put upon me as it was tonight."

"My dear boy, you take the matter too seriously," said his companion. "Your nerves are out of order with your work, and you make too much of it. How could such a thing as this stride about the streets of Oxford, even at night, without being seen?"

"It has been seen. There is quite a scare in the town about an escaped ape, as they imagine the creature to be. It is the talk of the place."

"Well, it's a striking chain of events. And yet, my dear fellow, you must allow that each incident in itself is capable of a more natural explanation."

"What! Even my adventure of tonight?"

"Certainly. You come out with your nerves all unstrung and your head full of this theory of yours. Some gaunt, half-famished tramp steals after you, and seeing you run, is emboldened to pursue you. Your fears and imagination do the rest."

"It won't do, Peterson; it won't do."

"And again, in the instance of your finding the mummy case empty, and then a few moments later with an occupant, you know that it was lamplight, that the lamp was half-turned down, and that you had no special reason to look hard at the case. It is quite possible that you may have overlooked the creature in the first instance."

"No, no; it is out of the question."

"And then Lee may have fallen into the river, and Norton been garroted. It is certainly a formidable indictment that you have against Bellingham; but if you were to place it before a police magistrate, he would simply laugh in your face."

"I know he would. That is why I mean to take the matter into my own hands."

"Eh?"

"Yes; I feel that a public duty rests upon me, and, besides, I must do it for my own safety, unless I choose to allow myself to be hunted by this beast out of the college, and that would be a little too feeble. I have quite made up my mind what I shall do. And first of all, may I use your paper and pens for an hour?"

"Most certainly. You will find all that you want upon that side table."

Abercrombie Smith sat down before a sheet of foolscap, and for an hour, and then for a second hour his pen traveled swiftly over it. Page after page was finished and tossed aside while his friend leaned back in his armchair, looking across at him with patient curiosity. At last, with an exclamation of satisfaction, Smith sprang to his feet, gathered his papers up into order, and laid the last one up on Peterson's desk.

"Kindly sign this as a witness," he said.

"A witness? Of what?"

"Of my signature, and of the date. The date is the most important. Why, Peterson, my life might hang upon it."

"My dear Smith, you are talking wildly. Let me beg you to go to bed."

"On the contrary, I never spoke so deliberately in my life. And I will promise to go to bed the moment you have signed it."

"But what is it?"

"It is a statement of all that I have been telling you tonight. I wish you to witness it."

"Certainly," said Peterson, signing his name under that of his companion. "There you are! But what is the idea?"

"You will kindly retain it, and produce it in case I am arrested."

"Arrested? For what?"

"For murder. It is quite on the cards. I wish to be ready for every event. There is only one course open to me, and I am determined to take it."

"For heaven's sake, don't do anything rash!"

"Believe me, it would be far more rash to adopt any other course. I hope that we won't need to bother you, but it will ease my mind to know that you have this statement of my motives. And now I am ready to take your advice and to go to roost, for I want to be at my best in the morning."

Abercrombie Smith was not an entirely pleasant man to have as an enemy. Slow and easy-tempered, he was formidable when driven to action. He brought to every purpose in life the same deliberate resoluteness which had distinguished him as a scientific student. He had laid his studies aside for a day, but he intended that the day would not be wasted. Not a word did he say to his host as to his plans, but by nine o'clock he was well on his way to Oxford.

In the High Street he stopped at Clifford's, the gunmaker's, and bought a heavy revolver, with a box of central-fire cartridges. Six of them he slipped into the chambers, and half cocking the weapon, placed it in the pocket of his coat. He then made his way to Hastie's rooms, where the big oarsman was lounging over his breakfast, with the *Sporting Times* propped up against the coffeepot.

"Hullo! What's up?" he asked. "Have some coffee?"

"No, thank you. I want you to come with me, Hastie, and do what I ask you."

"Certainly, my boy."

"And bring a heavy stick with you."

"Hullo!" Hastie stared. "Here's a hunting crop that would fell an ox."

"One other thing. You have a box of amputating knives. Give me the longest of them."

"There you are. You seem to be fairly on the war trail. Anything else?"

"No; that will do." Smith placed the knife inside his coat and led the way to the quadrangle. "We are neither of us chickens, Hastie," said he. "I think I can do this job alone, but I take you as a precaution. I am going to have a little talk with Bellingham. If I have only him to deal with, I won't, of course, need you. If I shout, however, up you come, and lam out with your whip as hard as you can lick. Do you understand?"

"All right. I'll come if I hear you bellow."

"Stay here, then. I may be a little time, but don't budge until I come down."

"I'm a fixture."

Smith ascended the stairs, opened Bellingham's door, and stepped in. Bellingham was seated behind his table, writing. Beside him, among his litter of strange possessions, towered the mummy case, with its sale number 249 still stuck upon its front and its hideous occupant stiff and stark within it. Smith looked very deliberately round him, closed the door, and then, stepping across to the fireplace, struck a match and set the fire alight. Bellingham sat staring, with amazement and rage upon his bloated face.

"Well, really now, you make yourself at home," he gasped.

Smith sat himself deliberately down, placing his watch upon the table, drew out his pistol, cocked it, and laid it in his lap. Then he took the long amputating knife from his bosom and threw it down in front of Bellingham.

"Now, then," said he, "just get to work and cut up that mummy."

"Oh, is that it?" said Bellingham with a sneer.

"Yes, that is it. They tell me that the law can't touch you. But I have a law that will set matters straight. If in five minutes you have not set to work, I swear by the God who made me that I will put a bullet through your brain!"

"You would murder me?"

Bellingham had half risen, and his face was the color of putty.

"Yes."

"And for what?"

"To stop your mischief. One minute has gone."

"But what have I done?"

"I know and you know."

"This is mere bullying."

"Two minutes are gone."

"But you must give reasons. You are a madman—a dangerous madman. Why should I destroy my own property? It is a valuable mummy."

"You must cut it up, and you must burn it."

"I will do no such thing."

"Four minutes are gone."

Smith took up the pistol and he looked toward Bellingham with an inexorable face. As the second hand stole round, he raised his hand, and the finger twitched upon the trigger.

"There! There! I'll do it!" screamed Bellingham.

In frantic haste he caught up the knife and hacked at the figure of the mummy, ever glancing round to see the eye and the weapon of his terrible visitor bent upon him. The creature crackled and snapped under every stab of the keen blade. A thick, yellow dust rose up from it. Spices and dried essences rained down upon the floor. Suddenly, with a rending crack, its backbone snapped asunder, and it fell, a brown heap of sprawling limbs, upon the floor.

"Now into the fire!" said Smith.

The flames leaped and roared as the dried and tinderlike debris was piled upon it. The little room was like the stokehole of a steamer and the sweat ran down the faces of the two men; but still the one stooped and worked, while the other sat watching him with a set face. A thick, fat smoke oozed out from the fire, and a heavy smell of burned resin and singed hair filled the air. In a quarter of an hour a few charred and brittle sticks were all that was left of Lot No. 249.

"Perhaps that will satisfy you," snarled Bellingham, with hate and fear in his little gray eyes as he glanced back at his tormentor.

"No; I must make a clean sweep of all your materials. We must have no more devil's tricks. In with all these leaves! They may have something to do with it."

"And what now?" asked Bellingham when the leaves also had been added to the blaze.

"Now the roll of papyrus which you had on the table that night. It is in that drawer, I think."

"No, no," shouted Bellingham. "Don't burn that. Why, man, you don't know what you do. It is unique, it contains wisdom which is nowhere else to be found."

"Out with it!"

"But look here, Smith, you can't really mean it. I'll share the knowledge with you. I'll teach you all that is in it. Or, stay, let me only copy it before you burn it!''

Smith stepped forward and turned the key in the drawer. Taking out the yellow, curled roll of paper, he threw it into the fire and pressed it down with his heel. Bellingham screamed and grabbed at it, but Smith pushed him back and stood over it until it was reduced to a formless, gray ash.

"Now, Master B.," said he, "I think I have pretty well drawn your teeth. You'll hear from me again, if you return to your old tricks. And now good morning, for I must go back to my studies.''

And such is the narrative of Abercrombie Smith as to the singular events which occurred in Old College, Oxford, in the spring of '84. As Bellingham left the university immediately afterward and was last heard of in the Sudan, there is no one who can contradict his statement. But the wisdom of men is small, and the ways of nature are strange, and who shall put a bound to the dark things which may be found by those who seek for them?

DONALD A. WOLLHEIM is one of the master creators of modern science fiction. He developed Ace Books' science-fiction program, starting in 1952. In 1971 he founded his own publishing company, DAW Books, which developed into one of the leading producers of quality SF and fantasy. Wollheim is also a noted anthologist and author of horror stories, some of the latter published under the pseudonym David Grinnell.

BONES

by Donald A. Wollheim

The Museum of Natural Sciences was not very far from the place where he was staying, so Severus found himself striding briskly through the dim, winding streets that night. He had come to Boston on a visit, renewed acquaintances with learned men with whom he had exchanged knowledge in years past; thus the letter he had received in this morning's mail inviting him to a private demonstration this night.

It was not a pleasant walk; already he was beginning to regret not having taken some other means of transportation. The buildings were old and loomed darkly over the narrow streets. Lights were few; for the most part, they came from flickering, dust-encrusted lampposts of last century's design. Large moths and other nocturnal insects fluttered over their surfaces, adding their moving shadows to the air of desolation which hung about these ways.

The moon was behind clouds that had streaked across the autumn skies all day and now blocked out the stars. The night about him was warm with that touch of unexpected chill which comes in autumn. Severus shuddered more than once as a wandering breeze slithered across his face unexpectedly around some dreary corner. He increased his pace, looked more suspiciously about him.

Boston, the oldest section of the city. Antique brick buildings dating back to the revolution, some much further. Dwelling places of the best families of two centuries ago. Now steadily advancing progress and life had left them derelict as upon deserted shores. Old, three- or four-story structures, narrow tottering dirty red-brick houses with yawning black windows that now looked out through filth-encrusted panes upon streets and byways that served to shelter only the poorest and most alien section of the city's people. Forgotten, the district imparted its despair and overhanging doom to the man who walked its ways that night.

Half-conquered by the smell of the antique houses, the subtle vibrations of past generations still pervading his spirit, Severus came at last out of the narrow streets into the open square where stood the museum.

The change surprised him. Here all was open. The dark, cloud-streaked sky loomed down overhead with a closeness that appalled him for a moment. The white marble facade of the structure glistened oddly in his view. It stood out, the cleanliness of it, as something exceedingly out of place, as something too new, too recent to have any right here. Its Neo-Grecian designs were horribly modern and crude for the eighteenth-century blocks that surrounded it.

He walked swiftly across the open square, up the wide stone steps to the entrance of the building. Quickly he thrust open the small side door, hurried through as if to escape the thoughts of forgotten streets outside.

How futile such hopes in a museum! He realized that the instant the door was closed. He stood in a dark hall, lit dimly by one bulb above the entrance, another one at the opposite end of the main passage. And at once his nostrils were assailed by the inescapable odor of all such institutions—age!

The musty air rushed over his body, took him into its folds. The silence assailed his ears with a suddenness that all but took his breath away. He looked about, trying to catch his bearings. Then he ventured a step, walked rapidly across the large chamber, down a wide corridor opening off it. Not a glance did he cast from side to side. The looming shadows of indescribable things were enough for him. His imagination supplied the rest.

Unavoidable glimpses of shadowy sarcophagi and grotesquely carven idols sent great cold chills thrilling down his spine.

Up a narrow staircase, a turn to the right. At last he was at the room set aside for the night's demonstration. He stood a moment trying to catch his breath and regain composure. Then he pushed the door open, stepped inside.

A bare room with scarcely any furnishings. About seven or eight other men were there. In low tones they greeted him, drew him over to their circle. All were standing; there were no chairs in the room. A couple of small instrument racks and the main object was all.

The room was dominated by a long, low table upon which rested a six-foot bundle of dull gray cloth like a giant cocoon. Severus stared at it a moment, then recognized it as an Egyptian mummy removed from its coffin case. It obviously awaited unwinding.

So this was what he'd been invited to, he thought, wishing he hadn't been so friendly to the Egyptologists attached to this particular museum.

Glancing around, Severus took note of the others present. He was surprised to recognize one as a medical doctor highly esteemed at a city hospital. The doctor indeed seemed to be one of the active participants in what was about to take place, for he wore a white smock that indicated action.

Bantling, the Egyptologist, held up a hand for silence.

"Most of you know what is about to take place tonight; therefore I will merely outline it for your convenience and for the one or two who know nothing about it." He nodded to Severus and smiled.

"This object, as you have all surmised, is an Egyptian mummy. But it is, we hope, different from all other such mummies previously examined.

"According to our painstaking translation of the hieroglyphics of the sarcophagus whence this body came, this marks an attempt of the priesthood of the Fourth Dynasty to send one of their number alive into the lands to come. The unique part of it, and that which occupies us tonight, is that this priest did not die, nor was his body in any way mutilated. Instead, according to the inscriptions, he was fed and bathed in certain compounds that would suspend, indefinitely, the actions of his body cells. He was then put to sleep and prepared for a slumber very like death, yet not true death. In this state he could remain for years, yet still be reawakened to walk again, a living man.

"In brief, and using modern terminology, these people of what we call ancient times, claim to have solved the secret of suspended animation. Whether or not they did is for us now to determine."

Severus felt himself grow cold as this knowledge penetrated his being. The past had indeed reached out to the present. He would witness this night the end of an experiment started thousands of years before. Perhaps he himself would yet speak to and hear speak an inhabitant of this lost age. Egypt, buried these hundreds of centuries, Egypt aged beyond belief—yet, a man of that time-lost empire lay here in this very room, in the North American city of Boston.

"Three thousand seven hundred B.C." he heard someone remark in answer to an unheard question.

Severus raised his eyes from the object on the table, let his gaze fall upon the window and what was revealed through it. Some of the clouds had cleared away and the cold, bright stars shone through. Far-off flickering spots of light that must surely have shown upon Ancient Egypt as coldly. The very light just passing through his cornea may have originated in the time when this thing upon the table was about to be plunged into life-in-death.

Far off, the dull clanging of a church bell drifted into the room.

"Buck up, old man." A hand patted Severus's shoulder as an acquaintance came over to him. "It isn't as bad as it looks. Why that fellow will be as hale as any of us before the night is out. You'll think he's just a new immigrant."

Bantling and an assistant were even now engaged in unwrapping the mummy. Rolls and rolls of old, crumbling cloth were carefully being unwound from the figure on the table. Dust of death and ages now filled the air. Several coughs were heard; the door was opened on the dark passage outside to let the air change.

A gasp as at last the windings fell away. The body now lay entirely uncovered. Quickly, quietly, the wrappings were gathered together and piled in a receptacle while all crowded about to observe the Egyptian.

All in all, it was in a fine state of preservation. The skin was not brownish; it had not hardened. The arms and legs were still movable, had never stiffened in rigor mortis. Bantling seemed much pleased.

With horror Severus noted the several grayish-blue patches on parts of the face and body which he recognized without asking as a kind of mold.

Dr. Zweig, the physician, bent over and carefully scraped off the fungoid growths. They left nasty reddish pitted scars in the body that made Severus feel sick. He wanted to rush out of the room, out of the building into the clean night air. But the fascination of the horrible kept his glance fixed in hypnosis on the gruesome object before him.

"We are ready." Dr. Zweig said in a low voice.

They began to bathe the body with a sharp-smelling antiseptic, taking off all remaining traces of the preservatives used.

"Remarkable how perfect this thing is," breathed the physician. "Remarkable!"

Now at last the way was open for the work of revival. Large electric pads were brought out, laid all over the body, face, and legs. Current was switched into them; the body surface was slowly brought up to normal warmth.

Then arteries and veins were opened, tubes clamped to them running from apparatus under the table. Severus understood that warm artificial blood was being pumped into the body to warm up the internal organs and open up the flow of blood again.

Shortly Dr. Zweig announced himself ready to attempt the final work toward actually bringing the now pliant and vibrant corpse to life. Already the body seemed like that of a living man, the flush of red tingling its skin and cheeks. Severus was in a cold sweat.

"Blood flows again through his veins and arteries," whispered the Egyptologist. "It is time to turn off the mechanical heart and attempt to revive his own."

A needle was plunged into the chest, a substance injected into the dormant, thousands-year-old cardiac apparatus of the body. Adrenaline, Severus assumed.

Over the mouth and nostrils of the former mummy a bellows was placed, air forced into the lungs at regular periods. For a while there was no result. Severus began fervently to hope that there would be no result. The air was supercharged with tension, horror mixed with scientific zeal. Through the chamber, the wheeze of the bellows was the only sound.

"Look!"

Someone cried out the word, electrifying all in the room of resurrection. A hand pointed shakily at the chest of the thing on the table. There was more action now; the chest rose and fell more vigorously. Quietly the doctor reached over and pulled away the face mask and stopped the pumps.

And the chest of the Egyptian still moved, up and down in a ghastly rhythm of its own. Now to their ears became noticeable an odd sound, a rattling soft wheezing sound as of air being sucked in and out of a sleeping man.

"He breathes." The doctor reached out and laid a finger on the body's wrists. "The heart beats."

"He lives again!"

Their eyes stared at what had been done. There, on the table, lay a man, a light brown-skinned, sharp Semitic-featured man, appearing to be in early middle age. He lay there as one quietly asleep.

"Who will waken him?" whispered Severus above the pounding of his heart.

"He will awaken soon," was the answer. "He will rise and walk as if nothing had happened."

Severus shook his head, disbelievingly. Then . . .

The Egyptian moved. His hand shook slightly; the eyes opened with a jerk.

Spellbound they stood, the eyes of the Americans fixed upon the eyes of the ancient. In shocked silence they watched one another.

The Egyptian sat up slowly, as if painfully. His features moved not a bit; his body moved slowly and jerkily.

The ancient's eyes roved over the assembly. They caught Severus full in the face. For an instant they gazed at one another, the Vermont man looking into pain-swept ages, into grim depths of agony and sorrow, into the aeons of past time itself.

The Egyptian suddenly wrinkled up his features, swept up an arm, and opened his mouth to speak.

And Severus fled from the room in frightful terror, the others closely following. Behind them rang out a terrible, hoarse bellow, cut off by a gurgling which they barely heard. The entire company, to a man, fought each other like terrified animals, each struggling to be the first out of that museum, out the doors into the black streets and away.

For there are parts of the human body which, never having

been alive, cannot be preserved in suspended life. They are the bones, the teeth—strong in death, but unable to defy the crushing millennia.

And when the Egyptian had moved his body and opened his mouth to speak, his face had fallen in like termite-infested wood, the splinters of fragile, age-crumbled bones tearing through the flesh. His whole body had shaken, and, with the swing of the arm, smashed itself into a shapeless mass of heaving flesh and blood through which projected innumerable jagged fragments of dark gray, pitted bones.

*The devoted readers of E. F. BENSON (1867–1940) know this
English author principally as the creator of the* Make Way for
Lucia *series. The mummy-inspired terror of "Monkeys" is quite
a departure from the urbane drollery of Queen Lucia and her
entourage.*

MONKEYS

by E. F. Benson

Dr. Hugh Morris, while still in the early thirties of his age,
had justly earned for himself the reputation of being one of the
most dexterous and daring surgeons in his profession, and both
in his private practice and in his voluntary work at one of the
great London hospitals his record of success as an operator was
unparalleled among his colleagues. He believed that vivisection
was the most fruitful means of progress in the science of surgery, holding, rightly or wrongly, that he was justified in causing
suffering to animals, though sparing them all possible pain, if
thereby he could reasonably hope to gain fresh knowledge about
similar operations on human beings which would save life or
mitigate suffering; the motive was good, and the gain already
immense. But he had nothing but scorn for those who, for their
own amusement, took out packs of hounds to run foxes to death,
or matched two greyhounds to see which would give the death
grip to a single terrified hare: that, to him, was wanton torture,
utterly unjustifiable. Year in and year out, he took no holiday at
all, and for the most part he occupied his leisure, when the day's
work was over, in study.

He and his friend Jack Madden were dining together one warm
October night at his house looking onto Regent's Park. The
windows of his drawing room on the ground floor were open,

and they sat smoking, when dinner was done, on the broad window seat. Madden was starting next day for Egypt, where he was engaged in archaeological work, and he had been vainly trying to persuade Morris to join him for a month up the Nile, where he would be engaged throughout the winter in the excavation of a newly discovered cemetery across the river from Luxor, near Medinet Habu. But it was no good.

"When my eye begins to fail and my fingers to falter," said Morris, "it will be time for me to think of taking my ease. What do I want with a holiday? I should be pining to get back to my work all the time. I like work better than loafing. Purely selfish."

"Well, be unselfish for once," said Madden. "Besides, your work would benefit. It can't be good for a man never to relax. Surely freshness is worth something."

"Precious little if you're as strong as I am. I believe in continual concentration if one wants to make progress. One may be tired, but why not? I'm not tired when I'm actually engaged on a dangerous operation, which is what matters. And time's so short. Twenty years from now I shall be past my best, and I'll have my holiday then, and when my holiday is over, I shall fold my hands and go to sleep forever and ever. Thank God, I've got no fear that there's an afterlife. The spark of vitality that has animated us burns low and then goes out like a windblown candle, and as for my body, what do I care what happens to that when I have done with it? Nothing will survive of me except some small contribution I may have made to surgery, and in a few years' time that will be superseded. But for that I perish utterly."

Madden squirted some soda into his glass.

"Well, if you've quite settled that—" he began

"I haven't settled it, science has," said Morris. "The body is transmuted into other forms, worms batten on it, it helps to feed the grass, and some animal consumes the grass. But as for the survival of the individual spirit of a man, show me one tittle of scientific evidence to support it. Besides, if it did survive, all the evil and malice in it must surely survive, too. Why should the death of the body purge that away? It's a nightmare to contemplate such a thing, and oddly enough, unhinged people like spiritualists want to persuade us for our consolation that the nightmare is true. But odder still are those old Egyptians of yours, who thought that there was something sacred about their bodies, after they were quit of them. And didn't you tell me that they covered their coffins with curses on anyone who disturbed their bones?''

"Constantly,'' said Madden. "It's the general rule in fact. Marrowy curses written in hieroglyphics on the mummy case or carved on the sarcophagus.''

"But that's not going to deter you this winter from opening as many tombs as you can find, and rifling from them any objects of interest or value.''

Madden laughed.

"Certainly it isn't,'' he said. "I take out of the tombs all objects of art, and I unwind the mummies to find and annex their scarabs and jewelry. But I make an absolute rule always to bury the bodies again. I don't say that I believe in the power of those curses, but anyhow a mummy in a museum is an indecent object.''

"But if you found some mummied body with an interesting malformation, wouldn't you send it to some anatomical institute?'' asked Morris.

"It has never happened to me yet,'' said Madden, "but I'm pretty sure I shouldn't.''

"Then you're a superstitious Goth and an antieducational Vandal,'' remarked Morris. . . . "Hullo, what's that?'' He leaned out of the window as he spoke. The light from the room vividly illuminated the square of lawn outside, and across it was crawling the small twitching shape of some animal. Hugh Morris vaulted out of the window and presently returned, carrying carefully in his spread hands a little gray monkey, evidently desperately injured. Its hind legs were stiff and outstretched as if it was partially paralyzed.

Morris ran his soft deft fingers over it.

"What's the matter with the little beggar, I wonder,'' he said. "Paralysis of the lower limbs: it looks like some lesion of the spine.''

The monkey lay quite still, looking at him with anguished appealing eyes as he continued his manipulation.

"Yes, I thought so,'' he said. "Fracture of one of the lumbar vertebrae. What luck for me! It's a rare injury, but I've often wondered. . . . And perhaps luck for the monkey, too, though that's not very probable. If he was a man and a patient of mine, I shouldn't dare to take the risk. But, as it is . . .''

Jack Madden started on his southward journey next day, and by the middle of November was at work on this newly discov-

ered cemetery. He and another Englishman were in charge of
the excavation, under the control of the Antiquity Department
of the Egyptian government. In order to be close to their work
and to avoid the daily ferrying across the Nile from Luxor, they
hired a bare roomy native house in the adjoining village of Gurnah. A reef of low sandstone cliff ran northward from here toward the temple and terraces of Deir-el-Bahari, and it was in
the face of this and on the level below it that the ancient grave-
yard lay. There was much accumulation of sand to be cleared
away before the actual exploration of the tombs could begin, but
trenches cut below the foot of the sandstone ridge showed that
there was an extensive area to investigate.

The more important sepulchers, they found, were hewn in the
face of this small cliff: many of these had been rifled in ancient
days, for the slabs forming the entrances into them had been
split, and the mummies unwound, but now and then Madden
unearthed some tomb that had escaped these marauders, and in
one he found the sarcophagus of a priest of the Nineteenth Dynasty, and that alone repaid weeks of fruitless work. There were
nearly a hundred *ushaptiu* figures of the finest blue glaze; there
were four alabaster vessels in which had been placed the viscera
of the dead man removed before embalming; there was a table
of which the top was inlaid with squares of variously colored
glass and the legs were of carved ivory and ebony; there were
the priest's sandals adorned with exquisite silver filagree; there
was his staff of office inlaid with a diaper-pattern of cornelian
and gold, and on the head of it, forming the handle, was the
figure of a squatting cat, carved in amethyst, and the mummy,
when unwound, was found to be decked with a necklace of gold
plaques and onyx beads. All these were sent down to the Gizeh
Museum at Cairo, and Madden reinterred the mummy at the
foot of the cliff below the tomb. He wrote to Hugh Morris de-
scribing this find, and laying stress on the unbroken splendor of
these crystalline winter days, when from morning to night the
sun cruised across the blue, and on the cool nights when the
stars rose and set on the vaporless rim of the desert. If by chance
Hugh should change his mind, there was ample room for him
in this house at Gurnah, and he would be very welcome.

A fortnight later Madden received a telegram from his friend.
It stated that he had been unwell and was starting at once by
long sea to Port Said, and would come straight up to Luxor. In
due course he announced his arrival at Cairo and Madden went
across the river next day to meet him; it was reassuring to find

him as vital and active as ever, the picture of bronzed health. The two were alone that night, for Madden's colleague had gone for a week's trip up the Nile, and they sat out, when dinner was done, in the enclosed courtyard adjoining the house. Till then Morris had shied off the subject of himself and his health.

"Now I may as well tell you what's been amiss with me," he said, "for I know I look a fearful fraud as an invalid, and physically I've never been better in my life. Every organ has been functioning perfectly except one, but something suddenly went wrong there just once. It was like this."

He paused a moment.

"After you left," he said, "I went on as usual for another month or so, very busy, very serene, and, I may say, very successful. Then one morning I arrived at the hospital when there was one perfectly ordinary but major operation waiting for me. The patient, a man, was wheeled into the theatre anesthetized, and I was just about to make the first incision into the abdomen, when I saw that there was sitting on his chest a little gray monkey. It was not looking at me, but at the fold of skin which I held between my thumb and finger. I knew, of course, that there was no monkey there, and that what I saw was a hallucination, and I think you'll agree that there was nothing much wrong with my nerves when I tell you that I went through the operation with clear eyes and an unshaking hand. I had to go on: there was no choice about the matter. I couldn't say: 'Please take that monkey away,' for I knew there was no monkey there. Nor could I say: 'Somebody else must do this, as I have a distressing hallucination that there is a monkey sitting on the patient's chest.' There would have been an end of me as a surgeon and no mistake. All the time I was at work it sat there absorbed for the most part in what I was doing and peering into the wound, but now and then it looked up at me and chattered with rage. Once it fingered a spring forceps which clipped a severed vein, and that was the worst moment of all. . . . At the end it was carried out still balancing itself on the man's chest. . . . I think I'll have a drink. Strongish, please . . . Thanks.

"A beastly experience," he said when he had drunk. "Then I went straightaway from the hospital to consult my old friend Robert Angus, the alienist and nerve specialist, and told him exactly what had happened to me. He made several tests, he examined my eyes, tried my reflexes, took my blood pressure: there was nothing wrong with any of them. Then he asked me questions about my general health and manner of life, and among these questions was one which I am sure has already occurred to you, namely, had anything occurred to me lately, or even remotely, which was likely to make me visualize a monkey. I told him that a few weeks ago a monkey with a broken lumbar vertebra had crawled onto my lawn, and that I had attempted an operation—binding the broken vertebra with wire—which had occurred to me before as a possibility. You remember the night, no doubt?''

"Perfectly," said Madden, "I started for Egypt next day. What happened to the monkey, by the way?''

"It lived for two days: I was pleased, because I had expected it would die under the anesthetic, or immediately afterward from shock. To get back to what I was telling you. When Angus had asked all his questions, he gave me a good wigging. He said that I had persistently overtaxed my brain for years, without giving it any rest or change of occupation, and that if I wanted to be of any further use in the world, I must drop my work at once for a couple of months. He told me that my brain was tired out and that I had persisted in stimulating it. A man like me, he said, was no better than a confirmed drunkard, and that, as a warning, I had had a touch of an appropriate delirium tremens. The cure was to drop work, just as a drunkard must drop drink. He laid it on hot and strong: he said I was on the verge of a breakdown, entirely owing to my own foolishness, but that I had wonderful physical health, and that if I did break down, I should be a disgrace. Above all—and this seemed to me awfully sound advice—he told me not to attempt to avoid thinking about what had happened to me. If I kept my mind off it, I should be perhaps driving it into the subconscious, and then there might be bad trouble. 'Rub it in: think what a fool you've been,' he said. 'Face it, dwell on it, make yourself thoroughly ashamed of yourself.' Monkeys, too: I wasn't to avoid the thought of monkeys. In fact, he recommended me to go straightaway to the Zoological Gardens, and spend an hour in the monkey house.''

"Odd treatment," interrupted Madden.

"Brilliant treatment. My brain, he explained, had rebelled against its slavery and had hoisted a red flag with the device of a monkey on it. I must show it that I wasn't frightened at its bogus monkeys. I must retort on it by making myself look at dozens of real ones which could bite and maul you savagely, instead of one little sham monkey that had no existence at all. At the same time I must take the red flag seriously, recognize there was danger, and rest. And he promised me that sham monkeys wouldn't trouble me again. Are there any real ones in Egypt, by the way?"

"Not so far as I know," said Madden. "But there must have been once, for there are many images of them in tombs and temples."

"That's good. We'll keep their memory green and my brain cool. Well, there's my story. What do you think of it?"

"Terrifying," said Madden. "But you must have got nerves of iron to get through that operation with the monkey watching."

"A hellish hour. Out of some disordered slime in my brain there had crawled this unbidden thing, which showed itself, apparently substantial, to my eyes. It didn't come from outside: my eyes hadn't told my brain that there was a monkey sitting on the man's chest, but my brain had told my eyes so, making fools of them. I felt as if someone whom I absolutely trusted had played me false. Then again I have wondered whether some instinct in my subconscious mind revolted against vivisection. My reason says that it is justified, for it teaches us how pain can be relieved and death postponed for human beings. But what if my subconscious persuaded by brain to give me a good fright, and reproduce before my eyes the semblance of a monkey, just when I was putting into practice what I had learned from dealing out pain and death to animals?"

He got up suddenly.

"What about bed?" he said. "Five hours' sleep was enough for me when I was at work, but now I believe I could sleep the clock round every night."

Young Wilson, Madden's colleague in the excavations, returned next day and the work went steadily on. One of them was on the spot to start it soon after sunrise, and either one or both of them were superintending it, with an interval of a couple of hours at noon, until sunset. Then the mere work of clearing the face of the sandstone cliff was in progress and of carting away the silted soil, the presence of one of them sufficed, for there was nothing to do but to see that the workmen shoveled industriously and passed regularly with their baskets of earth and sand on their shoulders to the dumping grounds, which stretched away from the area to be excavated, in lengthening peninsulas of trodden soil. But, as they advanced along the sandstone ridge, there would now and then appear a chiseled smoothness in the cliff and then both must be alert. There was great excitement to see if, when they exposed the hewn slab that formed the door into the tomb, it had escaped ancient marauders and still stood in place and intact for the modern to explore. But now for many days they came upon no sepulcher that had not already been opened. The mummy, in these cases, had been unwound in the search for necklaces and scarabs, and its scattered bones lay about. Madden was always at pains to reinter these.

At first Hugh Morris was assiduous in watching the excavations, but as day after day went by without anything of interest turning up, his attendance grew less frequent; it was too much of a holiday to watch the day-long removal of sand from one place to another. He visited the Tomb of the Kings, he went across the river and saw the temples at Karnak, but his appetite for antiquities was small. On other days he rode in the desert, or spent the day with friends at one of the Luxor hotels. He came home from there one evening in rare good spirits, for he had played lawn tennis with a woman on whom he had operated for a malignant tumor six months before and she had skipped about the court like a two-year-old. "God, how I want to be at work again!" he exclaimed. "I wonder whether I ought not to have stuck it out and defied my brain to frighten me with bogeys."

The weeks passed on, and now there were but two days left before his return to England, where he hoped to resume work at once; his tickets were taken and his berth booked. As he sat over breakfast that morning with Wilson, there came a workman from the excavation, with a note scribbled in hot haste by Madden, to say that they had just come upon a tomb which seemed to be unrifled, for the slab that closed it was in place and unbroken. To Wilson, the news was like the sight of a sail to a marooned mariner, and when, a quarter of an hour later, Morris followed him, he was just in time to see the slab prized away. There was no sarcophagus within, for the rock walls did duty for that, but there lay there, varnished and bright in hue as if painted yesterday, the mummy case roughly following the outline of the human form. By it stood the alabaster vases containing the entrails of the dead, and at each corner of the sepulcher there were carved out of the sandstone rock, forming, as it were, pillars to support the roof, thickset images of squatting apes. The mummy case was hoisted out and carried away by workmen on a bier of boards into the courtyard of the excavators' house at Gurnah, for the opening of it and the unwrapping of the dead.

They got to work that evening directly after they had fed;

the face painted on the lid was that of a girl or young woman, and presently deciphering the heiroglyphic inscription, Madden read out that within lay the body of A-pen-ara, daughter of the overseer of the cattle of Senmut.

"Then follow the usual formulas," he said. "Yes, yes . . . ah, you'll be interested in this, Hugh, for you asked me once about it. A-pen-ara curses any who desecrates or meddles with her bones, and should anyone do so, the guardians of her sepulcher will see to him, and he shall die childless and in panic and agony; also the guardians of her sepulcher will tear the hair from his head and scoop his eyes from their sockets and pluck the thumb from his right hand, as a man plucks the young blade of corn from its sheath."

Morris laughed.

"Very pretty little attentions," he said. "And who are the guardians of this sweet young lady's sepulcher? Those four great apes carved at the corners?"

"No doubt. But we won't trouble them, for tomorrow I shall bury Miss A-pen-ara's bones again with all decency in the trench at the foot of her tomb. They'll be safer there, for if we put them back where we found them, there would be pieces of her hawked about by half the donkey boys in Luxor in a few days. 'Buy a mummy hand, lady? . . . Foot of a 'Gyppy queen, only ten piasters, gentlemen' . . . Now for the unwinding."

It was dark by now, and Wilson fetched out a paraffin lamp, which burned unwaveringly in the still air. The lid of the mummy case was easily detached, and within was the slim, swaddled body. The embalming had not been very thoroughly done, for all the skin and flesh had perished from the head, leaving only bones of the skull stained brown with bitumen. Round it was a mop of hair, which with the ingress of the air subsided like a belated soufflé and crumbled into dust. The cloth that swathed the body was as brittle, but round the neck, still just holding together, was a collar of curious and rare workmanship: little ivory figures of squatting apes alternated with silver beads. But again a touch broke the thread that strung them together, and each had to be picked out singly. A bracelet of scarabs and cornelians still clasped one of the fleshless wrists, and then they turned the body over in order to get at the members of the neck-lace which lay beneath the nape. The rotted mummy cloth fell away altogether from the back, disclosing the shoulder blades and the spine down as far as the pelvis. Here the embalming had been better done, for the bones still held together with remnants of muscle and cartilage.

Hugh Morris suddenly sprang to his feet.

"My God, look there!" he cried. "One of the lumbar vertebrae, there at the base of the spine, has been broken and clamped together with a metal band. To hell with your antiquities; let me come and examine something much more modern than any of us!"

He pushed Jack Madden aside, and peered at this marvel of surgery.

"Put the lamp closer," he said, as if directing some nurse at an operation. "Yes: that vertebra has been broken right across and has been clamped together. No one has ever, as far as I know, attempted such an operation except myself, and I have only performed it on that little paralyzed monkey that crept into my garden one night. But some Egyptian surgeon, more than three thousand years ago, performed it on a woman. And look, look! She lived afterward, for the broken vertebra put out that bony efflorescence of healing which has encroached over the metal band. That's a slow process, and it must have taken place during her lifetime, for there is no such energy in a corpse. The woman lived long; probably she recovered completely. And my wretched little monkey only lived two days and was dying all the time."

Those questing hawk-visioned fingers of the surgeon perceived more finely than actual sight, and now he closed his eyes as the tip of them felt their way about the fracture in the broken vertebra and the clamping metal band.

"The band doesn't encircle the bone," he said, "and there are no studs attaching it. There must have been a spring in it, which, when it was clasped there, kept it tight. It has been clamped round the bone itself; the surgeon must have scraped the vertebra clean of flesh before he attached it. I would give two years of my life to have looked on, like a student, at that masterpiece of skill, and it was worthwhile giving up two months of my work only to have seen the result. And the injury itself is so rare, this breaking of a spinal vertbra. To be sure, the hangman does something of the sort, but there's no mending that! Good Lord, my holiday has not been a waste of time!"

Madden settled that it was not worthwhile to send the mummy case to the museum at Gizeh, for it was of a very ordinary type, and when the examination was over, they lifted the body back into it, for reinterment next day. It was now long after midnight and presently the house was dark.

Hugh Morris slept on the ground floor in a room adjoining the yard where the mummy case lay. He remained long awake marveling at that astonishing piece of surgical skill performed, according to Madden, some thirty-five centuries ago. So occupied had his mind been with homage that not till now did he realize that the tangible proof and witness of the operation would tomorrow be buried again and lost to science. He must persuade Madden to let him detach at least three of the vertebrae, the mended one and those immediately above and below it, and take them back to England as demonstration of what could be done; he would lecture on his exhibit and present it to the Royal College of Surgeons for example and incitement. Other trained eyes besides his own must see what had been successfully achieved by some unknown operator in the Nineteenth Dynasty. . . . But supposing Madden refused? He always made a point of scrupulously reburying these remains; it was a principle with him, and no doubt some superstition complex—the hardest of all to combat with because of its sheer unreasonableness— was involved. Briefly, it was impossible to risk the chance of his refusal.

He got out of bed, listened for a moment by his door, and then softly went out into the yard. The moon had risen, for the brightness of the stars was paled, and though no direct rays shone into the walled enclosure, the dusk was dispersed by the toneless luminosity of the sky, and he had no need of a lamp. He drew the lid off the coffin and folded back the tattered cerements which Madden had replaced over the body. He had thought that those lower vertebrae of which he was determined to possess himself would be easily detached, so far perished were the muscle and cartilage which held them together, but they cohered as if they had been clamped, and it required the utmost force of his powerful fingers to snap the spine, and as he did so the severed bones cracked as with the noise of a pistol shot. But there was no sign that anyone in the house had heard it, there came no sound of steps, nor lights in the windows. One more fracture was needed, and then the relic was his. Before he re-placed the ragged cloths he looked again at the stained fleshless bones. Shadow dwelt in the empty eye sockets, as if black sunken eyes still lay there, fixedly regarding him; the lipless mouth snarled and grimaced. Even as he looked some change came over its aspect, and for one brief moment he fancied that there lay staring up at him the face of a great brown ape. But instantly that illusion vanished, and replacing the lid, he went back to his room.

The mummy case was reinterred next day, and two evenings after Morris left Luxor by the night train for Cairo, to join a homeward-bound P. & O. at Port Said. There were some hours to spare before his ship sailed, and having deposited his luggage, including a locked leather despatch case, on board, he lunched at the Café Twefik near the quay. There was a garden in front of it with palm trees and trellises gaily clad in bougainvilleas; a low wooden rail separated it from the street, and Morris had a table close to this. As he ate he watched the polychromatic pageant of Eastern life passing by: there were Egyptian officials in broadcloth frock coats and red fezzes; barefoot splay-toed fellahin in blue gabardines; veiled women in white making stealthy eyes at passersby; half-naked guttersnipe, one with a sprig of scarlet hibiscus behind his ear; travelers from India with solar topees and an air of aloof British superiority; disheveled sons of the Prophet in green turbans; a stately sheik in a white burnous; French painted ladies of a professional class with lace-rimmed parasols and provocative glances; a wild-eyed dervish in an accordion-pleated skirt, chewing betel nut and slightly foaming at the mouth. A Greek bootblack with box adorned with brass plaques tapped his brushes on it to encourage customers, an Egyptian girl squatted in the gutter beside a gramophone, steamers passing into the Canal hooted on their sirens.

Then at the edge of the pavement there sauntered by a young Italian harnessed to a barrel organ. With one hand he ground out a popular air by Verdi; in the other he held out a tin can for the tributes of music lovers. A small monkey in a yellow jacket, tethered to his wrist, sat on the top of his instrument. The musician had come opposite the table where Morris sat; Morris liked the gay tinkling tune, and feeling in his pocket for a piaster, he beckoned to him. The boy grinned and stepped up to the rail.

Then suddenly the melancholy-eyed monkey leaped from its place on the organ and sprang onto the table by which Morris sat. It alighted there, chattering with rage in a crash of broken glass. A flower vase was upset, a plate clattered on to the floor. Morris's coffee cup discharged its black contents on the tablecloth. Next moment the Italian had twitched the frenzied little beast back to him, and it fell head downward on the pavement. A shrill hubbub arose, the waiter at Morris's table hurried up with voluble execrations, a policeman kicked out at the monkey as it lay on the ground, the barrel organ tottered and crashed on the roadway. Then all subsided again, and the Italian boy picked up the little body from the pavement. He held it out in his hands to Morris.

"E morto," he said.

"Serve it right, too," retorted Morris. "Why did it fly at me like that?"

He traveled back to London by long sea, and day after day that tragic little incident, in which he had had no responsible part, began to make a sort of coloring matter in his mind during those hours of lazy leisure on shipboard, when a man gives about an equal inattention to the book he reads and to what passes round him. Sometimes if the shadow of a sea gull overhead slid across the deck toward him, there leaped into his brain, before his eyes could reassure him, the ludicrous fancy that this shadow was a monkey springing at him. One day they ran into a gale from the west; there was a crash of glass at his elbow as a sudden lurch of the ship upset a laden steward, and Morris jumped from his seat thinking that a monkey had leaped onto his table again. There was a cinematograph show in the saloon one evening, in which some naturalist exhibited the films he had taken of wild life in Indian jungles; when he put on the screen the picture of a company of monkeys swinging their way through the trees, Morris involuntarily clutched the sides of his chair in hideous panic that lasted but a fraction of a second, until he recalled to himself that he was only looking at a film in the saloon of a steamer passing up the coast of Portugal. He came sleepy into his cabin one night and saw some animal crouching by the locked leather despatch case. His breath caught in his throat before he perceived that this was a friendly cat which rose with gleaming eyes and arched its back. . . .

These fantastic unreasonable alarms were disquieting. He had as yet no repetition of the hallucination that he saw a monkey, but some deep-buried "idea," to cure which he had taken two months' holiday, was still unpurged from his mind. He must consult Robert Angus again when he got home, and seek further advice. Probably that incident at Port Said had rekindled the obscure trouble, and there was this added to it, that he knew he was now frightened of real monkeys; there was terror sprouting in the dark of his soul. But as for it having any connection with his pilfered treasure, so rank and childish a superstition deserved only the ridicule he gave it. Often he unlocked his leather case and sat poring over that miracle of surgery which made practical again long-forgotten dexterities.

But it was good to be back in England. For the last three days of the voyage no menace had flashed out on him from the unknown dusks, and surely he had been disquieting himself in vain. There was a light mist lying over Regent's Park on this warm March evening, and a drizzle of rain was falling. He made an appointment for the next morning with the specialist, he telephoned to the hospital that he had returned and hoped to resume work at once. He dined in very good spirits, talking to his manservant, and, as subsequently came out, he showed him his treasured bones, telling him that he had taken the relic from a mummy which he had seen unwrapped and that he meant to lecture on it. When he went up to bed, he carried the leather case with him. Bed was comfortable after the ship's berth, and through his open window came the soft hissing of the rain onto the shrubs outside.

His servant slept in the room immediately over his. A little before dawn he woke with a start, roused by horrible cries from somewhere close at hand. Then came words yelled out in a voice that he knew:

"Help! Help!" it cried. "Oh my god, my god! Ahh—" and it rose to a scream again.

The man hurried down and clicked on the light in his master's room as he entered. The cries had ceased; only a low moaning came from the bed. A huge ape with busy hands was bending over it; then taking up the body that lay there by the neck and the hips, he bent it backward and it cracked like a dry stick. Then it tore open the leather case that was on a table by the bedside, and with something that gleamed white in its dripping fingers, it shambled to the window and disappeared.

A doctor arrived within half an hour, but too late. Handfuls of hair with flaps of skins attached had been torn from the head of the murdered man, both eyes were scooped out of their sockets, the right thumb had been plucked off the hand, and the back was broken across the lower vertebrae.

Nothing has since come to light which could rationally explain the tragedy. No large ape had escaped from the neighboring Zoological Gardens, or, as far ass could be ascertained, from elsewhere; nor was the monstrous visitor of that night ever seen again. Morris's servant had only had the briefest sight of it, and his description of it at the inquest did not tally with that of any known simian type. And the sequel was even more mysterious, for Madden, returning to England at the close of the season in Egypt, had asked Morris's servant exactly what it was that his master had shown him the evening before as having been taken by him from a mummy which he had seen unwrapped, and had got from him a sufficiently conclusive account of it. Next autumn he continued his excavations in the cemetery at Gurnah, and he disinterred once more the mummy case of A-pen-ara and opened it. But the spinal vertebrae were all in place and complete: one had round it the silver clip which Morris had hailed as a unique achievement in surgery.

Actor-playwright SCOTT PARSON here makes his debut as a short-story writer. Mr. Parson has extensive New York and regional-theatre acting credits, and his playscript Roombuddies *was a finalist for the 1987 Forest A. Robert Playwriting Award at Northern Michigan University. He lives in New York City.*

ASLEEP ON THE JOB

by Scott Parson

Just after midnight, under the amber lights of the school parking lot, Dell Ludy sat in his road-grimed Chevy. After turning off the engine, he checked his watch. He should've been inside the main library, at the guards' station, some twenty minutes ago. As one of the two men on night security, he was responsible for getting briefed on new exhibits, new floor plans. Dr. Diffley had asked him to come in early on account of the Egyptian arrangement.

He fumed at the low, scattered, sand-toned buildings of South Central Arizona Junior College, and its junior-college creeps looking down their noses sharpened by scorn. All those well-schooled snobs and book brats made his jaw ache with anger. Maybe it was time again to move, to point the Chevy at the nearest, longest piece of asphalt and go.

Eyes closed, listening to the dashboard radio, he was back on the corner stool, near the jukebox, at the Gila River Inn, polishing off another payday. The Mexican girls dancing. Indians, off the nearby reservation, shooting pool for beers.

So he was late. Nothing he could do. But he oughta have some excuse. Something good. Engine trouble? Maybe an accident on the highway? No, engine trouble was more believable. He sipped vodka from a pint he kept buried among loose shotgun shells in the glove box. Sipping made it last. Dr. Diffley, the curator of the endless exhibits, was easily disgusted by the smell of alcohol breath. Dell screwed the cap back on.

But what harm could Diffley do anyway? Blow the whistle on him? Go whining to Buster Sweeney, the other security guard? Dell slapped the glove box closed and grabbed his uniform cap. Then he slid out of the car and locked the door.

He paused at the little marquee that announced the treasures of Egypt, giving credit to some state and national cultural exchange.

Using his keys, he entered the main library. He passed the checkout desks and the information kiosks, then stopped at the double glass doors leading to the large utilitarian area, a chameleon room which—at the whim and budget of a progressive state institution—became an art gallery, a small music auditorium, or a museum wing.

Dead trees for books and, on the other side of the doors, dead Egyptians and tomb paintings. It all made Dell itchy to pack up and move. It hadn't taken much to wear the excitement off this part of the country. Too many practical jokes, too many unwelcome passes at the jock-teasing coeds, got him sentenced to midnight shift. A sentence to silence, Dell thought, that the old guy, Buster, actually likes. Dr. Diffley doesn't have the guts to go ahead and fire me, Dell continued to brood, relishing the arithmetic of an old score ripe for revenge. Maybe one really great joke. Give Diffley a heart attack. Nothing fatal. Something to remember the name Dell Ludy by. *Then* he'd split. Maybe someplace cooler. Oregon. He was sick of the desert.

Pushing through the door, Dell saw that the multipurpose room had once more been transformed. This time, the high fabric panels had been stored away, the floor filled with the display of ancient objects, sitting in pools of dim light. The center of the room was taken up with a dais of light gray carpeting, upon which were two gleaming granite sarcophagi, the lids propped open by inset steel rods. A third sarcophagus was made of lustrous wood, painted with scenes of Egyptian daily life and cultish visions of heaven and hell. The huge artifacts were laid in a circle, allowing visitors, held at bay by velvet ropes, to peer into the coffins, as they walked the circumference of the dais. Each sarcophagus had a sheet of Plexiglas bolted down over the opening. As Dell walked around, back to the guards' station, he could see by the mirrors angled against the lid of the sarcophagi, the gilt and painted anthropoid coffins laid within. However, in the wooden sarcophagus, clearly visible, was the mummified corpse. Dell paused, never having seen an actual decayed cadaver. Flower-decked, cosmetic-counter death was the closest he'd come, the sleeping remains of relatives.

He edged against the rope, closer, stretching, and looked into the face of the corpse. Its features showed clearly through the nearly transparent strips of fabric. Dell could see by the low security lights the arms lashed to the sides of the body, hipbones protruding, defining where viscera had once been. And the face. Darkened, papery, stretched into a groaning mask. The lids of the eyes bulged, straining to see in a once lightless tomb.

"Here." Dr. Diffley handed the watch clock to Dell. The black strapped object startled him. "Buster will handle the video board. You can walk the clock."

"I had engine trouble—"

"Mr. Ludy, I need someone reliable. I asked you to come in a little early."

"Hey, I can't help if I got engine—"

"It's okay, Dr. Diffley. We can still split the watch." Buster spoke up from the video board at the guards' station.

"He'll relieve you for breaks only," Dr. Diffley said back into the shadowy alcove. He turned again to Dell. "Walking is not sleeping."

As Dell chilled over in anger, he noticed how, in the distorted fluorescence, Dr. Diffley resembled the dusty stiff in the box. He wanted to stub out those bulging eyes. Or . . . maybe hand him that heart attack. Nothing fatal. Just some playful bon voyage gift to remember Dell Ludy by.

"I could use a regular stretch—" Buster was still peacemaker, stepping into a familiar breach.

"Only for your breaks." Dr. Diffley backed away from Dell's peevish menace and disappeared silently through the glass doors.

Only when he was sure the curator was gone did Dell grouse out loud. "Walking ain't sleeping. You hear that? He stuck me for no good reason. Me and you always split the watch."

"It was tough getting this all together, making it all fit in here."

"Walking ain't sleeping. Did he tell you I was sleeping? How's he know?"

"A lot of things going wrong—"

"Then let *him* walk all night. Baby-sit some dead rags."

"These ain't dead rags. Think of 'em as time travelers. Nearly three thousand years old." Buster didn't want Dell adding hours to the night in a stew of injustice.

"It looks like an old gunnysack. A little old gunnysack."

"That's his job—being small. Don't you ever read about the stuff they bring in here?"

Dell didn't mind Buster so much. But he thought the old geez could be a pest. Jawing off about the useless information he'd picked up around here. Like this mummy.

"Small is what you need," Buster said, patting the glass cover, "if you're robbing tombs for a living." Dell looked up. The morbid criminality reached Dell, which Buster took for genuine interest. "This guy used to dig his way on his belly through these narrow little tunnels, grab what he could carry, and skinny out the way he come. Until he got caught, that is."

"Caught." Even ages past, people couldn't leave you alone.

"Well, he was a tomb robber. Priests took a dim view of tomb robbing. Bad for the afterlife."

"He got caught, so they wrapped him up and buried him?"

"Kinda like. Maybe they killed him first."

"Like, alive, and being wrapped up, and then nailed into the box?" The malicious torment tantalized Dell.

"Probably not. It took days to wrap somebody. Chant the spells, mix up the resins. See these paintings on the side here? They show how they caught him and made an example of him." Dell actually stooped to look where Buster pointed. "Also, hieroglyphs here call on him being a talisman against other tomb robbers. See this strip right here?" He pointed out a narrow length of pictograms. "It says: *I am he, called out, now servant of the tomb, Amenupher.* This writing here binds him for all eternity. Say, Dell, that's a job for you, hey? Night watchman for a tomb? Then if they ask if you were asleep on the job, you could snap to, and say, 'Yes, sir. All night, sir.' " But Dell, recalling Diffley's accusation, didn't laugh with Buster. "Yep, still working for the rich folks, after all these years."

"Those two?" Dell asked, indicating the stone sarcophagi.

"Yeah. They're a set." Maybe he was dispelling the moodiness. "Dr. Diffley said they had the devil's own time getting them on schedule—"

"They wrap you up, kill you, and still expect you to work for some rich guy—is that their idea of hell or something?"

"Oh, no. He's doing all right. For a mummy. Look at all the stuff. The gold and jewelry. Rich stuff. That's their idea of heaven. And it's not like he's stuck, really. He can go anywheres he wants, like a bird. That's what afterlife was to them. Flying around the world. That's their soul. A bird with a human face. Like this.'' Buster pointed to wooden panels covered in faded colors: ancient ideas of idyllic life, of heavens and the distant alternatives of hell. And in motion, between the heavens and the Nile-fed earth, great soaring birds, with almond-eyed faces of handsome men and beautiful women. ''He'd just have to return to this body when the sun came up.''

''Don't even look real. That petrified Indian at Posey's Roadside Reservation Museum looks realer.''

''Posey carved that thing outta wood. These are the gen-yoo-wine article.''

The burden of the rich man's curse on the linen-wrapped face seemed to stir the muscles of recognition in Dell, enticing him into admitting Amenupher into his solitary brotherhood dedicated to repining and repaying injustice. ''So—is it a curse, like?'' An absurd idea of supernatural justice tickled at Dell. ''Like Posey's Indian?''

''You don't believe in Posey's curse, do ya?''

''I don't say I believe nothin'. I'm just asking if it's a curse on him.''

''I guess it's a curse. Having to guard his master forever.'' Buster patted a detailed painting of bare maidens who were serving a reclining male with platters of stylized foods. ''But I'd like to have a slice or two of his curse on *my* plate.''

''Maybe he'd rather kill a few beers at the Gila River Inn.''

''You could try reading the sacred symbols here. Play a few spooky tunes. Activate his active ingredients and you might have a walking, talking Egyptian mummy shuffling around in his house shoes.'' They laughed, and Buster was glad to be shaking Dell loose from the calcified interest in his agenda of wrongs.

''We could run him out to the reservation. Indians believe in stuff like that. They'd swear he walked in.'' Buster laughed a little too generously. ''We could sit him next to the water cooler in Diffley's office,'' Dell continued. ''We could say he was just looking for a drink—a big drink.'' Buster pushed the puff of laughter, the humor evaporating. ''*Or* we could stick him behind the wheel of Diffley's car and shove it out into the sand. Hey, he was just trying to drive home to Egypt.''

Suddenly Buster was no longer laughing. Dell, he realized now, was simply working out his malicious menu, and he wanted no part of such meanness of spirit. ''Look, Dell—'' he began.

''You believe there's such a thing as mummy curses?'' Dell's invidiously small mind began tinkering with the mechanics of revenge.

"Nah. I'm a Baptist."

"You think Diffley believes in 'em?"

Disappointed, Buster resumed his seniority. "Dr. Diffley ain't gonna believe some three-thousand-year-old mummy got a itch to drive his car. He'll know somebody—" But Dell wasn't listening to him. "Man, you got a vacuum up there," he said, tapping his forehead. "Just anything'll rush in to fill it." He turned, with a shrug, and went back to the monitors.

"Hey, it's not like *I* believe anything."

But Buster only shook his head. Picking up the clipboard, he gestured Dell to follow. "Come on. Let's go over the list."

"I know how to walk the circuit." Dell clunked the vinyl-clad security clock on the floor.

"You got to keep an eye on the AC, too."

"Get maintenance."

"I'm not kidding. Check the ducts outside, for gophers or jackrabbits crawling in to nest or die."

"The ducts ain't on the circuit."

"We got to make sure there's plenty of fresh air. Some of the powders or spices in these mummies make you go blind, or something. Give you headaches. Just watch the air."

In response, Dell whirled around and clomped through the gallery, irritation heavy in his shoes. Outside, he leaned against the building, staring out between the walls, to the desert beyond. A sound of unhurried wings came and receded. Owls, thought Dell, looking for kangaroo rats.

He'd decided to grab one of the mummies, sell it to Posey as an ancient Indian chief. That way he'd be having it back on Diffley, on the school, the jock-teasers. And he'd make a few bucks to get him down the road.

Of course he'd have to scram, he thought, maybe to Oregon finally. Another name change. Another job, but next time one with a lot less responsibility, people always on his back.

In the maintenance shed, behind the large air-conditioning units, Dell picked up a clear plastic sheet to cover the mummified corpse. Up at Posey's he might even pretend he was Diffley. But to make that work, he'd have to wear his sport coat. Diffley would be years living it down. They might even fire him. The complex scheme amused Dell. Into his pocket went several socket wrenches. He'd have to wait until Buster took his dinner break at four A.M.

* * *

Just at four, Dell tucked the plastic sheet down into his uniform shirt, and he went in to the gallery to relieve Buster. Walking past the dais, past the three time travelers, resting comfortably, Dell checked the line of sight with the guards' station. Amenupher's sarcophagus was hidden from direct view. And the cameras were set at the wrong angle to see down into the coffin. Dell smiled. He'd be long gone down the interstate before anyone wised up.

"Ol' Amenupher's asleep on the job," said Dell, taking Buster's place at the video board.

Buster merely grunted a suggestion of a laugh at Dell. He'd just as soon leave Dell to the venial little miseries that clogged his imagination. Buster felt sorry for Dell, but he was glad to be away from him for a whole thirty minutes. He gathered his things and, with a nod, departed by the side exit.

With a guilty glance about, Dell left the monitors and hurried to Amenupher's sarcophagus. After laying out the plastic on the floor, he found one of the wrenches to fit the black bolts and began twisting them out. He tucked the last of the bolts in his pocket and lifted the sheet of Plexiglas. He was assaulted by the odor of languid decay. The unpleasant aroma and Dell's imagination caused his rising gorge, hard-swallowed away.

Actually reaching into the box wasn't as revolting, and the corpse lighter than he'd been prepared for. Awkward, mostly. He struggled to get Amenupher's remains up where he could cradle them out and down onto the plastic sheet. Once the body was laid out, Dell shivered involuntarily, jerked, and dusted at the places on his clothes where the corpse had shed its tattery bits of fabric. Three swift folds and a flip of the corpse had it tucked into a convenient package.

Still certain of secrecy, Dell toted the bundle to his car. Anxious fumbling with the keys set his heart to racing, the weight of night and starlessness carrying an edge of fear. But after he got the door open he relaxed, deriding himself for his skittishness. Death wasn't anything to be scared of.

Striding, slowing, and then striding again, he got back to the video board with less time to spare then he'd have liked. He was still chuffing deeply when Buster returned by the side door.

As he pulled the door shut, there sounded, to Dell, that unhurried flap of wings he'd caught earlier on his rounds.

"Buster, you let that owl in."

"What owl?" he asked, figuring Dell was on to another joke.

"You let some bird in here," Dell griped. He was afraid Buster would make him get the ladder to give chase, delaying his head start. Or worse, that he would discover the theft.

"I didn't hear no bird." Buster looked at him, waiting for the punch line. But Dell was listening as the flapping swirled and receded. "Leave it for maintenance." Buster just wanted Dell to continue walking.

Dell edged away before Buster changed his mind and heard the intruder. Looking back, he watched Buster dial through the cameras. He registered nothing out of place when he looked across at Dell, waving him off. Dell, obliging, left.

With the exhilaration of temerity, he tossed the watch clock in the grass, flipped the wrenches on the front seat of the car, and slid behind the steering wheel. He ground the ignition and roared off, the punctured muffler throbbing. Leaving the pools of mercury-halogen light, he turned onto the access road that led to Interstate 10. In the distance ahead, he could see the lights along the highway, the exit signs lit against the night.

He could also hear that persistent owl, so close and loud, over the drone of the belching muffler. He glanced from the mirror to the road, and out of the headlights the bird slapped against his windshield at his face. Larger than any owl, an eagle almost. Dell ducked, pulling the wheel to the left. The car shimmied to a stop. Swearing and straightening the wheel, he continued, more slowly.

Once more the beating wings, the whisk of feathers cutting air. His heart hammering deep in the silence—then there slammed at the back window the indistinct figure of the bird, punishing the glass, flailing about for entry. Then it was at the side, increasing its furious blasts, hurling itself against the windows.

Dell, cranking madly, shut the window on his left as this avian curiosity slammed suicidally into his view, a pale white face, no beak, and gaping holes for eyes and mouth. Terror written on the face of the bird, features of almost human expression. Dell recoiled backward.

Being afraid made him angry. He reached over onto the floor of the backseat, unracking the shotgun. He eased open the door, listening for the wings, and stepped out a little way from the car, trying to hear over the engine. But there was now only silence. In the distance, the lights of the college. Beyond to his right, the glowing chain of light and the highway.

And then constriction. His chest was gripped in two huge,

clasping hands. Dark without stars or moon. He threw himself to the ground. But now there was a light. Small, flickering. Yards away. He had to crawl. He couldn't breathe. He was closed in. His toes doing the work to inch him along. He couldn't bring his arms up from his sides to pull himself forward. Palms inch-worming through a narrow rock passage, angling downward, but he couldn't make himself slide. He had to kick along with his toes. If only he could take more air into his strangled lungs.

And then he could. His head swam, eyes lifted out of a swampy murk of shadow and ill-light. Painfully, he rolled over. Curled on his side, he could see the taillights of his car some distance behind him. His head continued to clear. He sat up, then crawled toward the car. Supporting himself on the fender, he drew himself up. He no longer had his shotgun. Looking back out into the sandy ditch from which he'd crawled, he decided to leave it. He got back into the car and locked the doors.

Once more in the familiar, he was confident enough to lean over the backseat and look into the face of his cargo—wrapped as he'd left him. Dell reached over and gave Amenupher a shake, to see if after all these years, he was faking. Just to be certain.

He was going to get rid of this lump. No joke, no great ideas. He'd just drive up to his trailer, pack, and then dump this little tomb robber at Posey's. If Posey'd give him money for the stiff, fine. If not, then the wooden Indian would have himself a petrified partner free of charge.

As Dell started down the road, the stench seemed greater. He figured maybe he wouldn't even try waking Posey. Just dump the corpse on his doorstep and drive off. His heart began its tempest throb once more, a heat and burning light in his head. He lost the lights of the highway ahead. The glowing dots danced about him as he spun the steering wheel frantically to keep the car pointed at the retreating lights.

Through the haze and pain, Dell could not tell if he was any closer to the highway. Was he farther? He jammed the gear into park, without braking, coming to a bucking stop, and throwing himself out of the car. He grasped his head.

Again the pug-faced bird swooped on him, wings flashing around his face. He slapped back, windmilling his arms to no effect. He could only scramble under the car.

The chain of lights ahead were now one, small and flickering. Far away, through that narrow opening. Purpose swept over Dell. The light. If he could only get to the light. He'd have a way out. But out where? He had to crawl. Again the constriction of chest muscle, ribs scraping together. And the light ahead. It seemed closer, or he closer to it. But he had to squirm and wriggle, his arms pinioned by the stone walls that he could feel at his fingertips, now sanding knuckles raw. Where was up? Was he on his back? If he could just make it to the light. With each undulation, abraded by rock, it was nearer, and nearer still. But the air was gone. No air.

In the gallery, Buster sat, angry and concerned. Dell had not relieved him at six A.M., and now it was nearly eight.

Morning sun haloed Dr. Diffley's arrival through the library to the security alcove, where he greeted Buster.

Buster nodded in reply, certain he could not alibi Dell again.

"Seems stuffy in here. Does it to you?" Dr. Diffley asked, gesturing Buster to follow him into the main area.

"Some."

"Did Dell keep an eye on the air conditioner, like I asked?" To which Buster only shrugged, postponing confession.

With a sigh, Dr. Diffley began waving a hand about, searching for dead air.

"If it's not one thing, it's another. After this, only local history and Indian artists. I make a deal with the exhibition director for just the stone sarcophagi and a few items. We sign the papers, and he has a stroke. I go ahead and hire a truck, on my anemic budget, and the driver jams up under the only squatty overpass between here and Idaho." He'd located the faulty duct. With a versatile pocketknife he began unscrewing the grill. "The insurance company and I tremble. They finally send the entire exhibit, we're squeezed to the walls, and *now*, no AC. This just isn't my semester."

As the last screw came loose, the grill was pushed from Diffley's hands. Dell's head lolled backward onto the curator—who leaped away from that face, strained, mouth wide, teeth attempting to bite air into starved lungs. Dell's features were shaded by suffocation, constricted by the ducting, impossibly narrow for his frame sausaged into the conduit.

Dr. Diffley made gurgling, dry heaving sounds, processing this horrid information.

Buster, no less affected, divined an absurd motive, a simple ghastly practical joke, somehow gone nightmarishly wrong. He backed away, casting about the gallery for what could be missing, for what Dell might have planned—

The tomb robber! To be sported about at Dr. Diffley's expense. He threw himself at the wooden sarcophagus and looked directly into the box.

But Amenupher was there, resting comfortably. Asleep on the job.

SHARYN McCRUMB *is the celebrated author of the Elizabeth MacPherson comedy-mystery series, beginning with* Sick of Shadows *and continuing through (to date)* The Windsor Knot. *In 1988 her nonseries novel,* Bimbos of the Death Sun, *won the Edgar Allan Poe Award for best original paperback mystery.*

REMAINS TO BE SEEN

by Sharyn McCrumb

When the two elderly ladies from the Warm Hearth Community for Seniors saw the mummy on the top shelf of the army surplus store, one of them gasped, "Where did it come from?" The other one opened her purse and said, "How much?"

George Carr, the owner of the Craig Springs Army Surplus Store, decided to answer the first question before he worried about the second.

Every Thursday the van from Warm Hearth brought a group of its sprier residents on a shopping trip downtown. There wasn't much that anyone actually needed to buy—toothpaste, maybe, or the new *Cosmopolitan*—but they enjoyed the outing, and the chance to exercise and window-shop at the same time. George Carr was used to seeing some of the old gentlemen in his establishment. The World War II veterans loved to come in and reminisce about the old days, using his merchandise as visual aids for their war yarns. This was the first time, though, that any of the Warm Hearth ladies had paid him a visit. George thought it was strange that they had.

"We were tired of the usual round of drugstores and dress shops," said the dumpy one in the black dress.

Since he had just been wondering that very thing, George laughed and said, "You read my mind!"

73

She turned triumphantly to her friend. "There, Lucille! I told you I'd been working on it. A dab of chicken blood behind each earlobe, and that Latin phrase I learned."

Lucille Beaumont, whose silver hair did not seem to go with her sharp black eyes and her hawkbill nose, patted her friend's arm. "Yes, Clutie. You've told me," she said in patient, but repressive tones. "Wouldn't you like to look around?"

Clutie Campbell shook her head. She looked up at the mummy. "You were going to tell us about him."

"Oh, Herman. Don't know that that's his real name, of course. But that's what we call him. We've had him for the last twenty years."

The ladies turned and stared at the glass-sided wooden coffin resting on the top shelf of the far wall. Below it was a tangled assortment of knapsacks and canteens, and a hand-lettered sign that said: YOUR CHOICE—$5. Just visible through the dusty glass was the body of a man: a wrinkled, leathery face poking out from the folds of a tatty-looking black suit that seemed rather large for its owner.

"Is it real?" asked Lucille Beaumont, sounding as if she rather hoped *not*.

George Carr nodded. He was accustomed to the questions. Every time a stranger visited the store, the same conversation took place: *He real? How'd you get him?*

"How'd you get him?" asked Clutie Campbell.

George started his well-rehearsed tale at the beginning. "In the early Twenties, a traveling carnival came here to Greene County. You know how it was: they'd pitch a tent in the old fairgrounds, set up the booths and the rides and the girlie shows, and three days later they'd be gone, with the pocket money of every kid in town."

Clutie nodded impatiently. "So—what was *he*? A sideshow exhibit?"

"No. Herman up there was a working member of the carnival. I think he was one of the construction crew, setting up the booths and all."

"A roustabout," murmured Lucille, but she was shushed into silence by Clutie, who clearly did not want the conversation to be derailed into a discussion of vocabulary. In her youth Lucille had been in show business, and she was entirely too fond of showing off her expertise by correcting people's speech and by critiquing the performances on *Days of Our Lives*. Clutie, for one, was sick of it.

George Carr, well into his story by now, paid no attention to their bickering. "The way I heard it, Herman here died on the second night in town. I think maybe a beam knocked him in the head, or something. An accident, anyway." He looked a little nervously at the stiff, leathery figure on the high shelf. "I never checked. Anyhow, his body was sent to Culbertson's, the local funeral parlor. They got right to work embalming him, and they had him all ready for the funeral."

"I expect they provided the suit," said Clutie with an appraising glance upward.

"Culbertson's had him all ready for the funeral and drew up their bill for services—and they come to find out that the carnival had pulled up stakes and left town. Nobody claimed Herman, and nobody paid the mortuary."

Lucille Beaumont frowned. "Couldn't they have notified his next of kin?"

George Carr shrugged. "Didn't know who in Sam Hill he was. But Old Man Culbertson was firm on one point: no money, no funeral. So they kept him. As a floor model, you know. Showing what a good job they did at embalming. He was a curiosity around here when I was a kid. My pals and I used to love to go into Culbertson's to look at Herman."

"How did you get him?" Clutie wanted to know.

"Old Man Culbertson died back in '68, and the funeral home went out of business. So Herman here was auctioned off with the rest of the fixtures. I've had him here ever since."

Clutie pushed her gray bangs away from her glasses and peered up at the exhibit. "How much did you say he was?"

Her friend touched her arm. "Oh, Clutie, you know you don't—"

Clutie Campbell slid a credit card out of her pigskin wallet. "Can I put him on VISA?"

The Warm Hearth minivan had the usual fourteen passengers for the return trip to the retirement community. George Carr had agreed—after some negotiation—to deliver the purchase and to leave Herman in the tool shed behind Warm Hearth one hour after sunset. When he asked what the ladies wanted him for, Clutie had replied, "Religious reasons," in a tone that did not invite further discussion. In a way, it was true.

Lucille Beaumont had steered her friend to the back of the van, in hopes that Mr. Waldrop's snoring would drown out their ongoing discussion.

"You *cannot* purchase a corpse as a conversation piece!" Lucille whispered as the bus pulled away from the curb.

Clutie Campbell sniffed and directed her gaze out the window. "It is not a conversation piece. This is just what the organization needs. The book lists all kinds of spells that you can work with a deader."

"It's probably *illegal*!"

Clutie smiled vaguely. *"Do what thou wilt shalt be the whole of the law."*

Lucille shook her head. "I do wish you'd give this up, Clutie."

Her friend patted her broom-straw hair. "I think you ought to join us, Lucille. Emmie Walkenshaw thinks we're the oldest coven in the country."

"I am a Presbyterian!" hissed Lucille Beaumont between clenched teeth. "I *refuse* to join a group of Satanists!"

"Weren't Presbyterians once called *covenanters*?" asked Clutie in mock innocence. "I'd look into it if I were you, Lucille. There may be no conflict of interest after all." She smiled through a frosty silence for the duration of the ride.

Lucille Beaumont was so out of sorts that evening that she sat with the ancient Mrs. Hartnell at dinner, which was as close as you could come to eating alone at Warm Hearth. Annie Hartnell was fond of asking people, *"Did you have a nice life?"* And after that she pretty much ignored you until you went away. Usually people took pains to avoid her, but tonight Lucille decided that Mrs. Hartnell was the only company she was fit for.

Really, she thought, Clutie Campbell's Satanist business was getting out of hand. Clutie was a widowed schoolteacher who claimed that the routine of Warm Hearth bored her, and that the intellectual climate was nil. Her earlier attempts at culture—a poetry society and a debating team—had failed miserably, but the drama and secrecy of witchcraft had attracted a following. At first a group of folks had gone along with her because it made a nice change from square dancing and canasta, but now it was more than a game. The thirteen recruits had progressed from Ouija boards to table tapping to pentagrams and incantations. So far the staff was unaware of this diversion, and Lucille was determined not to be a snitch, but the coven was getting bolder (*sillier!* thought Lucille), and discovery seemed inevitable.

As she carried her dinner tray to the service hutch, Lucille could not resist a warning to the head witch. "Clutie," she said dramatically, not even bothering to lower her voice, "there is great danger in tampering with the forces of darkness!"

Just then Mrs. Hartnell was wheeled by in her chair, beaming and nodding at the table of Satanists. "Did you have a nice life?" she asked sweetly.

Tinker's Meadow was a quarter of a mile from the retirement community. It was bordered on three sides by piney woods and was fronted on the east by a little-used dirt road. High Priestess Clutie chose it for the ceremony for privacy—and because it was as far from the home as they could carry a mummy in a glass-fronted box.

A pale dime-sized moon shone on the long grass, and an autumn wind made the coven shiver. It was just after eight o'clock. Midnight would have been a better time for spells to work, but several folks had to be back by eleven to take medication, so they had to make do with the darkness, the full moon, and a real corpse.

Clutie wore a homemade Egyptian collar over her black evening gown, clumps of rings and bracelets, and a black pageboy wig reminiscent of Cher. But she was very dignified. She clutched her copy of *Ancient Spells & Rituals* with an air of solemn authority. At her direction, Mrs. Walkenshaw drew a pentagram on the ground (with chalk borrowed from the Warm Hearth billiard table). Mr. Waldrop and Mr. Junger took the mummy out of its shabby coffin and placed it faceup within the circle. There was a smell of mothballs from the vintage suit.

"He feels like the cover of a Bible," Mr. Junger whispered to Miss Fowler.

Clutie motioned for her followers to join hands and form a ring around the pentagram. She closed her eyes and threw back her head. "We are invoking the black angels with this once-living mortal—with this terrible sacrifice *from a gulf profound as that Serbonian bog Betwixt Damiata and Mount Casius old, Where armies whole have sunk; the parching air Burns frore, and cold performs the effect of fire.*" (The Warm Hearth's library copy of *Paradise Lost* had been missing for several months.)

"In exchange for our demonic offering, we ask for power—" Clutie clanked her bracelets and made her voice rise to a howl as she chanted a few Latin phrases from the magic book.

"Power!" murmured the coven members, swaying rhythmically as she chanted.

"I drop fresh blood upon this offering and command you, Demon, to reveal yourself unto your priestess!"

The circle began to writhe as the members turned and threaded their way to the left through the group, clasping each other's hand as they passed. This completed, they rejoined hands and paced solemnly to the right in one full rotation. *(Allemande left and circle right.)*

That was when the *thing* appeared at the edge of the woods. The coven members with better hearing had claimed to hear a snarl or a roar a few seconds before the apparition, but all eyes turned almost simultaneously to the dark clearing where a white shape had materialized. It was no more than a flash in the blackness, but suddenly—where its mouth ought to be—a long tongue of flames billowed forth like a fiery banner. Slowly, deliberately it began to move forward.

The thirteen members of the Warm Hearth coven thought they were screaming, "The Demon!" but in fact the sound came out more like "Aarggh!" Everybody got the message, though. In less time than you could say *amen*, the senior-citizen Satanists had dropped hands and were sprinting toward the road. Clutie Campbell, her black drapery hitched up around her knees, was leading the pack. As they headed off in the direction of the retirement community, several members paused for breath and announced their intention of disbanding the coven. Mrs. Walkenshaw recited the Lord's Prayer as one long word, refusing to look back. Clutie Campbell wondered if she ought to wait a week before she suggested a synchronized swimming team.

The book of magic and the tatty roustabout mummy lay forgotten in the dirt of Tinker's Meadow.

When the shouts of the departing coven had faded into the autumn night, a solitary figure stepped out of the woods and walked toward the abandoned pentagram. Its white robe rustled in the long grass as it stopped to retrieve a long wooden-handled implement from the ground. The mummy's leathery face remained impassive in the moonlight.

"Well, that's that," said Lucille Beaumont softly as she looked down at the erstwhile sacrifice. "Of course, you probably didn't know what was happening to you, but it was downright disrespectful, and I had to put a stop to it. Whoever you are, you deserve a proper funeral. All I can manage is a prayer and a few old hymns, though. I hope that will do."

Lucille rolled up the sleeves of her white Presbyterian choir robe and picked up the Warm Hearth gardener's shovel. "You deserve to get buried, too,'' she told the mummy. ''I was in a carnival when I was young, just like you, and us carnies have to stick together.'' Lucille Beaumont's second husband had been the fire-eater, and he'd taught her the tricks of his trade. Although she had much preferred being the fortune-teller, she never forgot her lessons in pyrotechnics. She had had to improvise the fire-eating materials for the Tinker's Meadow performance, but she had apparently been a most convincing demon. She smiled to herself, remembering the Satanists' screaming retreat. Good thing there weren't any heart patients in the coven.

''I reckon a lifetime in show business is long enough,'' she remarked. ''A person ought to be allowed to retire. And you sure don't want to keep on in show business when you're dead, do you, mister?''

Gently, but matter-of-factly, she placed the mummy back in his glass-fronted box, and she said a simple prayer for the repose of both body and soul. When that was done, she sank the shovel deep into the clay of Tinker's Meadow to begin the makeshift grave. As the spadefuls of earth plopped softly on the grass, Lucille Beaumont sang her second husband's favorite hymn— ''Give Me Oil in My Lamp, Keep Me Burning''—in a voice like a rusting calliope.

SEABURY QUINN (1889–1969) is best known as the creator of Jules de Grandin, perhaps the most famous occult detective in literary history. A mainstay of the magazine Weird Tales, *Quinn had well over one hundred stories published in its pages, some ninety of them featuring Jules de Grandin.*

THE MAN IN CRESCENT TERRACE

by Seabury Quinn

"But this is most pleasant, *vraiment*," Jules de Grandin told me as we reached the corner where the black-and-orange sign announced a bus stop. "The *moteur*, he is a convenience. Yes. *Whiz—pouf!* He takes you where you wish to go all quickly, and *sifflement!* he brings you back all soon. But where there is no need for haste—*non*. It is that we grow soft and lazy substituting gasoline for walking muscle, Friend Trowbridge. Is it not better that we walk on such a lovely evening?"

The brief October dusk had deepened into dark as if a curtain had been drawn across the sky, and in the east a star sprang out and a cluster of little stars blinked after it. A little breeze came up and rustled faintly in the almost leafless maples, but it seemed to me a faint sound of uneasiness came from them, not the comfortable cradle song of evening, but a sort of restrained moaning.

And with the sibilation of the wind there came the sound of running footsteps, high heels pounding in a sharp staccato on the sidewalk with a drumminglike panic made audible. The diffused glow of a street lamp showed her to us as she ran, hurrying with the awkward, knock-kneed gait of a woman unused to sprinting, casting fearful looks across her shoulder each few steps, but never slackening her terror-goaded pace.

It was not until she was almost within touching-distance that she saw us and gave vent to a gasp of relief mingled with fright.

"Help!" she panted, then, almost fiercely, "run—run! He—it's coming. . . ."

"*Tenez*, who is it comes, mademoiselle?" de Grandin asked. "Tell us who it is annoys you. I shall take pleasure in tweaking his nose—"

"*Run*—run, you fool!" the girl broke in hysterically, clutching at my lapel as a drowning person might clutch at a floating plank. "If it catches me—" Her breathless words blurred out and the stiffness seemed to go from her knees as she slumped against me, flaccid as a rag doll.

I braced her slight weight in my arms, half turning as I did so, and felt the warm stickiness of fresh blood soak through my glove. "De Grandin," I exclaimed, "she's been hurt—bleeding—"

"*Hein?*" He deflected the sharp gaze which he had leveled down the darkened street. "What is it that you say—*mordieu*, but you have right, Friend Trowbridge! We must see to her—*hola, taxi, à moi, tout vite!*" He waved imperatively at the rattletrap cab that providentially emerged from the tree-arched tunnel of the street.

"Sorry, gents." The driver slowed but did not halt his vehicle. "I'm off duty an' got just enough gas to git back to the garage—"

"*Pardieu*, then you must reassume the duty right away, at once, immediately!" de Grandin broke in. "We are physicians and this lady has been injured. We must convey her to the surgery for treatment, and I have five—*non*, three—dollars to offer as an incentive—"

"I heard you the first time, chief," the cabby interrupted. "For five dollars it's a deal. Hop in. Where to?"

Our impromptu patient had not regained consciousness when we reached my house, and while de Grandin concluded fiscal arrangements with the chauffeur I carried her up the front steps and into the surgery. She could not have weighed a hundred pounds, for she was slightly, almost boyishly built, and the impression of boyishness was heightened by the way in which her flaxen blonde hair was cropped closely at back and sides and combed straight back from her forehead in short soft waves. Her costume added little to her weight. It was a dress of black watered silk consisting of a sleeveless blouse cut at the neckline in the Madame Chiang manner and a pleated skirt that barely reached her knees. She wore no hat, but semi-elbow-length gloves of black suede fabric were on her hands and her slim, small, unstockinged feet were shod with black suede sandals crisscrossed with straps of gold. If she had had a handbag it had been lost or thrown away in her panic-stricken flight.

"Ah—so, let us see what is to be done," de Grandin ordered as I laid my pretty burden on the examination table. Deftly he undid the row of tiny jet buttons that fastened the girl's blouse at the shoulder, and with a series of quick, gentle tweaks and twitches drew the garment over her head. She wore neither slip nor bandeau, only the briefest of sheer black-crêpe step-ins; we had only to turn her on her side to inspect her injury.

This was not very extensive, being an incised wound some four inches long beginning just beneath the right scapula and slanting toward the vertebral aponeurosis at an angle of about sixty degrees. At its commencement it was quite deep, striking through the derma to the subcutaneous tissue, but at termination it trailed off to a mere superficial skin wound. It was bleeding freely and its clean-cut edges gaped widely owing to the elasticity of the skin and the retraction of the fibrous tissue. "Hmm," de Grandin murmured as he bent above the wound. "From the cleanness of its lips this cut was evidently inflicted by a razor or a knife that had been honed to razorsharpness. Do not you agree, Friend Trowbridge?"

I looked across his shoulder and nodded.

"*Précisément*. And from the way it slants and from the fact it is so much deeper at commencement than at termination, one may assume the miscreant who inflicted it stole up behind her, hoping to take her by surprise, but struck a split second too late. The blow was probably directed with a slicing motion at her neck, but she was already in flight when her assailant struck. *Tiens*, as things are, she had luck with her, this little pretty poor one. A little deeper and the weapon might have struck into the rhomboideus, a little to the right, it might have sliced an artery. As it is—" He wiped the welling blood away, sponged the wound and surrounding epidermis with alcohol, and pinched the gaping lips of the incision together in perfect apposition, then laid a pad of gauze on the closed wound and secured it with a length of adhesive plaster. "Voilà." He looked up with an elfin grin. "She are almost good like new now I damn think, Friend Trowbridge. Her gown is still too wet with blood for wearing, but—"

He paused a moment, eyes narrowed in thought, then: "Excuse me one small, little second, if you please," he begged, and rushed from the surgery.

I could hear him rummaging about upstairs, and wondered what amazing notion might have taken possession of his active, unpredictable French brain, but before I had a chance to call to him he came back with a pleased smile on his lips and a Turkish towel from the linen closet draped across his arm. "Regard me, Friend Trowbridge," he ordered. "See what a fellow of infinite resource I am." He wrapped the soft, tufted fabric about the girl's slim torso, covering her from armpits to knees, and fastened the loose end of the towel with a pair of safety pins. "*Morbleu*, I think perhaps a brilliant couturier was lost when I decided to become a physician," he announced as he surveyed his handiwork. "Does she not look *très chic* in my creation? By damn it, I shall say she does!"

"Humph," I admitted, "she's adequately covered, if that's any satisfaction to you."

"I had expected more enthusiastic praise," he told me as he drew the corners of his mouth down, "but—*que voulez-vous?*—the dress designer like the prophet must expect to be unhonored in his own country. Yes." He nodded gloomily and lifted the girl from the table to an easy chair, taking care to turn her so her weight would not impinge upon her injured shoulder.

He passed a bottle of ammonium carbonate beneath her nostrils, and as the pungent fumes made her nose wrinkle in the beginnings of a sneeze and her pale lids fluttered faintly: "So, mademoiselle, you are all better now? But certainly. Drink this, if you will be so kind." He held a glass of brandy to her lips. "Ah, that is good, *n'est-ce-pas? Morbleu*, I think it is so good that I shall have a small dose of the same!"

"And now"—with small fists on his hips and arms akimbo he took his stand before her—"will you have the kindness to tell us all about it?"

She cowered back in the chair and we could see a pulse flutter in her throat. Her eyes were almost blank, but fear stared from them like a death's head leering from a window. "Who are—where am I?" she begged piteously. "Where is it? Did you see it?" As her fingers twisted and untwisted themselves in near hysteria then came in contact with the towel swathed round her. They seemed to feel it unbelievingly, as if they had an intelligence separate from the rest of her. Then she looked down, gave a startled, gasping cry, and leaped from the chair. "Where am

I?'' she demanded. "What has happened to me? Why am I dressed in—in this?''

De Grandin pressed her gently back in the chair. "One question and one answer at a time, if you please, mademoiselle. You are in the house of Dr. Samuel Trowbridge. This is he''—he bowed in my direction—"and I am Dr. Jules de Grandin. You have been injured, though not seriously, and that is why you were brought here when you swooned in the street. The garment you are wearing is fashioned from a bath towel. I am responsible for it, and thought it quite chic, though neither you nor Dr. Trowbridge seem to fancy it, which is a great pity and leaves your taste in dress open to question. You have it on because your gown was disfigured when you were hurt; also it is a little soiled at present. That can and will be remedied shortly.

"Now''—his little round blue eyes twinkled and he laughed reassuringly—"I have answered your questions. Will not you be so kind as to answer ours?''

Some of the fear went out of her eyes and she managed to contrive a little smile. People usually smiled back at de Grandin. "I guess I've been seeing too many horror films," she confessed. "I saw the operating table and the bandages and instruments, and smelled the medicines, then when I realized I was dressed in this, my first thought was that I'd been kidnapped and—''

De Grandin's shout of laughter drowned her half-ashamed confession. "*Mordieu*, you thought that you were in the house of Monsieur Dracula J. Frankenstein, and that the evil, mad surgeons were about to make a guinea pig or white rabbit of you, *n'est-ce-pas*, mademoiselle? I assure you that fear is quite groundless. Dr. Trowbridge is an eminently respectable practitioner, and while I have been accused of many things, human vivisection is not one of them.

"Some three-quarters of an hour ago Dr. Trowbridge and I stood at Colfax and Dorondo streets, waiting for an omnibus. We observed you coming toward us, running like Atalanta racing from the suitors, and obviously very much afraid. When you reached us, you cried out for us to run also, then swooned in Dr. Trowbridge's arms. It was then we saw that you had been injured. *Alors*, we did the proper thing. We bundled you into a taxi and brought you here for treatment. You know why we removed your dress, and why you wear my own so smart creation.

"That puts you in possession of the facts, mademoiselle. It is for you to tell us what transpired before we met. You may speak freely, for we are physicians, and anything you say will be held in strict confidence. Also, if we can, we shall be glad to help you.''

She gave him a small grateful smile. ''I think you've done a lot to help me already, sir. I am Edina Laurace and I live with my aunt, Mrs. Dorothy Van Artsdalen at 1840 Pennington Parkway. This afternoon I called on some friends living in Clinton Avenue and walked through Crescent Terrace to Dorondo Street to take a number-four bus. I was almost through the Terrace when—'' she stopped, and we could see the flutter of a little blue vein at the base of her throat as her heart action quickened— ''when I heard someone running.''

''*Parbleu*, another runner?'' murmured Jules de Grandin. Aloud he ordered: ''Proceed, if you please, mademoiselle.''

''Naturally, I looked around. It was getting dark, and I was all alone—''

''One understands. And then what was it that you saw?''

''A man was running toward me. Not exactly toward me, but in the same direction I was going. He was a poor-looking man; that is, his clothes were out of press and seemed too loose for him, and his shoes scuffed on the pavement as he ran—you know how a bum's shoes sound—as if they were about two sizes too large? He seemed almost out of breath and scared of something, for every few steps he'd glance back across his shoulder. Then I saw what he was running from, and started to run, too. It was—'' her hands went up to her eyes, as if to shut some frightful vision out, and she trembled as if a sudden draft of cold air had blown on her—''it was a mummy!''

''A *what*?'' I demanded.

''*Comment?*'' Jules de Grandin almost barked.

''All right,'' she answered as a faint flush strained her pale cheeks, ''tell me I'm crazy. I still say it was a mummy; one of those things you see in museums, you know. It was tall, almost six feet, and bone-thin. As far as I could make out it was about the color of a tan shoe and seemed to be entirely unclothed. It ran in a peculiar sort of way, not like a man, but sort o' jerkily, like a marionette moved by unseen wires; but it ran fast. The man behind me ran with all his might, but it kept gaining on him without seeming to exert itself at all.''

Her recitation seemed to recall her terror, for her breathing quickened as she spoke and she paused to swallow every few words. ''At first I thought the mummy had a cane in its hand, but as it came nearer I saw it was a stick about two—maybe three—feet long, tipped with a long, flat spearhead made of gold, or perhaps copper.

"You know how it is when you're frightened that way. You run for all you're worth, yet somehow you have to keep looking back. That's the way I was. I'd run a little way, then feel I *had* to look back. Maybe I couldn't quite convince myself it was a mummy. It was, all right, and it was gaining steadily on the man behind me.

"Just as I reached Dorondo Street I heard an awful cry. Not exactly a scream, and not quite a shout, but a sort of combination of the two, like *'ow-o-o-oh!'* and I looked back just in time to see the mummy slash the man with its spear. It didn't stab him. It chopped him with the edge of its weapon. That's when he yelled." She paused a moment and let her breath out in a long, quivering sigh. "He didn't fall; not right away. He sort o' staggered, stumbling over his own feet, or tripping over something that wasn't there, then reeled forward a few steps, with his arms spread out as if he reached for something to break his fall. Then he went down upon his face and lay there on the sidewalk perfectly still, with his arms and legs spread out like an X."

"And then?" de Grandin prompted softly as she paused again.

"Then the thing stood over him and began sticking him with its spear. It didn't move fast nor seem in any hurry; it just stood over him and stuck the spear into him again and again, like—like a woman testing a cake with a broom straw, if that means anything to you."

De Grandin nodded grimly. "It does, indeed, mademoiselle. And then?"

"Then I *did* start to run, and presently I saw it coming after me. I kept looking back, like I told you, and for a while I didn't see it; then all at once there it was, moving jerkily, and sort o' weaving back and forth across the sidewalk, almost as if it weren't quite sure which way I'd gone. That gave me an idea. I ran until I came to a dark spot in the road, the point between two street lamps where the light was faintest, and rushed across the street, running on tiptoes. Then I ran quietly as I could down the far side of the road, keeping to the shadows as much as possible. For a time I thought I'd shaken it, for when it came to where I'd crossed the street it seemed to pause and look about. Then it seemed to realize what I'd done and came across to my side. Three times I crossed the street, and each time I gained a few yards on it; but I was getting out of breath and knew I couldn't keep the race up much longer.

"Then I had another idea. From the way the creature ran it seemed to me it must be blind, or almost so, and followed me by sound more than sight. So next time I crossed the street, instead of running I hid behind a big tree. Sure enough, when the thing came over, it seemed at fault, and stood there, less than ten feet from me, turning round and round, pointing its spear first one way, then another, like a blind man feeling with his cane for some familiar object.

"It might have missed me altogether if I could have stayed stock-still, but when I got a close-up look at it—it was so terrible I couldn't keep a gasp of terror back. That did it. In an instant it was after me again, and I was dodging round and round the tree.

"You can't imagine how horrible it was. The thing was blind, all right. Once I got a good look at its face—its lips were like tanned leather and I could see the jagged line of its teeth where the dried-up mouth had come a little open, and both its eyes were tightly shut. But blind or not, it could hear me, and it was like a dreadful game of blind man's buff, I dodging back to keep the tree between us, then crouching for a sprint to the next tree and doubling and turning around that, and all the time that dreadful thing following, sometimes thrusting at me with the spear, sometimes chopping at me with it, but never hurrying. If it had rushed or sprung or jumped at me, it wouldn't have seemed half so terrifying. But it didn't. It just kept after me, seeming to know that sooner or later it would find me.

"I'd managed to get back my breath while we were dodging back and forth around the trees, and finally I made another break for freedom. That gave me a short respite, for when I started running this time I kept on the parking, and my feet made no noise on the short grass, but before I'd run a hundred feet I trod on a dried, curled-up leaf. It didn't make much noise, just the faintest crackling, but that was enough to betray me, and in another second the mummy was after me. D'ye remember that awful story in Grimms' Fairy Tales where the prince is captured by a giant, and manages to blind him, but finds that the charmed ring upon his finger forces him to keep calling, 'Here am I,' each time he eludes his pursuer? That's the way it was with me. The thing that followed me was blind, but any slightest sound was all it needed for direction, and no matter how still I tried to be I couldn't help making some small noise to betray my position.

"Twice more I halted to play blind man's buff with it around the streetside trees, and the last time it slashed me with its spear. I felt the cut like a switch on my shoulder, it didn't hurt so much as smart, but in a moment I could feel the blood run down my back and knew that I'd been wounded. Then I lost my head completely and rushed straight down the sidewalk, running for my life. That would have been the end of me had it not been for the cat."

"The cat, mademoiselle?" de Grandin asked.

"Yes, sir. It—the mummy—was about a hundred and fifty feet behind me, and gaining every step, when a big black cat came across the sidewalk. I don't know where it came from, but I hope that it has cream for dinner and two nice, fat mice for dessert every day for the rest of its life. You know how cats act sometimes when they see something coming at them—how they sort o' crouch down and stay still, as if they hope whatever it is that threatens 'em won't seem 'em if they don't move? That's the way this cat did—at first. But when the mummy was almost on it, it jumped up and arched its back, puffed out its tail, and made every hair along its spine stand straight up. Then it let out a miaul almost loud enough to wake the dead.

"That stopped the mummy in its tracks. You know how deceptive a caterwaul can be—how it rises and falls like a banshee's howl and seems to come from half a dozen places at once? I think that's what must have happened. The mummy was attuned to catch the slightest sound vibration, like a delicate radio instrument, but it couldn't seem to locate the exact place whence the cat's miaul came.

"I glanced back once, and if it hadn't been so horrible, it would have seemed ludicrously funny, that murderous blind mummy standing there, swaying back and forth as if the unseen strings that moved it had suddenly come loose, turning its leathery, unseeing face this way and that, and that big black tomcat standing stiff-legged in its path, its back arched up, its tail fluffed out, and its eyes blazing like two little spots of green fire. They might have stayed that way for two minutes, maybe more. I didn't stop to watch, but kept on running for dear life. The last I saw of them the puss was circling round the mummy, walking slowly and stiff-kneed, the way cats do before they close for a fight, never taking its eyes off the thing, and growling those deep belly growls that angry cats give. I think the mummy slashed at it with its spear, but I can't be sure of that. I know the cat did not give a scream as it almost certainly would have if it had been struck. Then I saw you and Dr. Trowbridge standing by the bus stop, and''—she spread her slim hands in a gesture of finality—"here we are.''

"We are, indeed," de Grandin conceded with a smile, "but we cannot remain so. It grows late and Tante Dorothée will worry. Come, we will take you to her and tomorrow you may come to have your wound dressed, or if you prefer you may go to your own family physician.'' He took his chin between his thumb and forefinger and looked thoughtfully at her. "I fear your dress is not yet quite dry, mademoiselle, and from my own experience I know blood-wet garments are most uncomfortable. We shall ride in Dr. Trowbridge's *moteur*—do you greatly mind retaining the garment I devised for you, wearing one of my topcoats above it? No one would notice—"

"Why, of course, sir.'' The girl smiled up into his eyes. "This is really quite a scrumptious dress; I'm sorry I said horrid things about it.''

"*Tiens*, the compliment is much appreciated, mademoiselle, even though it is a bit late," he returned with a bow. "Now, if we are all ready . . .'' He stood aside to let her precede us to the hall.

"Perhaps it would be best if you did not tell Tante Dorothée all your adventure," he advised as I drew up before the modest but attractive little house where she lived with her aunt. "She might not understand—"

"You mean she'd never believe me!'' the girl broke in with what was more than the suggestion of a giggle. "I don't think I'd believe a person who told me such a story.'' Her air of gaiety dropped from her and her laughing eyes became serious. "I know it really couldn't have happened," she admitted. "Mummies just don't run around the streets killing people like that—but all the same, it's so!''

"*Tu parles, ma petite.*'' De Grandin chuckled. "When you have grown as old as I, which will not be for many years, you'll know as I do that most of the impossible things are quite true. Yes, I say it.''

"You mean you actually believe that cock-and-bull yarn she told us,'' I demanded as we drove home.

"But certainly.''

"But it's so utterly fantastic. Mummies, as she herself admitted, don't run about the streets and kill people—"

"Mummies ordinarily do not run about the streets at all," he corrected. "Nevertheless, I believe her."

"Humph. Next thing, I suppose, you'll be calling Costello in on the case."

"If I am not much more mistaken that I think the good Costello will not need my summons," he returned as we reached my driveway. "Is not that he at our front door?"

"Hola, mon lieutenant," he called as he leaped from the car. "What fortunate breeze has wafted you hither?"

"Good evenin' gentlemen," Detective-Lieutenant Jeremiah Costello answered as he stepped back from the door. " 'Tis luck I'm in, fer Mrs. McGinnis wuz just afther tellin' me as how ye'd driv away, wid yer dinner practic'ly on th' table, an' hadn't said a word about when ye'd come back."

"But now that we are so well met, you will have dinner with us?" asked the Frenchman.

"Thank ye kindly, sor. I've had me supper, an' I'm on duty—"

"Ah bah," de Grandin interrupted, "I fear you are deteriorating. Since when have you not been competent to eat two dinners, then smack your lips and look about for more? But even if you have no appetite, you will at least lend us your company and share a cup of coffee, a liqueur, and a cigar?"

"Why, yes, sor, I'll be glad o' that," Costello returned. "An' would ye be afther listenin' to me tale o' woe th' while?"

"Assuredly, *mon vieux.* Your shoptalk is invariably interesting."

"Well, sors," Costello told us as he drained his demitasse and took a sip from the glass of old whiskey de Grandin had poured for him. "It's like this way: I wuz about to lave th' office an' call it a day, fer this bein' a lootenant ain't as easy as it wuz when I wuz sergeant, d'ye understand, an' I'd been hard at it since eight o'clock this mornin', when all to onct me tellyphone starts ringin' like a buzz saw cuttin' through a nail, an' Dogherty o' th' hommyside squad's on th' other end. He an' Schmelz, as fine a lad as never ate a bite o' bacon wid his breakfast eggs an' fasted all day on Yom Kippur, had been called to take a look into th' killin' o' Louis Westbrook, also known as Looie th' Louse. He wuz a harmless sort o' bum, th' Louse, never doin' much agin th' law except occasionally gettin' drunk an' maybe just a mite disorderly, an' actin' as a stooly fer th' boys sometimes—"

"A stooly?" echoed de Grandin. "And what is that, if you please?"

"Sure, sor, ye know. A stool pigeon."

"Ah, yes, one comprehends. A *dénonciateur*, we use them in the *Sûreté*, also."

"Yes, sor. Just so. Well, as I wuz sayin', Looie'd been found dead as a mackerel in Crescent Terrace, an'—"

"*Morbleu*, do you say it? In Crescent Terrace?"

"That same, sor. An', like I says—"

"One moment, if you please. He was dead by a wound inflicted from the rear, possibly in the head, but more likely in the neck, and on his body were numerous deep punctured wounds—"

"Howly Mither! He wuz all o' that, sor. How'd ye guess it?"

"I did not guess, my friend. I knew. Proceed with your description of the homicide."

"Well, sor, like ye said, Looie had been cut down from th' rear, swiped acrost th' neck wid a sword or sumpin' like that. His spinal column wuz hacked through just about here—" He turned his head and held his finger to his neck above the second cervical vertebra. "I've seen men kilt just so when I was in th' Fillypines. They're willin' workers wid th' bolo, those Fillypino johnnies, as many a bloody Jap can certify. An' also like ye said, sor, he wuz punctured full o' deep, wide wounds all up his back an' down his legs. Like a big, wide-bladed knife or sumpin' had been pushed into him.

"Ever see th' victim o' one o' them Comorra torture-killin's— the' *Sfregio* or Death o' the' Seventy Cuts, as they calls it? Well, th' way this pore Joe had been mangled reminded me o' them, on'y—"

"A moment, if you please," de Grandin interrupted. "This Joseph of whom you speak? We were discussing the unhappy demise of Monsieur Louis the Louse; now you introduce a new victim—"

"Arrah, Dr. de Grandin, sor, be aisy," Costello cut in, half-way between annoyance and laughter, "when I say Joe I mean Looie—"

"*Ha?* It is that they are identical?"

"Yes, sor. Ye might say so."

De Grandin glanced at me with quizzically raised brows then lifted narrow shoulders in the sort of a shrug a Frenchman gives when he wants to indicate complete dissociation with the matter. "Say on, my friend," he ordered in a weary voice. "Tell us more of this Monsieur Joseph-Louis and his so tragic dissolution.''

''Well, sor, like I wuz tellin' ye, Looie'd done a bit o' stoolin' now an' then, but it wuz mostly small-fry, unimportant stuff, puttin' th' finger on dips an' dope peddlers, or tippin' th' department off when a pawnbroker acted as a fence; sometimes slippin' us th' office when a loft burglary wuz cookin', an' th' like o' that. We hadn't heard that he'd been mixed up with any of these now black-handers, so when he turns up dead an' all butchered like I said, we're kind o' wondering who kilt him, an' why.''

''I have the answer to one part of your question, *mon Lieutenant*,'' de Grandin informed him with a grave nod.

''An' have ye, now, sor? That's just grand. Would ye be afther tellin' me who done it, just for old times' sake? That is, if it's not a military secret.''

''*Mais non. Pas du tout.* He was killed by a mummy.''

''A—glory be to God!'' Costello drained his glass of whiskey at a gulp. ''Th' man says he wuz kilt be a mummy! Sure, Dr. de Grandin, sor, ye wuz always a great one for kiddin', but this is business.''

De Grandin's little round blue eyes were hard and cold as ice as they looked into Costello's. ''I am entirely serious, my friend. I who speak to you say he was slain by a mummy.''

''Okay, sor. If ye say so, I s'pose it's so. I've never known ye to give me a bum steer, but sayin' a gink's been kilt be a mummy is pretty close to tryin' to tell me that pigs fly an' tomcats sing grand op'ry. Now, th' question is, 'How're we gonna find this murderin' mummy?' Do they kape him in a museum, or does he run loose in th' streets?''

''*Le bon Dieu* only knows,'' the little Frenchman answered with a shrug, ''but perhaps we can narrow down our search. Tomorrow I shall go to the morgue and inspect the corpse of Monsieur Joseph-Louis. Meantime there is something you can do to aid the search. This Crescent Terrace, as I recall it, is a little street. Secure the names of every householder and compile as complete a dossier on each as is possible: what his habits are, whence he comes, how long he has lived there—everything. The smallest little detail is important. There are no unimportant things in such a case as this. You comprehend?''

''I do, sor.''

''*Très bien.*'' He cast a speculative look at the decanter of whiskey. "There is at least three-quarters of a quart left in the bottle, my friends. Let us do a little serious drinking."

The streetlights were coming on and the afterglow was faint in the west under the first cold stars when we gathered in my study for a council of war next evening. De Grandin tapped a sheaf of neatly typed pages lying on the table before him. "This Monsieur Grafton Loftus is our most likely suspect," he announced. "This is the dossier compiled on him by your department, Friend Costello:

No. 18 Crescent Terrace—Loftus, Grafton. Unmarried, about fifty. Born in England. Came to this country from London four years ago. No occupation, maintains fair account in the Clifton Trust Co., periodically replenished by foreign bank drafts. Pays all bills promptly. Goes out very little, has no intercourse with neighbors. Few visitors. Nothing known of personal habits, hobbies, etc. No pets. Neighbors on each side speak of having heard low, peculiar whistle, no tune, coming from his home at night, sometimes continuing for half hour at a time, have also noted strong smell like that of Chinese incense coming from his house at times."

"Perhaps I am a trifle dull," I said sarcastically, "but I fail to see where anything in that dossier gives ground for suspicion. We haven't any personal description of Mr. Loftus. Does he look like a mummy?"

"I would not say so," de Grandin replied. "I took occasion to call on him this afternoon, pretending to ask direction to the house of an entirely mythical Monsieur John Garfield. Monsieur Loftus came to the door—after I had rung his doorbell unremittingly for half an hour—and seemed considerably annoyed. He is a big man, most decidedly stout, bald-headed, with a red face and fat cheeks threatening to engulf his small eyes. His lips are very red, his mouth is small, and pouts like that of a petulant child. Also, he was distressingly uncivil when I asked most courteously for the nonexistent Monsieur Garfield's address. I did not like his looks. I do not like him. No. Not at all."

"All the same, there's nothing in what you've told us to indicate he goes around disguised as a mummy and murdering inoffensive bums," I persisted.

"Ah bah!" he answered. "You vex me, Friend Trowbridge. Attend me, if you please. When I had seen this Monsieur Loftus, I called New Scotland Yard on Transatlantic telephone and talked with my friend Inspector Grayson, formerly of the British intelligence. He told me much I wished to know. By example: Monsieur Loftus served with the British troops in Egypt and Mesopotamia during the First World War. While there he foregathered with decidedly unsavory characters and was three times court-martialed for being absent without leave when native pow-wows were in progress. Of no importance, you say? Very well, to continue: When he returned to England, he became identified with several malodorous secret societies. The first of these was the Gorgons, ostensibly a nature-worship cult, but actually concerned with diabolism. He appears to have grown tired of these and joined the cult of Lokapala, which comprised as sinister a company of blackguards as could be found anywhere. They were known to have sacrificed animals with revolting cruelties, and were suspected of having indulged in human sacrifice at least on one occasion. The police broke this gang up and Loftus, with several others, was sentenced to a short term in the workhouse.

"We next hear of him as a member of the gang known as Los Leopardos, the Human Leopards, whose headquarters in the Shooter's Hill locality of Blackheath was raided by the police in 1938. Again the estimable Monsieur Loftus served a short term in jail. He was also implicated in the deviltries of Rowely Thorne, whose nemesis our mutual friend John Thunstone is. Now''—he swept us with a cold, challenging stare—''you will admit the company he kept was something less than desirable.''

"That may be so,'' I conceded, "but all the same—''

"But all the same he was a member of the Esoteric Society of the Resurrection. You comprehend?''

"I can't say that I do. Was that society one of those half-baked religious organizations?''

"Neither half-baked nor religious, in the true sense of the term, my friend. They were drawn from every stratum of society, from every country, every race. Scientists some of them were, men and women who had perverted their knowledge to base ends. Others were true mystics, Indian, Egyptian, Syrian, Druse, Chinese, English, French, Italian, even some Americans. They brought together the wisdom—all the secret, buried knowledge—of the East, and mated—not married—it to the science of the West. The offspring was a dreadful, illegitimate monster. Here, let me read you a transcription of an eyewitness's account of a convocation of the society:

The members of the cult, all robed in flowing white draperies, gathered in the courtyard of the society's headquarters around the replica of an Egyptian tomb with heavy doors like those of an icebox held fast with triple locks and bolts of solid silver. After a brief ceremony of worship four members of the society wearing black and purple draperies came out of the house, led by the Grand Hierophant robed in red vestments. They halted before the tomb and at a sign from the high priest all members of the congregation stopped their ears with their fingers while the Hierophant and his acolytes mumbled the secret formula while the silver locks and bolts were being unfastened. Then the high priest cried the Secret Word of Power while his assistants threw incense on the brazier burning before the tomb.

In a moment they emerged bearing a black-painted bier or stretcher on which lay the unwrapped body of an Egyptian mummy. Three times they bore the embalmed corpse around the courtyard that every member of the congregation might look on it and know that it was dead. Then they went back into the tomb.

More incense was burned while everybody knelt on the bare earth and stared fixedly at the entrance of the tomb. Minutes passed, then at the gaping doorway of the tomb appeared the mummy, standing upright and moving slowly and mechanically, like a marionette moved by invisible wires. In its right hand it held a short spear tipped with the tempered copper that only the ancient Egyptians knew how to make.

The chief hierophant walked before the mummy, blowing softly on a silver whistle each few steps, and the revivified litch seemed to hear and follow the sound of the whistle. Three times the mummy followed the high priest in a circuit of the courtyard, then priest and living corpse went back into the tomb. The priest came out in a few moments and quickly fastened the silver locks of the tomb door. He was perspiring profusely, although the night was cold.

The strictest silence was enjoined during the entire ceremony, and instant dismissal from the society was the penalty decreed for any member making even the slightest sound while the mummy was out of the tomb. Once, it was said, a woman member became hysterical when the mummy emerged from the tumulous, and burst into a fit of weeping. The litch leaped on her in an instant and struck her down with its spear, then hacked her body to ribbons as she lay writhing on the earth.

It was only by the shrilling of the high hierophant's whistle that the thing was finally persuaded to give over its bloody work and lured back to the tomb.

"What do you think from that, *hein*?" he demanded as he finished reading.

"It sounds like the ravings of a hashish-eater, or the recollection of a most unpleasant dream," I volunteered.

There was no hint of impatience in the smile he turned on me. "I agree, Friend Trowbridge. It are assuredly *extra ordinem*—outside things' usual and accepted order—as the lawyers say; but most of us make the mistake of drawing the line of the possible too close. When I read this transcription over the phone to our friend Monsieur Manly Wade Wellman this afternoon, he agreed it was entirely possible for such things to be.

"Now"—once more he swept us with his fixed, unwinking cat stare—"me, I have evolved an hypothesis; this so odious Loftus, who had been a member of this altogether detestable society, has made use of opportunity to cheat. While others stopped their ears as the hierophant pronounced the secret invocation—the Word of Power as the witness to the ceremony calls it—he listened and became familiar with it. He anticipated making similar experiments, I have no doubt, but the onset of the war and the bombings of London interfered most seriously with his plans. *Alors*, he came to this country, took up residence in the quietly respectable Crescent Terrace, and proceeded with his so unholy trials. That would account for the incense his neighbors smelled at night, also for the whistlings they heard. Do not you agree?"

"I don't agree," I answered, "but if we grant your premises, I see the logic of your conclusions."

"Triomphe!" he exclaimed with a grin. "At last good skeptical Friend Trowbridge agrees with me, even though he qualifies his agreement. We make the progress.

"And now, my friends"—he turned from me to Costello, Dogherty and Schmelz—"if you are ready, let us go. The darkness comes and with it—*eh bien*, who shall say what will eventuate?"

Crescent Terrace was a short semilunar byway connecting Clinton Avenue and Dorondo Street built up on the west side with neat houses. There were only twenty of them in the block, and their numbers ran consecutively, since a small park faced the east curb of the street.

We drew up at the far side of the park and walked across its neatly clipped lawns between beds of coleus and scarlet sage. At the sidewalk we halted and scanned the blank-faced houses opposite. "The second building from the end is Number 18," Jules de Grandin whispered. "Do you take station behind yonder clump of shrubs, Friend Costello, and Sergeants Dogherty and Schmelz will form an ambuscade just behind that hedge of hemlock. Friend Trowbridge, it is best that you remain with the lieutenant so that we shall have two parties of two each for reserves."

"An' where will you be, sor?" Costello asked.

"Me, I shall be the lure, the bait, the stalking horse. I shall parade as innocently as an unborn lamb before his lair."

"But we can't let ye take th' risk all by yerself, sor," Costello objected, only to be cut short by de Grandin's sharp:

"*Zut!* You will do exactly as I say, *mon ami*. Me, I have worked this strategy out mathematically and know what I am doing. Also, I was not born yesterday, or even day before. *A bientôt, mes amis.*" He slipped into the shadows silently as a bather letting himself down into dark water. In a moment we saw him emerge from the far side of the park into Clinton Avenue, turn left, and enter Crescent Terrace. Somehow, as he strode along the footway with an air of elaborate unconcern, his silver-headed ebony stick tucked beneath his left elbow, he reminded me of a drum major strutting before a band, and we heard him humming to himself as if he had not a care in the world.

He had almost traversed the three hundred yards of the short half-moon of the Terrace, walking slower and more slowly as he approached Dorondo Street. "Nothin' doin' yet," breathed Dogherty. "I been lookin' like a tomcat at a mouse hole, an' don't see nothin'—"

"Zat so?" whispered Costello sharply. "If ye'd kape yer eyes on th' street an' not on Dr. de Grandin, maybe ye'd see more than ye have. What's that yonder in th' doorway o' Number 18, I dunno?"

Dogherty, Schmelz, and I turned at his sharp question. We had, as he said, been watching Jules de Grandin, not the street behind him. Now, as we shifted our glances, we saw something stirring in the shadow that obscured the doorway of Number 18. At first it seemed to be no more than a chance ray of light beamed into the vestibule by the shifting of a tree bough between house and street lamp, but as we kept our eyes glued to it we saw that it was a form—a tall, attenuated, skeletally thin form moving stealthily in the shadow.

Slowly the thing emerged from the gloom of the doorway, and despite the warning I had had, I felt a prickling sensation at the back of my neck just above my collar, and a feeling as of sudden chill ran through my forearms. It was tall, as we had been told, fully six feet from its bare-boned feet to hairless, parchment-covered skull, and the articulation of its skeleton could be seen plainly through the leathery skin that clung to the gaunt, staring bones. The nose was large, high-bridged, and haughty, like the beak of a falcon or eagle, and the chin was prominent beneath the brownish sheath of skin that stretched drum-tight across it. The eyes were closed and showed only as twin depressions in the skull-like countenance, but the mummified lips had retracted to show a double line of teeth in a mirthless grin. Its movements were irregular and stiff, like the movements of some monstrous mechanical doll or, as Edina Laurace had expressed it, like a marionette worked by unseen wires. But once it had emerged from the doorway it moved with shocking quickness. Jerkily, and with exaggeratedly high knee action, it crossed the lawn, came to the sidewalk, turned on its parchment-soled feet as if on a pivot, and started after de Grandin.

The luckless bum it had pursued the night before had run from it. De Grandin waited till the scraping of its fleshless feet against the flagstones was almost at his elbow, then wheeled to face it, little round blue eyes ablaze, small teeth showing in a grin as mirthless and menacing as the mummy's own. *"Sa-ha, Monsieur le Cadavre"*—he spoke almost pleasantly—"it seems we meet to try conclusions, *hein*? Monsieur Joe-Louis the Louse you killed, but me you shall not kill. Oh, no!"

Glinting like a flash of silver lightning in the street lamp's glow, the blade of his sword came ripped from its sheath, and he fell into guard position.

The mummy paid no more attention to his sword than if it had been a straw. It never faltered in its advance, but pressed upon him, broad-bladed spear raised like an ax. Down came the chopping spearhead, up went de Grandin's rapier, and for a moment steel and spear haft locked in an impasse. Then nimbly as an eel escaping from a gloved hand, the Frenchman's weapon disengaged and he leaped back beyond the reach of the spear.

But the mummy came on relentlessly, or more exactly, insensately, with the utter lack of caution of an automaton. The rapier played lightninglike, weaving glittering patterns in the pale light of the street lamps; de Grandin danced as agilely as the shadow of a windblown leaf, avoiding heavy slash and devastating lunge, then closed in quickly as a winking eye, thrusting, stabbing, driving with a blade that seemed more quicksilver than steel. Once, twice, three times we saw his rapier pass clear through the litch, its point emerging four full inches from the leather-skinned back, but for all the effect his thrusts had, he might have been driving a pin into a pincushion.

The mummy could not have weighed much more than fifty pounds, and the little Frenchman's devastating thrusts drove it back on its heels like blows from a fist, socking it from perpendicular until it leaned at an angle of forty degrees to the earth, but it seemed endowed with a devilish equilibrium and righted itself like a gyroscope each time he all but forced it off its balance.

"*Mais c'est l'enfantillage*—this is childishness!" we heard de Grandin pant as we closed in and sought a chance to seize his skeletonlike antagonist. "He who fights an imp of Satan as if he were human is a fool!

"Stand back, my friends," he called to us as we approached, "this is my task, and I will finish it, by blue!" He dodged back from the chopping of the mummy's spear, fumbling in his pocket with his left hand, then once more drove in savagely, his rapier slipping past the weapon of his adversary to pierce clear through the bony body.

And as the sword hilt struck against the mummy's ribs and swayed it backward, he thrust forward with his left hand. There was a click, a spurt of sparks, and the blue point of a little cone of flame as the wick of his cigarette lighter kindled.

The tiny blue flame touched the mummy's wrinkled skin, a flickering tongue of yellow fire bloomed like a golden blossom from the point of contact, and in an instant the whole bony, bitumen-smeared body of the litch was ablaze. If it had been composed of oil-soaked cotton waste, it could not have caught fire more quickly or blazed more fiercely. The flame licked up its wasted torso, seized greedily upon emaciated limbs, burned scrawny neck and scraggy, parchment-covered head as if they had been tinder. The stiffness went from thigh- and shin-bones as they crumbled into ashes, and the blazing torso fell with a horrifying thud to the flagstones, flame crackling through its dryness.

"*Ha*, that was a trick you had not thought of, *Monsieur le Cadavre*!" De Grandin thrust the tip of his sword into the fast-crumbling remnants of the litch, stirring them as he might have stirred a coal fire with a poker. "You were invulnerable to my steel, for you had no life in you to be let out with a sword, but fire you could not stand against. Oh, no, my old and very naughty one, you could kill poor Monsieur Joe-Louis the Louse, you could frighten poor Mademoiselle Edina, and wound her most sorely in the shoulder, but me you could not overcome, for Jules de Grandin is one devilish clever fellow and more than a match for all the mummies ever made in Egypt. Yes, certainly; of course!

"And now, my friends"—he turned to us—"there is unfinished business on the agendum. Let us have some pointed conversation with this so offensive Monsieur Loftus."

A brass knocker hung on the door of Number 18 Crescent Terrace, and de Grandin seized its ring and beat a thunderous tattoo. For some time there was no response, but finally a shuffling step came in the hall, and the door opened a few inches. The man who stared at us was big in every way, tall, broad, and thick. His fat cheeks hung down like the dewlaps of a hound, his little mouth was red and full-lipped, like that of a spoiled child or willful woman, and he stared at us through the thick lenses of rimless spectacles with that expression of vague but vast kindliness which extreme shortsightedness often confers. "Yes?" he asked in a soft oleaginous voice.

"Monsieur Loftus, one assumes?" de Grandin countered.

The man looked at him searchingly. "Oh, so it's you?" he replied. "You're the man who came here today—"

"*Assurément*, Monsieur, and I have returned with these gentlemen of the police. We would speak with you if you can spare us a few minutes. If you find it inconvenient—*eh bien*, we shall speak with you nevertheless."

"With me? About what?"

"Oh, various matters. The matter of the so abominable mummy you endowed with pseudo-life by means of certain charms you learned as a member of *la Société de la Résurrection Esotérique*, by example. Also about the death of Monsieur Joe-Louis the Louse which was occasioned yesternight by that same mummy, and of the attack of Mademoiselle Edina Laurace by your utterly detestable mummy-creature—"

The fat face looking at us underwent sudden transformation. The childish, peevish mouth began to twist convulsively and little streams of saliva dribbled from its corners. "You can't do anything to me!" Loftus exclaimed. "I deny everything. I never had a mummy; never raised it from the dead; never sent it out to kill—who would believe you if you tried to bring me into court on such a charge? No judge would listen to you; no jury would convict me—"

"Silence *cochon!*" cried de Grandin sharply. "Go up the stairs and pack a valise. We take you to the *bureau de police* all soon."

The fat man stepped back, looking at him with an almost pitying smile. "If you wish to make a fool of yourself—"

"*Allez vous-en!*" The Frenchman pointed to the stairs. "Go pack your things, or we shall take you as you stand. Your execrable mummy we have burned to ashes. For you the fire of the electric chair awaits. Yes."

As Loftus turned to mount the stairs the little Frenchman whispered to Costello: "He has right, by damn it! He could not be convicted in a modern court of law, especially in this country. We might as well charge him with riding on a broomstick or turning himself into a wolf."

"Be dad, sor, ye've got sumpin' there," Costello admitted gloomily. "We seen th' whole thing wid our own ten eyes; we seen ye fight wid it an' finally make a bonfire out o' it, but if we tried to tell it to a judge, he'd have all five o' us in th' bughouse quicker'n ye could say 'Scat!' so he would."

"*Précisément.* For that reason I ask that you will go out on the porch and await me. I have a plan."

"I don't see how ye're goin' to work it, sor—"

"It is not necessary that you see, my friend. Indeed, it is far better that you do not. Be swift and do as I say. In a moment he will be among us; then it will be too late."

We filed out the door and waited on the little roofless porch before the house. "If this ain't screwy," Dogherty began but got no further, for a sharp cry, half of protest, half of terror, sounded from the house, and we rushed back into the vestibule. The door had swung to behind us and the lock hand snapped, so while Costello and Dogherty beat on it Schmelz and I raced to a window.

"We're coming!" I called as Sergeant Schmelz broke the glass, thrust his hand through the opening, and undid the lock. "We're coming, de Grandin!"

Costello and Dogherty forced the front door as Schmelz and I broke through the window, and the four of us charged into the hall together. "Howly Mither!" exclaimed Costello. Loftus lay at the foot of the stairs as oddly and grotesquely lifeless as an overstuffed scarecrow. His head was bent at an utterly impossible angle, and his arms and legs splayed out from his gross body, unhinged and nastily limp at knees and elbows.

De Grandin stood above him, and from the expression on his face I could not determine whether laughter fought with weeping or weeping with laughter. "*Je suis désolé*—I am completely desolated, my friends!" he told us. "Just as Monsieur Loftus was about to descend the stairs his foot slipped and he fell heavily. *Hélas*, I fear his neck is broken. Indeed, I am quite sure of it. He are completely dead. Is it not deplorable?"

Costello looked at Jules de Grandin, Jules de Grandin looked at Costello, and nothing moved in either of their faces. "Ye wouldn't 'a' helped him be any chanct, would ye, sor?" the Irishman asked at length.

"Helped him, *mon lieutenant*? Alas, no. He was below me when he fell. I could not possibly have caught him. It is unfortunate, disastrous, most regrettable—but that is how things are. Yes."

"Yes, sor," Costello answered in a toneless, noncommittal voice. "I had a hunch that's how things would turn out.

"Schmelz, Dogherty, why th' divil are ye standin' there gapin' like ye'd never seen a dead corpse before, an' ye both members o' th' hommyside squad? Git busy, ye omadhauns. Tellyphone th' coroner an' tell him we've a customer for him.

"An' now, sor, what's next?" he asked de Grandin.

"*Eh bien*, my old and rare, what should men do when they have finished a good day's work?"

"Sure, Dr. de Grandin, sor, ye'd never be advisin' that we take a wee dhrap o'th' potheen, would ye?"

They exchanged a long, solemn wink.

The father of the modern detective story, EDGAR ALLAN POE (1809–1849), a century and a half after his death, still retains his reputation for constructing the most beautiful and grotesque tales of gothic terror. "Some Words with a Mummy," which first appeared in the April 1845 American Whig Review, offers a contrast with most of Poe's oeuvre; it is a spoof of elements that are usually horrific in his stories.

SOME WORDS WITH A MUMMY

by Edgar Allan Poe

The symposium of the preceding evening had been a little too much for my nerves. I had a wretched headache, and was desperately drowsy. Instead of going out, therefore, to spend the evening, as I had proposed, it occurred to me that I could not do a wiser thing than just eat a mouthful of supper and go immediately to bed.

A *light* supper, of course. I am exceedingly fond of Welsh rabbit. More than a pound at once, however, may not at all times be advisable. Still, there can be no material objection to two. And really between two and three, there is merely a single unit of difference. I ventured, perhaps, upon four. My wife will have it five—but, clearly, she has confounded two very distinct affairs. The abstract number, five, I am willing to admit; but, concretely, it has reference to bottles of Brown Stout, without which, in the way of condiment, Welsh rabbit is to be eschewed.

Having thus concluded a frugal meal, and donned my nightcap, with the sincere hope of enjoying it till noon the next day, I placed my head upon the pillow, and, through the aid of a capital conscience, fell into a profound slumber forthwith.

But when were the hopes of humanity fulfilled? I could not

have completed my third snore when there came a furious ringing at the street-door bell, and then an impatient thumping at the knocker, which awakened me at once. In a minute afterward, and while I was still rubbing my eyes, my wife thrust in my face a note, from my old friend, Dr. Ponnonner. It ran thus:

> *Come to me, by all means, my dear good friend, as soon as you receive this. Come and help us to rejoice. At last, by long persevering diplomacy, I have gained the assent of the Directors of the City Museum, to my examination of the mummy— you know the one I mean. I have permission to unswathe it and open it, if desirable. A few friends only will be present— you, of course. The mummy is now at my house, and we shall begin to unroll it at eleven tonight.*
>
> > *Yours ever,*
> >
> > > *Ponnonner*

By the time I had reached the "Ponnonner," it struck me that I was as wide-awake as a man need be. I leaped out of bed in an ecstasy, overthrowing all in my way; dressed myself with a rapidity truly marvelous; and set off, at the top of my speed, for the doctor's.

There I found a very eager company assembled. They had been awaiting me with much impatience; the mummy was extended upon the dining table; and the moment I entered, its examination was commenced.

It was one of a pair brought, several years previously, by Captain Arthur Sabretash, a cousin of Ponnonner's, from a tomb near Eleithias, in the Lybian mountains, a considerable distance above Thebes on the Nile. The grottos at this point, although less magnificent than the Theban sepulchers, are of higher interest, on account of affording more numerous illustrations of the private life of the Egyptians. The chamber from which our specimen was taken, was said to be very rich in such illustrations—the walls being completely covered with fresco paintings and bas-reliefs, while statues, vases, and mosaic work of rich patterns, indicated the vast wealth of the deceased.

The treasure had been deposited in the museum precisely in the same condition in which Captain Sabretash had found it— that is to say, the coffin had not been disturbed. For eight years it had thus stood, subject only externally to public inspection. We had now, therefore, the complete mummy at our disposal; and to those who are aware how very rarely the unransacked antique reaches our shores, it will be evident at once that we had great reason to congratulate ourselves upon our good fortune.

Approaching the table, I saw on it a large box, or case, nearly seven feet long, and perhaps three feet wide, by two feet and a half deep. It was oblong—not coffin-shaped. The material was at first supposed to be the wood of the sycamore *(platanus)*, but, upon cutting into it, we found it to be pasteboard, or, more properly, papier-mâché, composed of papyrus. It was thickly ornamented with paintings, representing funeral scenes and other mournful subjects—interspersed among which, in every variety of position, were certain series of hieroglyphical characters, intended, no doubt, for the name of the departed. By good luck, Mr. Gliddon formed one of our party; and he had no difficulty in translating the letters, which were simply phonetic, and represented the word *Allamistakeo*.

We had some difficulty in getting this case open without injury; but, having at length accomplished the task, we came to a second, coffin-shaped, and very considerably less in size than the exterior one, but resembling it precisely in every other respect. The interval between the two was filled with resin, which had, in some degree, defaced the colors of the interior box.

Upon opening this latter (which we did quite easily), we arrived at a third case, also coffin-shaped, and varying from the second one in no particular, except in that of its material, which was cedar, and still emitted the peculiar and highly aromatic odor of that wood. Between the second and the third case there was no interval—the one fitting accurately within the other.

Removing the third case, we discovered and took out the body itself. We had expected to find it, as usual, enveloped in frequent rolls, or bandages, of linen; but, in place of these, we found a sort of sheath, maybe of papyrus, and coated with a layer of plaster, thickly gilt and painted. The paintings represented subjects connected with the various supposed duties of the soul, and its presentation to different divinities, with numerous identical human figures, intended, very probably, as portraits of the persons embalmed. Extending from head to foot was a columnar, or perpendicular, inscription, in phonetic hieroglyphics, giving again his name and titles, and the names and titles of his relations.

Around the neck thus unsheathed, was a collar of cylindrical glass beads, diverse in color, and so arranged as to form images

of deities, of the scarabeus, etc., with the winged globe. Around
the small of the waist was a similar collar or belt.

Stripping off the papyrus, we found the flesh in excellent preservation, with no perceptible odor. The color was reddish. The
skin was hard, smooth, and glossy. The teeth and hair were in
good condition. The eyes (it seemed) had been removed, and
glass ones substituted, which were very beautiful and wonder-
fully lifelike, with the exception of somewhat too determined a
stare. The fingers and the nails were brilliantly gilded.

Mr. Gliddon was of opinion, from the redness of the epidermis, that the embalmment had been effected altogether by asphaltum; but, on scraping the surface with a steel instrument,
and throwing into the fire some of the powder thus obtained,
the flavor of camphor and other sweet-scented gums became
apparent.

We searched the corpse very carefully for the usual openings
through which the entrails are extracted, but, to our surprise,
we could discover none. No member of the party was at that
period aware that entire or unopened mummies are not infre-
quently met. The brain it was customary to withdraw through
the nose; the intestines through an incision in the side; the body
was then shaved, washed, and salted; then laid aside for several
weeks, when the operation of embalming, properly so called,
began.

As no trace of an opening could be found, Dr. Ponnonner
was preparing his instruments for dissection when I observed
that it was then past two o'clock. Hereupon it was agreed to
postpone the internal examination until the next evening; and
we were about to separate for the present, when someone suggested an experiment or two with the voltaic pile.

The application of electricity to a mummy three or four thousand years old at the least, was an idea, if not very sage, still
sufficiently original, and we all caught it at once. About one-
tenth in earnest and nine-tenths in jest, we arranged a battery in
the doctor's study and conveyed thither the Egyptian.

It was only after much trouble that we succeeded in laying
bare some portions of the temporal muscle which appeared of
less stony rigidity than other parts of the frame, but which, as
we had anticipated, of course, gave no indication of galvanic
susceptibility when brought in contact with the wire. This, the
first trial, indeed, seemed decisive, and, with a hearty laugh at
our own absurdity, we were bidding each other good night, when
my eyes, happening to fall upon those of the mummy, were there

immediately riveted in amazement. My brief glance, in fact, had sufficed to assure me that the orbs which we had all supposed to be glass, and which were originally noticeable for a certain wild stare, were now so far covered by the lids, that only a small portion of the *tunica albuginea* remained visible.

With a shout I called attention to the fact, and it became immediately obvious to all.

I cannot say that I was *alarmed* at the phenomenon, because "alarmed" is, in my case, not exactly the word. It is possible, however, that, but for the Brown Stout, I might have been a little nervous. As for the rest of the company, they really made no attempt at concealing the downright fright which possessed them. Dr. Ponnonner was a man to be pitied. Mr. Gliddon, by some peculiar process, rendered himself invisible. Mr. Silk Buckingham, I fancy, will scarcely be so bold as to deny that he made his way, upon all fours, under the table.

After the first shock of astonishment, however, we resolved, as a matter of course, upon further experiment forthwith. Our operations were now directed against the great toe of the right foot. We made an incision over the outside of the exterior *os sesamoideum pollicis pedis*, and thus got at the root of the abductor muscle. Readjusting the battery, we now applied the fluid to the bisected nerves—when, with a movement of exceeding lifelikeness, the mummy first drew up its right knee so as to bring it nearly in contact with the abdomen, and then, straightening the limb with inconceivable force, bestowed a kick upon Dr. Ponnonner, which had the effect of discharging that gentleman, like an arrow from a catapult, through a window into the street below.

We rushed out en masse to bring in the mangled remains of the victim, but had the happiness to meet him upon the staircase, coming up in an unaccountable hurry, brimful of the most ardent philosophy, and more than ever impressed with the necessity of prosecuting our experiment with vigor and with zeal.

It was by his advice, accordingly, that we made, upon the spot, a profound incision into the tip of the subject's nose, while the doctor himself, laying violent hands upon it, pulled it into vehement contact with the wire.

Morally and physically—figuratively and literally—was the effect electric. In the first place, the corpse opened its eyes and winked very rapidly for several minutes, as does Mr. Barnes in the pantomime; in the second place, it sneezed; in the third, it sat upon end; in the fourth, it shook its fist in Dr. Ponnonner's

face; in the fifth, turning to Messieurs Gliddon and Buckingham, it addressed them, in very capital Egyptian, thus:

"I must say, gentlemen, that I am as much surprised as I am
mortified at your behavior. Of Dr. Ponnonner nothing better
was to be expected. He is a poor little fat fool who *knows* no
better. I pity and forgive him. But you, Mr. Gliddon—and you,
Silk—who have traveled and resided in Egypt until one might
imagine you to the manor born—you, I say, who have been so
much among us that you speak Egyptian fully as well, I think,
as you write your mother tongue—you, whom I have always
been led to regard as the firm friend of the mummies—I really
did anticipate more gentlemanly conduct from *you*. What am I
to think of your standing quietly by and seeing me thus unhand-
somely used? What am I to suppose by your permitting Tom,
Dick, and Harry to strip me of my coffins, and my clothes, in
this wretchedly cold climate? In what light (to come to the point)
am I to regard your aiding and abetting that miserable little
villain, Dr. Ponnonner, in pulling me by the nose?"

It will be taken for granted, no doubt, that upon hearing this
speech under the circumstances, we all either made for the
door, or fell into violent hysterics, or went off in a general swoon.
One of these three things was, I say, to be expected. Indeed,
each and all of these lines of conduct might have been very
plausibly pursued. And, upon my word, I am at a loss to know
how or why it was that we pursued neither the one nor the other.
But, perhaps, the true reason is to be sought in the spirit of the
age, which proceeds by the rule of contraries altogether, and is
now usually admitted as the solution of everything in the way of
paradox and impossibility. Or, perhaps, after all, it was only the
mummy's exceedingly natural and matter-of-course air that di-
vested his words of the terrible. However this may be, the facts
are clear, and no member of our party betrayed any very particular trepidation or seemed to consider that anything had gone
very especially wrong.

For my part I was convinced it was all right, and merely
stepped aside, out of the range of the Egyptian's fist. Dr. Ponnonner thrust his hands into his breeches pockets, looked hard
at the mummy, and grew excessively red in the face. Mr. Gliddon stroked his whiskers and drew up the collar of his shirt. Mr.
Buckingham hung down his head and put his right thumb into
the left corner of his mouth.

The Egyptian regarded him with a severe countenance for
some minutes and at length, with a sneer, said:

"Why don't you speak, Mr. Buckingham? Did you hear what I asked you or not? *Do* take your thumb out of your mouth!"

Mr. Buckingham, hereupon, gave a slight start, took his right thumb out of the left corner of his mouth, and, by way of indemnification, inserted his left thumb in the right corner of the aperture above-mentioned.

Not being able to get an answer from Mr. B., the figure turned peevishly to Mr. Gliddon, and, in a peremptory tone, demanded in general terms what we all meant.

Mr. Gliddon replied at great length, in phonetics; and but for the deficiency of American printing offices in hieroglyphical type, it would afford me much pleasure to record here, in the original, the whole of his very excellent speech.

I may as well take this occasion to remark that all the subsequent conversation in which the mummy took a part was carried on in primitive Egyptian, through the medium (so far as concerned myself and other untraveled members of the company)—through the medium, I say, of Messieurs Gliddon and Buckingham, as interpreters. These gentlemen spoke the mother tongue of the mummy with inimitable fluency and grace; but I could not help observing that (owning, no doubt, to the introduction of images entirely modern, and, of course, entirely novel to the stranger) the two travelers were reduced, occasionally, to the employment of sensible forms for the purpose of conveying a particular meaning. Mr. Gliddon, at one period, for example, could not make the Egyptian comprehend the term "politics," until he sketched upon the wall, with a bit of charcoal, a little carbuncle-nosed gentleman, out at elbows, standing upon a stump, with his left leg drawn back, right arm thrown forward, with his fist shut, the eyes rolled up toward heaven, and the mouth open at an angle of ninety degrees. Just in the same way Mr. Buckingham failed to convey the absolutely modern idea "wig," until (at Dr. Ponnonner's suggestion) he grew very pale in the face and consented to take off his own.

It will be readily understood that Mr. Gliddon's discourse turned chiefly upon the vast benefits accruing to science from the unrolling and disemboweling of mummies; apologizing, upon this score, for any disturbance that might have been occasioned *him*, in particular, the individual mummy called Allamistakeo; and concluding with a mere hint (for it could scarcely be considered more) that, as these little matters were now explained, it might be as well to proceed with the investigation intended. Here Dr. Ponnonner made ready his instruments.

In regard to the latter suggestions of the orator, it appears that Allamistakeo had certain scruples of conscience, the nature of which I did not distinctly learn; but he expressed himself satisfied with the apologies tendered, and, getting down from the table, shook hands with the company all around.

When this ceremony was at an end, we immediately busied ourselves in repairing the damages which our subject had sustained from the scalpel. We sewed up the wound in his temple, bandaged his foot, and applied a square inch of black plaster to the tip of his nose.

It was now observed that the Count (this was the title, it seems, of Allamistakeo) had a slight fit of shivering—no doubt from the cold. The doctor immediately repaired to his wardrobe, and soon returned with a black dress coat, made in Jennings's best manner, a pair of sky-blue-plaid pantaloons with straps, a pink gingham chemise, a flapped vest of brocade, a white sack overcoat, a walking cane with a hook, a hat with no brim, patent-leather boots, straw-colored kid gloves, an eyeglass, a pair of whiskers, and a waterfall cravat. Owing to the disparity of size between the Count and the doctor (the proportion being as two to one), there was some little difficulty in adjusting these habiliments upon the person of the Egyptian; but when all was arranged, he might have been said to be dressed. Mr. Gliddon, therefore, gave him his arm, and led him to a comfortable chair by the fire, while the doctor rang the bell upon the spot and ordered a supply of cigars and wine.

The conversation soon grew animated. Much curiosity was, of course, expressed in regard to the somewhat remarkable fact of Allamistakeo's still remaining alive.

"I should have thought," observed Mr. Buckingham, "that it is high time you were dead."

"Why," replied the Count, very much astonished, "I am little more than seven hundred years old! My father lived a thousand, and was by no means in his dotage when he died."

Here ensued a brisk series of questions and computations, by means of which it became evident that the antiquity of the mummy had been grossly misjudged. It had been five thousand and fifty years and some months since he had been consigned to the catacombs at Eleithias.

"But my remark," resumed Mr. Buckingham, "had no reference to your age at the period of interment; (I am willing to grant, in fact, that you are still a young man), and my allusion was to the immensity of time during which, by your own showing, you must have been done up in asphaltum.''

"In what?'' said the Count.

"In asphaltum,'' persisted Mr. B.

"Ah, yes; I have some faint notion of what you mean; it might be made to answer, no doubt—but in my time we employed scarcely any thing else than the bichloride of mercury.''

"But what we are especially at a loss to understand,'' said Dr. Ponnonner, "is how it happens that, having been dead and buried in Egypt five thousand years ago, you are here today all alive and looking so delightfully well.''

"Had I been, as you say, *dead*,'' replied the Count, "it is more than probable that dead I should still be; for I perceive you are yet in the infancy of galvanism and cannot accomplish with it what was a common thing among us in the old days. But the fact is, I fell into catalepsy, and it was considered by my best friends that I was either dead or should be; they accordingly embalmed me at once—I presume you are aware of the chief principle of the embalming process?''

"Why, not altogether.''

"Ah, I perceive—a deplorable condition of ignorance! Well, I cannot enter into details just now: but it is necessary to explain that to embalm (properly speaking) in Egypt, was to arrest indefinitely *all* the animal functions subjected to the process. I used the word 'animal' in its widest sense, as including the physical not more than the moral and *vital* being. I repeat that the leading principle of embalmment consisted, with us, in the immediately arresting, and holding in perpetual *abeyance*, *all* the animal functions subjected to the process. To be brief, in whatever condition the individual was, at the period of embalmment, in that condition he remained. Now, as it is my good fortune to be of the blood of the Scarabæus, I was embalmed *alive*, as you see me at present.''

"The blood of the Scarabæus!'' exclaimed Dr. Ponnonner.

"Yes. The Scarabæus was the *insignium*, or the 'arms,' of a very distinguished and very rare patrician family. To be 'of the blood of the Scarabæus,' is merely to be one of that family of which the Scarabæus is the *insignium*. I speak figuratively.''

"But what has this to do with your being alive?''

"Why, it is the general custom in Egypt to deprive a corpse, before embalmment, of its bowels and brains; the race of the Scarabæi alone did not coincide with the custom. Had I not been a Scarabæus, therefore, I should have been without bowels and brains; and without either it is inconvenient to live.''

"I perceive that,'' said Mr. Buckingham, "and I presume that all the *entire* mummies that come to hand are of the race of Scarabæi.''

"Beyond doubt.''

"I thought,'' said Mr. Gliddon, very meekly, "that the Scarabæus was one of the Egyptian gods.''

"One of the Egyptian *what*?'' exclaimed the mummy, starting to its feet.

"Gods!'' repeated the traveler.

"Mr. Gliddon, I really am astonished to hear you talk in this style,'' said the Count, resuming his chair. "No nation upon the face of the earth has ever acknowledged more than one *god*. The Scarabæus, the Ibis, etc. were with us (as similar creatures have been with others) the symbols, or *media*, through which we offered worship to the Creator too august to be more directly approached.''

There was here a pause. At length the colloquy was renewed by Dr. Ponnonner.

"It is not improbable, then, from what you have explained,'' said he, "that among the catacombs near the Nile there may exist other mummies of the Scarabæus tribe, in a condition of vitality.''

"There can be no question of it,'' replied the Count. "All the Scarabæi embalmed accidentally while alive, are alive. Even some of those *purposely* so embalmed, may have been overlooked by their executors, and still remain in the tomb.''

"Will you be kind enough to explain,'' I said, "what you mean by 'purposely so embalmed'?''

"With great pleasure,'' answered the mummy, after surveying me leisurely through his eyeglass—for it was the first time I had ventured to address him a direct question.

"With great pleasure,'' he said. "The usual duration of man's life, in my time, was about eight hundred years. Few men died, unless by most extraordinary accident, before the age of six hundred; few lived longer than a decade of centuries; but eight were considered the natural term. After the discovery of the embalming principle, as I have already described it to you, it occurred to our philosophers that a laudable curiosity might be gratified, and, at the same time, the interests of science much advanced, by living this natural term in installments. In the case of history, indeed, experience demonstrated that something of this kind was indispensable. An historian, for example, having attained the age of five hundred, would write a book with great labor and then get himself carefully embalmed; leaving instructions to his executors pro tem that they should cause him to be revivified after the lapse of a certain period—say five or six hundred years. Resuming existence at the expiration of this time, he would invariably find his great work converted into a species of haphazard notebook—that is to say, into a kind of literary arena for the conflicting guesses, riddles, and personal squabbles of whole herds of exasperated commentators. These guesses, etc., which passed under the name of annotations, or emendations, were found so completely to have enveloped, distorted, and overwhelmed the text, that the author had to go about with a lantern to discover his own book. When discovered, it was never worth the trouble of the search. After rewriting it throughout, it was regarded as the bounden duty of the historian to set himself to work immediately in correcting, from his own private knowledge and experience, the traditions of the day concerning the epoch at which he had originally lived. Now this process of rescription and personal rectification, pursued by various individual sages from time to time, had the effect of preventing our history from degenerating into absolute fable.''

''I beg your pardon,'' said Dr. Ponnonner at this point, laying his hand gently upon the arm of the Egyptian—''I beg your pardon, sir, but may I presume to interrupt you for one moment?''

''By all means, *sir*,'' replied the Count, drawing up.

''I merely wished to ask you a question,'' said the doctor. ''You mentioned the historian's personal correction of *traditions* respecting his own epoch. Pray, sir, upon an average, what proportion of these Kabbala were usually found to be right?''

''The Kabbala, as you properly term them, sir, were generally discovered to be precisely on a par with the facts recorded in the unrewritten histories themselves—that is to say, not one individual iota of either was ever known, under any circumstances, to be not totally and radically wrong.''

''But since it is quite clear,'' resumed the doctor, ''that at least five thousand years have elapsed since your entombment, I take it for granted that your histories at that period, if not your traditions, were sufficiently explicit on that one topic of universal interest, the Creation, which took place, as I presume you are aware, only about ten centuries before.''

''Sir!'' said the Count Allamistakeo.

The doctor repeated his remarks, but it was only after much additional explanation that the foreigner could be made to comprehend them. The latter at length said, hesitatingly:

"The ideas you have suggested are to me, I confess, utterly novel. During my time I never knew any one to entertain so singular a fancy as that the universe (or this world if you will have it so) ever had a beginning at all. I remember once, and once only, hearing something remotely hinted, by a man of many speculations, concerning the origin *of the human race*; and by this individual, the very word *Adam* (or Red Earth), which you make use of, was employed. He employed it, however, in a generical sense, with reference to the spontaneous germination from rank soil (just as a thousand of the lower genera of creatures are germinated)—the spontaneous germination, I say, of five vast hordes of men, simultaneously upspringing to five distinct and nearly equal divisions of the globe."

Here, in general, the company shrugged their shoulders, and one or two of us touched our foreheads with a very significant air. Mr. Silk Buckingham, first glancing slightly at the occiput and then at the sinciput of Allamistakeo, spoke as follows:

"The long duration of human life in your time, together with the occasional practice of passing it, as you have explained, in installments, must have had, indeed, a strong tendency to the general development and conglomeration of knowledge. I presume, therefore, that we are to attribute the marked inferiority of the old Egyptians in all particulars of science, when compared with the moderns, and more especially with the Yankees, altogether to the superior solidity of the Egyptian skull."

"I confess again," replied the Count, with much suavity, "that I am somewhat at a loss to comprehend you; pray, to what particulars of science do you allude?"

Here our whole party, joining voices, detailed, at great length, the assumptions of phrenology and the marvels of animal magnetism.

Having heard us to an end, the Count proceeded to relate a few anecdotes, which rendered it evident that prototypes of Gall and Spurzheim had flourished and faded in Egypt so long as to have been nearly forgotten, and that the maneuvers of Mesmer were really very contemptible tricks when put in collation with the positive miracles of the Theban *savans*, who created lice and a great many other similar things.

I here asked the Count if his people were able to calculate eclipses. He smiled rather contemptuously, and said they were.

This put me a little out, but I began to make other inquiries in regard to his astronomical knowledge, when a member of the company, who had never as yet opened his mouth, whispered in my ear that for information on this head, I had better consult Ptolemy (whoever Ptolemy is), as well as one plutarch *de facie lunæ*.

I then questioned the mummy about burning glasses and lenses, and, in general, about the manufacture of glass; but I had not made an end of my inquiries before the silent member again touched me quietly on the elbow and begged me for God's sake to take a peep at Diodorus Siculus. As for the Count, he merely asked me, in the way of reply, if we moderns possessed any such microscopes as would enable us to cut cameos in the style of the Egyptians. While I was thinking how I should answer this question, little Dr. Ponnonner committed himself in a very extraordinary way.

"Look at our architecture!" he exclaimed, greatly to the indignation of both the travelers, who pinched him black and blue to no purpose.

"Look," he cried with enthusiasm, "at the Bowling Green Fountain in New York! Or if this be too vast a contemplation, regard for a moment the Capitol at Washington, D.C.!"—and the good little medical man went on to detail, very minutely, the proportions of the fabric to which he referred. He explained that the portico alone was adorned with no less than four and twenty columns, five feet in diameter, and ten feet apart.

The Count said that he regretted not being able to remember, just at that moment, the precise dimensions of any one of the principal buildings of the city of Aznac, whose foundations were laid in the night of time, but the ruins of which were still standing, at the epoch of his entombment, in a vast plain of sand to the westward of Thebes. He recollected, however, (talking of the porticos) that one affixed to an inferior palace in a kind of suburb called Carnac, consisted of a hundred and forty-four columns, thirty-seven feet in circumference, and twenty-five feet apart. The approach to this portico, from the Nile, was through an avenue two miles long, composed of sphynxes, statues, and obelisks, twenty, sixty, and a hundred feet in height. The palace itself (as well as he could remember) was, in one direction, two miles long, and might have been altogether about seven in circuit. Its walls were richly painted all over, within and without, with hieroglyphics. He would not pretend to *assert* that even fifty or sixty of the doctor's Capitols might have been built within these walls, but he was by no means sure that two or three hundred of them might not have been squeezed in with some trouble. That palace at Carnac was an insignificant little building after all. He (the Count), however, could not conscientiously refuse to admit the ingenuity, magnificence, and superiority of the Fountain at the Bowling Green, as described by the doctor. Nothing like it, he was forced to allow, had ever been seen in Egypt or elsewhere.

I here asked the Count what he had to say to our railroads.

"Nothing," he replied, "in particular." They were rather slight, rather ill-conceived, and clumsily put together. They could not be compared, of course, with the vast, level, direct, iron-grooved causeways upon which the Egyptians conveyed entire temples and solid obelisks of a hundred and fifty feet in altitude.

I spoke of our gigantic mechanical forces.

He agreed that we knew something in that way, but inquired how I should have gone to work in getting up the imposts on the lintels of even the little palace of Carnac.

This question I concluded not to hear, and demanded if he had any idea of artesian wells; but he simply raised his eyebrows; while Mr. Gliddon winked at me very hard and said, in a low tone, that one had been recently discovered by the engineers employed to bore for water in the Great Oasis.

I then mentioned our steel; but the foreigner elevated his nose and asked me if our steel could have executed the sharp carved work seen on the obelisks, and which was wrought altogether by edge tools of copper.

This disconcerted us so greatly that we thought it advisable to vary the attack to metaphysics. We sent for a copy of a book called the *Dial*, and read out of it a chapter or two about something which is not very clear, but which the Bostonians call the Great Movement of Progress.

The Count merely said that great movements were awfully common things in his day, and as for progress, it was at one time quite a nuisance, but it never progressed.

We then spoke of the great beauty and importance of democracy and were at much trouble in impressing the Count with a due sense of the advantages we enjoyed in living where there was suffrage ad libitum, and no king.

He listened with marked interest, and in fact seemed not a little amused. When we had done, he said that a great while ago, there had occurred something of a very similar sort. Thirteen Egyptian provinces determined all at once to be free and to set a magnificent example to the rest of mankind. They assembled their wise men and concocted the most ingenious constitution it is possible to conceive. For a while they managed remarkably well; only their habit of bragging was prodigious. The thing ended, however, in the consolidation of the thirteen states, with some fifteen or twenty others, in the most odious and insupportable despotism that was ever heard of upon the face of the earth.

I asked what was the name of the usurping tyrant.

As well as the Count could recollect, it was *Mob*.

Not knowing what to say to this, I raised my voice and deplored the Egyptian ignorance of steam.

The Count looked at me with much astonishment, but made no answer. The silent gentleman, however, gave me a violent nudge in the ribs with his elbows—told me I had sufficiently exposed myself for once—and demanded if I was really such a fool as not to know that the modern steam engine is derived from the invention of Hero, through Solomon de Caus.

We were now in imminent danger of being discomfited; but, as good luck would have it, Dr. Ponnonner, having rallied, returned to our rescue and inquired if the people of Egypt would seriously pretend to rival the moderns in the all-important particular of dress.

The Count, at this, glanced downward to the straps of his pantaloons, and then taking hold of the end of one of his coattails, held it up close to his eyes for some minutes. Letting it fall, at last, his mouth extended itself very gradually from ear to ear; but I do not remember that he said anything in the way of reply.

Hereupon we recovered our spirits, and the doctor, approaching the mummy with great dignity, desired it to say candidly, upon its honor as a gentleman, if the Egyptians had comprehended, at *any* period, the manufacture of either Ponnonner's lozenges or Brandreth's pills.

We looked, with profound anxiety, for an answer—but in vain. It was not forthcoming. The Egyptian blushed and hung down his head. Never was triumph more consummate; never was defeat borne with so ill a grace. Indeed, I could not endure the spectacle of the poor mummy's mortification. I reached my hat, bowed to him stiffly, and took leave.

Upon getting home I found it past four o'clock and went immediately to bed. It is now ten A.M. I have been up since seven, penning these memoranda for the benefit of my family and of mankind. The former I shall behold no more. My wife is a shrew. The truth is, I am heartly sick of this life and of the nineteenth century in general. I am convinced that everything is going wrong. Besides, I am anxious to know who will be president in 2045. As soon, therefore, as I shave and swallow a cup of coffee, I shall just step over to Ponnonner's and get embalmed for a couple of hundred years.

*TARLETON FISKE is a revered crime and suspense novelist—
appearing here under an assumed name.*

BEETLES

by Tarleton Fiske

When Hartley returned from Egypt, his friends said he had
changed. The specific nature of that change was difficult to detect, for none of his acquaintances got more than a casual glimpse
of him. He dropped around to the club just once, and then retired to the seclusion of his apartments. His manner was so
definitely hostile, so markedly antisocial, that very few of his
cronies cared to visit him, and the occasional callers were not
received.

It caused considerable talk at the time—gossip rather. Those
who remembered Arthur Hartley in the days before his expedition abroad were naturally quite cut up over the drastic metamorphosis in his manner. Hartley had been known as a keen
scholar, a singularly erudite field-worker in his chosen profession of archaeology; but at the same time he had been a peculiarly charming person. He had the worldly flair usually
associated with the fictional characters of E. Phillips Oppen-
heim, and a positively devilish sense of humor which mocked
and belittled it. He was the kind of fellow who could order the
precise wine at the proper moment, at the same time grinning
as though he were as much surprised by it all as his guest of the
evening. And most of his friends found this air of culture without
ostentation quite engaging. He had carried this urbane sense of
the ridiculous over into his work; and while it was known that
he was very much interested in archaeology, and a notable figure

in the field, he inevitably referred to his studies as "pottering around with old fossils and the old fossils that discovered them."

Consequently, his curious reversal following his trip came as a complete surprise.

All that was definitely known was that he had spent some eight months on a field trip to the Egyptian Sudan. Upon his return he had immediately severed all connections with the institute he had been associated with. Just what had occurred during the expedition was a matter of excited conjecture among his former intimates. But something had definitely happened; it was unmistakable.

The night he spent at the club proved that. He had come in quietly, too quietly. Hartley was one of those persons who usually made an entrance, in the true sense of the word. His tall, graceful figure, attired in the immaculate evening dress so seldom found outside of the pages of melodramatic fiction; his truly leonine head with its Stokowski-like bristle of gray hair; these attributes commanded attention. He could have passed anywhere as a man of the world, or a stage magician awaiting his cue to step onto the platform.

But this evening he entered quietly, unobtrusively. He wore dinner clothes, but his shoulders sagged, and the spring was gone from his walk. His hair was grayer, and it hung pallidly over his tanned forehead. Despite the bronze of Egyptian sun on his features, there was a sickly tinge to his countenance. His eyes peered mistily from amidst unsightly folds. His face seemed to have lost its mold; the mouth hung loosely.

He greeted no one and took a table alone. Of course cronies came up and chatted, but he did not invite them to join him. And oddly enough, none of them insisted, although normally they would gladly have forced their company upon him and jollied him out of a black mood, which experience had taught them was easily done in his case. Nevertheless, after a few words with Hartley, they all turned away.

They must have felt it even then. Some of them hazarded the opinion that Hartley was still suffering from some form of fever contracted in Egypt, but I do not think they believed this in their hearts. From their shocked descriptions of the man they seemed one and all to sense the peculiar *alien* quality about him. This was an Arthur Hartley they had never known, an aged stranger, with a querulous voice which rose in suspicion when he was questioned about his journey. Stranger he truly was, for he did not even appear to recognize some of the men who greeted him, and when he did it was with an abstracted manner—a clumsy way of wording it, but what else is there to say when an old friend stares blankly into silence upon meeting, and his eyes seem to fasten on far-off terrors that affright him?

That was the strangeness they all grasped in Hartley. He was afraid. Fear bestrode those sagging shoulders. Fear breathed a pallor into that ashy face. Fear grinned into those empty, far-fixed eyes. Fear prompted the suspicion in the voice.

They told me, and that is why I went round to see Arthur Hartley in his rooms. Others had spoken of their efforts, in the week following his appearance at the club, to gain admittance to his apartment. They said he did not answer the bell, and complained that the phone had been disconnected. But that, I reasoned, was fear's work.

I wouldn't let Hartley down. I had been a rather good friend of his—and I may as well confess that I scented a mystery here. The combination proved irresistible. I went up to his flat one afternoon and rang.

No answer. I went into the dim hallway and listened for footsteps, some sign of life from within. No answer. Complete, utter silence. For a moment I thought crazily of suicide, then laughed the dread away. It was absurd—and still, there had been a certain dismaying unanimity in all the reports I had heard of Hartley's mental state. When the stolidest, most hardheaded of the club bores concurred in their estimate of the man's condition, I might well worry. Still, suicide . . .

I rang again, more as a gesture than in expectations of tangible results, and then I turned and descended the stairs. I felt, I recall, a little twinge of inexplicable relief upon leaving the place. The thought of suicide in that gloomy hallway had not been pleasant.

I reached the lower door and opened it, and a familiar figure scurried past me on the landing. I turned. It was Hartley.

For the first time since his return I got a look at the man, and in the hallway shadows he was ghastly. Whatever his condition at the club, a week must have accentuated it tremendously. His head was lowered, and as I greeted him he looked up. His eyes gave me a terrific shock. There was a stranger dwelling in their depths—a haunted stranger. I swear he shook when I addressed him.

He was wearing a tattered topcoat, but it hung loosely over

his gauntness. I noticed that he was carrying a large bundle done up in brown paper.

I said something, I don't remember what; at any rate, I was at some pains to conceal my confusion as I greeted him. I was rather insistently cordial, I believe, for I could see that he would just as soon have hurried up the stairs without even speaking to me. The astonishment I felt converted itself into heartiness. Rather reluctantly he invited me up.

We entered the flat, and I noticed that Hartley double-locked the door behind him. That, to me, characterized his metamorphosis. In the old days, Hartley had always kept open house, in the literal sense of the word. Studies might have kept him late at the institute, but a chance visitor found his door open wide. And now, he double-locked it.

I turned around and surveyed the apartment. Just what I expected to see I cannot say, but certainly my mind was prepared for some sign of radical alteration. There was none. The furniture had not been moved; the pictures hung in their original places; the vast bookcases still stood in the shadows.

Hartley excused himself, entered the bedroom, and presently emerged after discarding his topcoat. Before he sat down he walked over to the mantel and struck a match before a little bronze figurine of Horus. A second later the thick gray spirals of smoke arose in the approved style of exotic fiction, and I smelled the pungent tang of strong incense.

That was the first puzzler. I had unconsciously adopted the attitude of a detective looking for clues—or, perhaps, a psychiatrist ferreting out psychoneurotic tendencies. And the incense was definitely alien to the Arthur Hartley I knew.

"Clears away the smell," he remarked.

I didn't ask "What smell?" Nor did I begin to question him as to his trip, his inexplicable conduct in not answering my correspondence after he left Khartoum, or his avoidance of my company in this week following his return. Instead, I let him talk.

He said nothing at first. His conversation rambled, and behind it all I sensed the abstraction I had been warned about. He spoke of having given up his work and hinted that he might leave the city shortly and go up to his family home in the country. He had been ill. He was disappointed in Egyptology, and its limitations. He hated darkness. The locust plagues had increased in Kansas.

This rambling was—insane.

I knew it then, and I hugged the thought to me in the perverse delight which is born of dread. Hartley was mad. "Limitations" of Egyptology. "I hate the dark." "The locusts of Kansas."

But I sat silently when he lighted the great candles about the room; sat silently staring through the incense clouds to where the flaming tapers illuminated his twitching features. And then he broke.

"You are my friend?" he said. There was a question in his voice, a puzzled suspicion in his words that brought sudden pity to me. His derangement was terrible to witness. Still, I nodded gravely.

"You are my friend," he continued. This time the words were a statement. The deep breath which followed betokened resolution on his part.

"Do you know what was in that bundle I brought in?" he asked suddenly.

"No."

"I'll tell you. Insecticide. That's what it was. Insecticide!"

His eyes flamed in triumph which stabbed me.

"I haven't left this house for a week. I dare not spread the plague. They follow me, you know. But today I thought of the way—absurdly simple, too. I went out and bought insecticide. Pounds of it. And liquid spray. Special formula stuff, more deadly than arsenic. Just elementary science, really—but its very prosaicness may defeat the Powers of Evil."

I nodded like a fool, wondering whether I could arrange for him to be taken away that evening. Perhaps my friend, Dr. Sherman, might diagnose. . . .

"Now let them come! It's my last chance—the incense doesn't work, and even if I keep the lights burning, they creep about the corners. Funny the woodwork holds up; it should be riddled."

What was this?

"But I forgot," said Hartley. "You don't know about it. The plague, I mean. And the curse." He leaned forward and his white hands made octopus shadows on the wall.

"I used to laugh at it, you know," he said. "Archaeology isn't exactly a pursuit for the superstitious. Too much groveling in ruins. And putting curses on old pottery and battered statues never seemed important to me. But Egyptology—that's different. It's human bodies, there. Mummified, but still human. And the Egyptians were a great race—they had scientific secrets we haven't yet fathomed, and of course we cannot even begin to approach their concepts in mysticism."

Ah! There was the key! I listened, intently.

"I learned a lot, this last trip. We were after the excavation job in the new tombs up the river. I brushed up on the dynastic periods, and naturally the religious significance entered into it. Oh, I know all the myths—the Bubatis legend, the Isis resurrection theory, the true names of Ra, the allegory of Set—

"We found things there, in the tombs—wonderful things. The pottery, the furniture, the bas-reliefs we were able to remove. But the expeditionary reports will be out soon; you can read of it then. We found mummies, too. Cursed mummies."

Now I saw it, or thought I did.

"And I was a fool. I did something I never should have dared to do—for ethical reasons, and for other, more important reasons. Reasons that may cost me my soul."

I had to keep my grip on myself, remember that he was mad, remember that his convincing tones were prompted by the delusions of insanity. Or else, in that dark room I might have easily believed that there was a power which had driven my friend to this haggard brink.

"Yes, I did it, I tell you! I read the Curse of the Scarabæus—sacred beetle, you know—and I did it anyway. I couldn't guess that it was true. I was a skeptic; everyone is skeptical enough until things happen. Those things are like the phenomenon of death; you read about it, realize that it occurs to others, and yet cannot quite conceive of it happening to yourself. And yet it does. The Curse of the Scarabæus was like that."

Thoughts of the Sacred Beetle of Egypt crossed my mind. And I remembered, also, the seven plagues. And I knew what he would say. . . .

"We came back. On the ship I noticed them. They crawled out of the corners every night. When I turned the light on they went away, but they always returned when I tried to sleep. I burned incense to keep them off, and then I moved into a new cabin. But they followed me.

"I did not dare tell anyone. Most of the chaps would have laughed, and the Egyptologists in the party wouldn't have helped much. Besides, I couldn't confess my crime. So I went on alone."

His voice was a dry whisper.

"It was pure hell. One night on the boat I saw the black things crawling in my food. After that I ate in the cabin, alone. I dared not see anyone now, for fear they might notice how the things followed me. They did follow me, you know—if I walked in shadow on the deck, they crept along behind. Only the sun kept them back, or a pure flame. I nearly went mad trying to account logically for their presence; trying to imagine how they got on the boat. But all the time I knew in my heart what the truth was. They were a sending—the Curse!

"When I reached port, I went up and resigned. When my guilt was discovered there would have been a scandal, anyway, so I resigned. I couldn't hope to continue work with those things crawling all over, wherever I went. I was afraid to look anyone up. Naturally, I tried. That one night at the club was ghastly, though—I could see them marching across the carpet and crawling up the sides of my chair, and it took all there was in me to keep from screaming and dashing out.

"Since then I've stayed here, alone. Before I decide on any course for the future, I must fight the Curse and win. Nothing else will help."

I started to interject a phrase, but he brushed it aside and continued desperately.

"No, I couldn't go away. They followed me across the ocean; they haunt me in the streets. I could be locked up and they would still come. They come every night and crawl up the sides of my bed and try to get at my face and I must sleep soon or I'll go mad, they crawl over my face at night, they crawl—"

It was horrible to see the words ooze out between his set teeth, for he was fighting madly to control himself.

"Perhaps the insecticide will kill them. It was the first thing I should have thought of, but of course panic confused me. Yes, I put my trust in the insecticide. Grotesque, isn't it? Fighting an ancient curse with insect powder?"

I spoke at last. "They're beetles, aren't they?"

He nodded. "Scarabæus beetles. You know the curse. The mummies under the protection of the Scarab cannot be violated."

I knew the curse. It was one of the oldest known to history. Like all legends, it has had a persistent life. Perhaps I could reason.

"But why should it affect you?" I asked. Yes, I would reason with Hartley. Egyptian fever had deranged him, and the colorful curse story had gripped his mind. If I spoke logically, I might get him to understand his hallucination. ''Why should it affect you?'' I repeated.

He was silent for a moment before he spoke, and then his words seemed to be wrung out of him.

''I stole a mummy,'' he said. ''I stole the mummy of a temple virgin. I must have been crazy to do it; something happens to you under that sun. There was gold in the case, and jewels, and ornaments. And there was the Curse, written. I got them—both.''

I stared at him, and knew that in this he spoke the truth.

''That's why I cannot keep up my work. I stole the mummy, and I am cursed. I didn't believe, but the crawling things came just as the inscription said.

''At first I thought that was the meaning of the Curse, that wherever I went the beetles would go, too, that they would haunt me and keep me from men forever. But lately I am beginning to think differently. I think the beetles will act as messengers of vengeance. I think they mean to kill me.''

This was pure raving.

''I haven't dared open the mummy case since. I'm afraid to read the inscription again. I have it here in the house, but I've locked it up and I won't show you. I want to burn it—but I must keep it on hand. In a way, it's the only proof of my sanity. And if the things kill me—''

''Snap out of it,'' I commanded. Then I started. I don't know the exact words I used, but I said reassuring, hearty, wholesome things. And when I finished, he smiled the martyred smile of the obsessed.

''Delusions? They're real. But where do they come from? I can't find any cracks in the woodwork. The walls are sound. And yet every night the beetles come and crawl up the bed and try to get at my face. They don't bite, they merely crawl. There are thousands of them—black thousands of silent, crawling things, inches long. I brush them away, but when I fall back asleep they come back; they're clever, and I can't pretend. I've never caught one; they're too fast-moving. They seem to understand me—or the power that sends them understands.

''They crawl up from hell night after night, and I can't last much longer. Some evening I'll fall completely asleep and they will creep over my face, and then—''

He leaped to his feet and screamed.

"The corner—in the corner now—out of the walls—"

The black shadows were moving, marching.

I saw a blur, fancied I could detect rustling forms advancing, creeping, spreading before the light.

Hartley sobbed.

I turned on the electric light. There was, of course, nothing there. I didn't say a word, but left abruptly. Hartley continued to sit huddled in his chair, his head in his hands.

I went straight to my friend, Dr. Sherman.

2

He diagnosed it as I thought he would: phobia, accompanied by hallucinations. Hartley's feeling of guilt over stealing the mummy haunted him. The visions of beetles resulted.

All this Sherman studded with the mumbo-jumbo technicalities of the professional psychiatrist, but it was simple enough. Together we phoned the institute where Hartley had worked. They verified the story, insofar as they knew Hartley had stolen a mummy.

After dinner Sherman had an appointment, but he promised to meet me at ten and go with me again to Hartley's apartment. I was quite insistent about this, for I felt that there was no time to lose. Of course, this was a mawkish attitude on my part, but the strange afternoon session had deeply disturbed me.

I spent the early evening in unnerving reflection. Perhaps that was the way all so-called Egyptian curses worked. A guilty conscience on the part of a tomb looter made him project the shadow of imaginary punishment on himself. He had hallucinations of retribution. That might explain the mysterious Tutankhamen deaths; it certainly accounted for the suicides.

And that was why I insisted on Sherman seeing Hartley that same night. I feared suicide very much, for if ever a man was on the verge of complete mental collapse, Arthur Hartley surely was.

It was nearly eleven, however, before Sherman and I rang the bell. There was no answer. We stood in the dark hallway as I vainly rapped, then pounded. The silence only served to augment my anxiety. I was truly afraid, or else I never would have dared using my skeleton key.

As it was, I felt the end justified the means. We entered.

The living room was bare of occupants. Nothing had changed since the afternoon—I could see that quite clearly, for all the lights were on, and the guttering candle stumps still smoldered.

Both Sherman and I smelled the reek of the insecticide quite strongly, and the floor was almost evenly coated with thick white insect powder.

We called, of course, before I ventured to enter the bedroom. It was dark, and I thought it was empty until I turned on the lights and saw the figure huddled beneath the bedclothes. It was Arthur Hartley, and I needed no second glance to see that his white face was twisted in death.

The reek of insecticide was strongest here, and incense burned; and yet there was another pungent smell—a musty odor, vaguely animallike.

Sherman stood at my side, staring.

"What shall we do?" I asked.

"I'll get the police on the wire downstairs," he said. "Touch nothing."

He dashed out, and I followed him from the room, sickened. I could not bear to approach the body of my friend—that hideous expression on the face affrighted me. Suicide, murder, heart attack—I didn't even wish to know the manner of his passing. I was heartsick to think that we had been too late.

I turned from the bedroom and then that damnable scent came to my nostrils redoubled, and I knew. "Beetles!"

But how could there be beetles? It was all an illusion in poor Hartley's brain. Even his twisted mind had realized that there were no apertures in the walls to admit them; that they could not be seen about the place.

And still the smell rose on the air—the reek of death, of decay, of ancient corruption that reigned in Egypt. I followed the scent to the second bedroom, forced the door.

On the bed lay the mummy case. Hartley had said he locked it up in here. The lid was closed, but ajar.

I opened it. The sides bore inscriptions, and one of them may have pertained to the Scarabæus Curse. I do not know, for I stared only at the ghastly, unshrouded figure that lay within. It was a mummy, and it had been sucked dry. It was all shell. There was a great cavity in the stomach, and as I peered within I could see a few feebly crawling forms—inch-long, black buttons with great writhing feelers. They shrank back in the light, but not before I saw the scarab patterns on the outer crusted backs.

The secret of the Curse was here—the beetles had dwelt within the body of the mummy! They had eaten it out and nested within, and at night they crawled forth. It was true then!

I screamed once the thought hit me, and dashed back to Hartley's bedroom. I could hear the sound of footsteps ascending the outer stairs; the police were on their way, but I couldn't wait. I raced into the bedroom, dread tugging at my heart.

Had Hartley's story been true, after all? Were the beetles really messengers of a divine vengeance?

I ran into that bedroom where Arthur Hartley lay, stooped over his huddled figure on the bed. My hands fumbled over the body, searching for a wound. I had to know how he had died.

But there was no blood, there was no mark, and there was no weapon beside him. It had been shock or heart attack, after all. I was strangely relieved when I thought of this. I stood up and eased the body back again on the pillows.

I felt almost glad, because during my search my hands had moved over the body while my eyes roved over the room. I was looking for beetles.

Hartley had feared the beetles—the beetles that crawled out of the mummy. They had crawled every night, if his story was to be believed; crawled into his room, up the bedposts, across the pillows.

Where were they now? They had left the mummy and disappeared, and Hartley was dead. Where were they?

Suddenly I stared again at Hartley. There was something wrong with the body on the bed. When I had lifted the corpse, it seemed singularly light for a man of Hartley's build. As I gazed at him, now, he seemed empty of more than life. I peered into that ravaged face more closely, and then I shuddered. For the cords on his neck moved convulsively, his chest seemed to rise and fall, his head fell sideways on the pillow. He lived—or something inside him did!

And then as his twisted features moved, I cried aloud, for I knew how Hartley had died, and what had killed him; knew the secret of the Scarab Curse and why the beetles crawled out of the mummy to seek his bed. I knew what they had meant to do—what, tonight, they had done. I cried aloud as I saw Hartley's face move, in hopes that my voice would drown that dreadful rustling sound which filled the room and came from *inside Hartley's body*.

I knew that the Scarab Curse had killed him, and I screamed quite wildly as his mouth gaped slowly open. Just as I fainted, I saw Arthur Hartley's dead lips part, allowing a rustling swarm of *black Scarabæus beetles* to pour out across the pillow.

EDWARD D. HOCH *has published seven hundred short stories in a career that has spanned more than thirty years. His story "The Oblong Room" won an Edgar Award from the Mystery Writers of America in 1967—and his monthly contribution to* Ellery Queen's Mystery Magazine *is eagerly awaited by his legion of fans.*

THE WEEKEND MAGUS

By Edward D. Hoch

"He goes up to Scotland every weekend," Sir Richard's secretary had told me. "Nobody knows what he does there."

I'd come to London to obtain an interview with Sir Richard Forbish for an American newsmagazine, and if I had to follow him to Scotland to get it, that was all right with me, too. I flew up to Glasgow on the afternoon plane and rented a car at the airport, getting out just before the weekend rush.

Sir Richard's Scottish retreat was fifty miles northwest of Glasgow, on the banks of Loch Awe. The sun was low in the sky by the time I reached it, and my first impression was only of a country house of modest proportions. The bell was answered not by a gaunt mysterious butler but by a pert young blonde in a tennis tunic. I was beginning to learn what Sir Richard did with his weekends.

"Come in! You must be that American writer who's come to interview Rich."

"Guilty," I admitted. "Is Sir Richard about?"

"Oh, yes." Her accent wasn't quite British. "He's working downstairs. I'll call him." She paused and said, almost as an afterthought, "I'm Minerva Athens. Pleased to meet you."

131

Glancing down at her short white tunic and bare legs she added, "Rich and I had a game of tennis earlier."

"Charming," I remarked, leaving her to take it however she would.

She vanished through a door to the basement, and when she reappeared after a moment she was followed by a tall, slender man who was both younger and handsomer than I'd expected him to look at forty-eight. "Good to see you here," he said, extending his hand.

"It's an honor, Sir Richard," I assured him.

"I don't usually receive journalists here on weekends, you know. I come up here with Minerva to get away from the pressures of London."

Minerva cleared her throat. "Let me slip into something else and I'll get us all a drink."

Sir Richard led me into a massive book-lined study in the best tradition of British manor houses. Seated behind his wide oak desk, he seemed to assume the role of eminent man of science for the first time. "I was a bit baffled by your request for an interview," he said. "Is your publication doing a series on nonwinners of the Nobel Prize?"

"You must know you're in line for that any year now."

"Perhaps."

"My editors in New York are mainly interested in your experiments with the radioactive dating of archaeological sites."

"An interesting field," Sir Richard said. "We've made some astonishing discoveries right here in Scotland."

I reached for my briefcase. "Mind if I record this?"

"I wasn't aware the formal interview had begun. Let us relax with a drink first. Good Scotch always tastes best right here in Scotland."

In a moment Minerva Athens was back, wearing a gold lounging robe. While she went off to fix our drinks, I asked Forbish, "Just as general background, what is your marital status?"

"My wife and I are separated. Minerva has been a great help to me in this trying time." His words seemed well rehearsed, as if he'd recited them many times in past months.

"She's a lovely young woman."

"She is that," he agreed.

Minerva returned with the Scotch and sat down to join us. Sir Richard left his desk and took one of the other chairs, reinforcing the informality of the session. "Are these weekends strictly for relaxation or do you manage to get some work in?" I asked.

"I'm working on something downstairs. A hobby of sorts."

"You've been especially successful in dating Egyptian artifacts."

Forbish warmed to his favorite subject. "My technique goes a step beyond carbon dating as practiced elsewhere. Interestingly enough, I've found some artifacts from Roman times right here in Scotland."

"This far north?"

Sir Richard smiled. "Hadrian's Wall was near the Scottish border, but the Wall of Antoninus was well into Scotland. And the Romans certainly ventured north of their walls, or they would not have realized the need for them."

"To keep out the barbarians from the north?"

He nodded and sipped his Scotch. "I have found evidence that Egyptians accompanied the Romans this far."

"What would Egyptians be doing here?"

He motioned toward the woman at his side. "Minerva is one-quarter Egyptian and she is here."

"But—"

"Seriously, Cleopatra lived in Rome as Caesar's mistress, and the ties between the two people were very great. I believe Egyptian specialists sometimes traveled with the Roman legions."

"Specialists in what?"

"Astronomy, embalming, the building of pyramids."

Minerva interrupted with a snort. "This solemn talk bores me. Do you play tennis?"

"Hardly at all," I answered.

"We have an indoor court around back. The house is much larger than it appears at first glance. I'll show you around tomorrow. You will be staying the weekend, won't you?"

"I hadn't planned—"

"Nonsense!" Sir Richard said. "Of course you'll stay!" He gave instructions for Minerva to prepare the guest room.

Later, after an excellent dinner of freshly killed pheasant, she showed me to the room. "He's pleased to have you here," she told me. "He has something very special to show you tomorrow."

In the morning after breakfast Sir Richard and I strolled down the hill to the edge of Loch Awe. I noticed that the rear of the large house overhung the hill, and big double doors provided a level access to the basement. "Is that a garage?" I asked.

"It was built as a boat house. The previous owner had a ramp running down to the water. I've put the space to other use."

"It's a fine clear lake for boating."

"All Scottish lochs are. That's why I love the country so much." He tossed a pebble far into the lake, and I watched the ripples break the calm mirrored surface.

"You're a weekend laird," I suggested.

"More of a weekend magus." His eyes twinkled at the words.

"Just what is it you're doing up here?"

Forbish stared out over the water. "Shortly after I purchased this house I made an amazing discovery. What I found was confirmation of an Egyptian presence here—confirmation in the most vivid manner. It was an earthen burial mound in the shape of a pyramid, containing the mummified remains of a man."

"A mummy? In Scotland?"

"Exactly."

"That's quite a discovery."

"There were the usual personal objects buried with him, and even what I took to be a pet. The Egyptians often buried mummified dogs and cats—even baboons—with their dead rulers."

"You found another tomb of King Tut!"

Sir Richard chuckled. "Hardly! There were no treasures of gold or precious gems. But my experiments with the mummified remains could make the Nobel Prize committee sit up and take notice."

I was beginning to see why this interview was so important to him. He would use it to make some important announcement. Before I could comment he hurried on. "Are you familiar with the experiments of the Americans Harris and Weeks in X-raying the mummies at the Cairo museum?"

"Vaguely."

"The work was carried out ten years ago by the University of Michigan School of Dentistry and yielded a wealth of new information. I attempted to carry the X-ray and radiation experiments a step further."

"With what result?"

He shrugged casually and tossed another pebble. "There is evidence of some reanimation in the bones of one of the subjects."

"What?" I couldn't believe my ears. "Are you talking about bringing a mummy back to life? Shades of Dr. Frankenstein!"

Forbish laughed. "Hardly anything like that. You won't encounter Boris Karloff lurching around the place trailing his wrappings."

"I hope not."

"Part of the Egyptian mummification technique involved the removal of brain matter, usually by metal hooks inserted through the nostrils. After such a procedure any resurrection would be quite impossible."

"Then what—"

He held up a hand. "All in good time. Do you have a camera?"

"I have a small one in my briefcase, but my editor usually arranges to send a photographer if it's necessary."

"Never mind. Your camera will serve very well. And I've been teaching Minerva to operate my little movie camera."

"When will all this photography take place?"

Sir Richard smiled. "Perhaps this evening."

After lunch I watched them play tennis on the indoor court around the back of the house. Minerva was quite good, and more than a match for Sir Richard. While he disappeared downstairs, I went for a stroll with her on the grounds of the estate, along the wooded hill that overlooked Loch Awe.

"What does he have in the basement?" I asked, coming right to the point.

She made a face. "Mummies. He'll show you tonight. That's what he lured you up here for."

"Mummies in Scotland! I can't get over it!"

"Neither can he. It's become an obsession with him—though only a weekend obsession, thank heavens!"

"He spoke of himself as a weekend magus."

"He is that, I suppose. A magus, a necromancer who would communicate with the dead."

"He wants to communicate?"

"Figuratively speaking."

"He mentioned reanimation."

"Yes."

"That implies a return to life."

"Sir Richard is a great man, a great scientist. You must know from your short time with him that he is no madman surrounded by bubbling test tubes and sparking generators."

"He seems quite sane," I agreed cautiously.

"The sanest man I've ever known. He has something here— a discovery whose very existence would be enough to make him famous around the world. And yet he's kept it secret for nearly a year while he's spent his weekends trying for the ultimate breakthrough. You see, he doesn't just want to be famous. He wants the recognition of his colleagues. He wants that prize."

"The Nobel. I gathered as much."

"Will you help him get it?"

"I'm only a poor journalist."

"But your magazine is one of the most important in America! This is not just any story he's giving you. It's the story of a lifetime!" She took a deep breath. "Can you get him a cover photograph?"

"If he can make a mummy walk, I'll get him his cover."

She turned to stare at me. "It will not walk, but I don't think you'll be disappointed."

We dined as we had the night before, by candlelight in the ornate dining room. Minerva proved to be a versatile cook, and this time the meal was French. As I finished my dessert and complimented her, Sir Richard pushed back his chair. "We must be about our business," he announced. "Let me show you to my laboratory."

Descending the basement steps reminded me of all the horror films of my youth, and only the light chatter of Forbish and Minerva relieved the tension. The basement room, behind the big double doors that led down to the water, was large enough to have accommodated several boats in its day. Now, however, it was given over to an array of electrical equipment. I recognized a large X-ray machine and some radiation gear of the sort sometimes found in hospitals for the treatment of tumors.

"This is expensive apparatus," I commented.

"But quite necessary." He led me to a table where a flat stone lay displayed beneath an overhead light. There was a line of hieroglyphics at the top, and beneath it a sentence in Latin.

Forbish translated it for me. *"Here is entombed the remains of the Egyptian Satni along with his favorite Gavia who perished here together in the third summer of the reign of Antoninus Pius."*

"What date would that be?" I asked.

"Probably A.D. 141. Antoninus Pius was the adopted son of Hadrian, and like Hadrian he built a wall of his own across the country, quite close to here. He was attempting to extend Roman rule further into what is now Scotland, but he had little success. His own adopted son, Marcus Aurelius, was a much better emperor."

"So the mummies you uncovered belong to Satni and Gavia?"

"It would seem so." Sir Richard walked to another table and pulled away a sheet, revealing the traditional form of a wrapped mummy. "This is Satni. I uncovered a portion of the head for testing purposes. Carbon-dating techniques confirm the date sometime in the middle of the second century."

"An Egyptian mummy in Scotland." There was a tone of wonder in my voice that I couldn't conceal. "It's quite a discovery."

"But only the beginning. After all, what's one more mummy in the world? Every big museum has a few on display."

"And this Gavia? Was it a woman?"

"More of a pet, I believe. The inscription speaks of his favorite. The word itself, 'Gavia,' is Latin for sea gull—but it was loosely used here as a graceful name, a pet name, for a sea creature."

As he spoke he moved to the back of the large room and pulled aside a long drape.

And then I saw it, stretched across the basement floor for a distance of perhaps forty feet, its great scaled body intertwined with electric wires and the remains of the mummy wrappings. "This," Sir Richard announced with a flourish, "is Gavia."

"It's some sort of giant serpent!" I exclaimed. "A python, perhaps?"

"Not at this size! Look again, sir—you are gazing upon a creature of the sea, an inhabitant of this very loch. I suspect it might be an ancestor of the one seen to the north of here, in Loch Ness."

"But—this is fantastic! You're telling me you've uncovered

the mummy of some sea serpent that was buried along with an Egyptian in the second century? Why in heaven's name would they be buried together?''

Sir Richard was smiling at my bafflement. ''The evidence indicates the Egyptian may have been riding on the back of Gavia when he died.'' He showed me another stone, and there upon it was a crude drawing of a man who seemed to be riding a serpent through the waves.

''I—I'm speechless!''

Minerva was at my elbow with a chuckle. ''So was Rich when he first found this thing. I wanted him to phone the police, the government, anyone. I wanted to shout it from the rooftops what he'd discovered. But he was wise to wait.''

''What are all these wires?'' I asked.

''Naturally I was trying to date and X-ray the serpent as I'd done with the other mummy. In the process of administering a massive doze of radiation I detected some movement.''

''You mean you've brought it back to life?''

''Hardly that! I mean the creature was never really dead. It went into some sort of shock to its nervous system at the time Satni died. We'll never know exactly what happened, but I believe it's been in a state of suspended animation—a sort of prolonged hibernation—ever since. Naturally the embalmers did not use the same technique on this monster that they used on humans. As near as I can tell, its brain and internal organs are intact. The embalming and mummification process only served to keep it alive.''

''How much movement has there been?''

''Only a bit of thrashing when the radiation is applied. If you'll get your camera, I'll give a demonstration. And Minerva—the movie camera, please.''

I took the camera from my briefcase with shaking hands and brought out the tape recorder, too. It was as near a moment of pure fantasy as I'd ever experienced, and I had to remind myself over and over that it was really happening. This was no pot-induced dream or movie shocker. It was happening, and to me.

''Go ahead,'' I said, moving as far back as I could to fit the sleeping monster in my lens. Minerva raised the movie camera and turned on her lights.

Sir Richard checked the wiring and then twisted his dials. There was a sudden thrashing of the serpent's tail that threatened to overturn a table. "Stop it!" Minerva warned. "You're giving him too much."

The old head lifted then from the floor, and the eyes seemed to stare into Sir Richard's eyes. He stepped backward and cut the power. I could see the little beads of sweat on his brow. "You see?" he asked me. "Everything I have told you is true."

Minerva took a sudden step forward. "It's still moving, Richard!"

"Of course. It's alive, after all."

"Let's go upstairs."

"Doesn't it need water?" I asked, still somewhat shaken by what I'd seen.

"The loch is its natural home, but it is an air-breathing creature." He turned out the lights and closed the drape over the serpent. Then we followed Minerva upstairs. "Is that worth a cover story?" he asked.

"I'll get you on the cover. I'll do better than that—I'll get you on the front page of every newspaper in the world!"

"Fine!"

"I'll phone our London office in the morning and have them send a photographic team up here. This is too big a story to handle by myself."

But when Sir Richard left us alone, Minerva expressed misgivings. "I'm worried about him," she admitted. "And now I'm worried about that thing in the basement, too. Richard is never satisfied. He's always striving to top himself. He found the earthen pyramid but that wasn't enough. He had to dig into it until he found the mummy, but that wasn't enough either. Then he found the coiled mummy of that serpent and I thought surely this would satisfy him. It did, for about a week. Then he was back up here on the weekend, talking about carbon dating and radiation doses. He brought the thing back to life, for God's sake, and I still don't think he's satisfied!"

"Well, the publicity he'll get should certainly satisfy him."

"I wonder."

Though I went to bed early, I found I couldn't sleep. The excitement of the story I was about to break kept me tossing and turning in the big old bed, composing new leads and even picture captions. And through it all one question kept bothering me. When the truth was out, when the world knew what Sir Richard Forbish had done on his weekends, would they give him the Nobel Prize or destroy him as a satanic sorcerer?

I must have finally dozed, because Minerva had to shake me awake. "Come quickly," she urged. "There are terrible noises from the basement."

I pulled on a robe and followed her downstairs, wishing I'd brought some sort of weapon. But when we reached the laboratory, all was quiet, and it wasn't until I felt the cool night mist on my face that I realized the big double doors were standing open. The mummy of Satni still rested on its table, but there was no sign of the serpent Gavia. The wires which had coupled it to the various electrical devices lay in a tangle on the floor.

"Richard!" she cried out.

But there was no answer.

We searched through the darkness outside the doors and by the first light of dawn we could make out the track in the dirt where Gavia had slithered down the hill to the waiting waters of Loch Awe. "We have to face it," I told her finally. "The serpent must have attacked and killed Sir Richard, then carried his body into the loch. There's no other explanation."

She thought about it for a long time, and when we returned to the big house, she said, "There is one other explanation. Remember that drawing he found in the pyramid? Rich was never satisfied. He was always trying for something more. I believe he might have urged the serpent down that hill to the water, making the noises I heard to frighten it. Certainly Gavia didn't open that double door by itself."

"But why . . . ?"

"Don't you see? I think Richard wanted to ride it, just as Satni had done all those centuries ago."

We didn't find either of them, and thought I still had the mummy of Satni for my story, somehow it wasn't enough—not with what I could have had. So I haven't written it yet, but I keep waiting. Sooner or later Sir Richard's body will wash up on the shore of the Loch Awe, or Gavia will come to the surface once more.

I've gotten myself transferred to the magazine's London bureau, and every weekend I go up to Scotland and join Minerva at the big house. The police have given up trying to explain Sir Richard's disappearance, but the two of us still search. We know what we're looking for, and sooner or later we'll find it. Then I'll have the biggest news break of the century.

It should certainly bring me a Pulitzer Prize.

VICTOR ROUSSEAU (1879–1960) was born in Great Britain, but resided in America for most of his life. A noted contributor to many of the pulp magazines of his day, Rousseau published a number of Western and mainstream novels in the 1920s, but he is best known for his novels The Sea Demons *(1916),* The Messiah of the Cylinder *(1917), and* Draught of Eternity *(1918).*

THE CURSE OF AMEN-RA

by Victor Rousseau

The scene all around me was about as repulsive a one as I had ever set eyes upon. On every side the flat, dun marshes, with their heavy growth of sedge, stretched away. In front of me—yes, that must be Pequod Island, for a strip of foul and sluggish water separated it from the mainland.

Pequod Island, in the lower reaches of Chesapeake Bay, was barely a hundred feet distant; I could have waded waist-high to it, but for the sucking quick-mud which, I knew, would engulf me if I attempted any such thing.

And there was no need to attempt it, for an ancient ferryman was already poling his antediluvian bark across the narrow channel in my direction. I stopped at the edge of the trail and waited for him.

He hailed me, using indistinguishable words in a local dialect that was unintelligible to me. Then, just out of reach, he held the punt with his pole and peered at me out of his deep-set eyes under their white thick eyebrows, while he chewed and worked his chin with its stained shaggy gray beard.

"Well, what are you waiting there for?" I asked impatiently. "Don't you see I want to cross?"

"Aye, ye want to cross, do ye? But what do ye want to cross for? Who d'ye want to see?" I managed to make out.

"I want to see Mr. Neil Farrant, if you've got to know," I answered. "I didn't know this island was private, though."

"Neil Farrant? What, him that's got the mummies down to Tap's Point?" There was a look of fear in the old ferryman's eyes. "He won't see ye. Won't see nobody. There was scores turned away when he first brung them here. Pestered the life out of him, they did. University perfessors and all—but he wouldn't see none of them."

"Well, this is different," I answered. "My name's Jim Dewey, and Mr. Farrant has especially requested me to call and help him with his work."

"Jim Dewey?" The ferryman turned the quid of tobacco in his mouth. "Yeah, I seem ter remember Mr. Farrant saying you could come."

But he still stood there, leaning upon his pole, eyeing me with ruminating, brooding suspicion.

"Well, why don't you bring the boat near enough for me to step down?" I asked.

"See here, mister, how'd I know you ain't come to try to help one of Dr. Coyne's loonies to escape?" he asked.

"What the devil do you mean? Who's he?" I answered. But before the old man could speak again, it flashed across my mind that Neil had told me the island was occupied principally by the house and extensive grounds of Dr. Rolf Coyne's private sanitarium, where some of the wealthiest and most hopelessly insane of Virginia and other states were housed.

That was why Neil, who had been associated with Dr. Coyne for three or four years before his departure for Egypt, as assistant to the University of North Virginia Excavation Fund, had chosen this lonely spot in which to work out certain experiments with the mummies that he had brought back. And I, because we had been friends through our four years at the university together, was to be permitted to assist in his task.

He had written me in guarded terms that had aroused my curiosity, had asked me to wire him whether I could come, and I had wired back my acceptance.

The old ferryman winked at me. "There's fellers wouldn't stop at helping the most desp'rit of them loonies to git away, if they was well paid for it," he said. "And they got away more than once. That's why we don't have no bridge between the island and the mainland. I'm Old Incorruptible, I am. That's what the doctor calls me. If you're a friend of Mr. Farrant's, I reckon you got the right to cross, but if you're thinking of gittin' some of them poor devils away, lemme tell you Dr. Coyne's bloodhounds will run ye down and tear ye to pieces.''

"Well, I'm not going to wait here all day while you're making up your mind whether I'm a fit person to cross," I retorted. "So bring your boat up to the bank, or get back where you came from, and I'll phone Mr. Farrant you refused to take me over."

The ancient chewed a minute or two on that, then reluctantly poled up to the bank. Clutching my suitcase, I stepped aboard, and the old man pushed back through the muddy water toward the opposite shore.

"How much to pay?" I asked as we finally landed.

"Ye can make it what ye like, mister," he answered. "Money don't mean nothing to me. Old Incorruptible, the doctor called me, and that's what I am. Ye can make it a quarter, or ye can make it fifty cents."

Having no change, I handed him a dollar and told him to keep it. His eyes bulged avariciously as he pocketed the bill. "Now which way to Mr. Farrant's house?" I asked.

"Down to Tap's Point," replied the ancient. "Foller that road through the village, and you'll come to the house a quarter mile or so beyond. But listen, mister." He seized me by the arm as I was about to stride down the weed-grown road. "Ye won't never come back. None of them done, who opened the graves in which them mummies lay. Only Mr. Farrant, and that was because he was a healer. Mr. Burke and Mr. Watrous, and that English lord whose name I fergit—all of them died, because of the curse that was put upon anyone opening them dead princes' and princesses' graves.

"Folks think we don't know down to Tap's Point, but we seen it all in the Sunday newspapers, and we ain't minded to have them dead mummies prowling round our homes and killing our children. I'm warning you, mister, the first person who's killed on Pequod Island, there's going to be a reckoning. Excepting you. If you want to commit suicide, you're welcome to it. But keep them mummies out of our homes."

He leaned forward and tapped me on the shoulder. "When you see them hawks, look out for trouble," he whispered. "The hounds knows, and we knows. You'd better not have come."

"You talk like a madman," I retorted. It irked me to think that the silly legend of a curse, fostered by the admittedly strange deaths of so many members of the expedition, had become known among these clowns. But the old man only went on chewing tobacco and grinning at me derisively; I turned from him and, with my suitcase in my hand, went striding down the track of a road that ran toward Tap's Point.

Pequod Island was more picturesque than I had supposed from the sight I had obtained of it from the flat shore opposite. In a few minutes I was passing between stretches of juniper and stunted cypress. Then I saw, far back through the trees, a great building, a cluster of buildings, which I knew must be Dr. Coyne's private sanitarium. There was an open space with tennis nets, and men were playing. Others were strolling in the grounds. Everything was open and unfenced—why shouldn't it be, with the bay on one side, and that stretch of muddy water on the other, and the bloodhounds?

I passed the grounds of the sanitarium and came to a straggling village beside the water, where a few fishing boats, drawn up, proclaimed the nature of the livelihood of the occupants. Two or three men, slouching about, stared at me sullenly, and a woman glared defiantly from an open doorway and muttered something as I went by. Another clutched a small child to her, as if I were some kidnapper.

I passed them, head erect, carrying my suitcase. I was still filled with indignation at the monstrous stories in circulation, all due to the fact that Neil Farrant had managed to bring back, in some unauthorized way, three or four of the mummy cases from the tomb of the kings that had recently been opened in Upper Egypt. And from what I remembered of Neil, I didn't for a moment suppose that he placed any stock in the absurd stories of a curse.

I had never known a more hardheaded fellow than my classmate. In fact, I had wondered a good deal at the guarded nature of his letter, and his remarks about certain experiments.

Well, the village was past me, and Tap's Point lay behind. The thread of foul water had broadened into a bay, on which three or four of the fishing boats were engaged in hauling in their booty. The sun was quite low in the west. The scene had suddenly become wild and beautiful. In front of me was a grove of trees, but there was sea debris right up to their edge, and I guessed that at times storms had submerged this corner of the island.

Then unexpectedly I saw Neil's house. It was an old farmhouse, extending over quite a large stretch of ground and built solidly of stone. At some early date it had probably been the country home of some colonial gentleman.

The edge of the sun had dipped down into the bay. Nothing was stirring in the quiet of the evening; the sails of the boats hung listlessly. I could no longer see the fishermen aboard, but something was hanging overhead. It was a hawk. And another hawk joined it, coming apparently from the direction of the sanitarium. Then a third and fourth came into view.

Fish hawks, I thought; nothing remarkable about their presence there. But what was it that the old fool had said about hawks? "When you see them hawks, look out for trouble!"

Well, I saw them, and a fifth, and a sixth, and I had no presentiment of trouble—only a sense of pleasure in the mildness of the evening as I approached the door of Neil's house. I noticed that the windows were all tightly shuttered in front and on both sides of the house, and wondered at that a little, for Neil had been a fresh-air fiend in our early days. I passed up the worn, crazy-stone path and tapped at the door.

I was conscious that the hawks had been following me, but I thought nothing of that. I knew that hawks would follow fishermen—at least, fishing hawks; and the fact that some eight or nine of them were circling above my head aroused no particular emotion in me. I tapped at the door of the shack, anticipating the moment of Neil's delighted recognition of me.

No answer came, and I tapped again, more loudly. Then I heard Neil's voice inside. "Who is it? What do you want here?"

Strangely harsh and uncouth it sounded; but I guessed that he had been made the victim of the crazy suspicious of the villagers.

"It's Jim Dewey. Didn't you expect me?" I called.

"Jim Dewey? Why didn't you wire me, man, as I asked you to do?"

"I did wire. I guess the telegraph system is a little slow in this part of the world," I answered. "Aren't you going to let me in?"

"Sure, but—you're alone, Jim? There's nothing with you?"

"Of course not," I answered.

There sounded the shuffling of Neil's feet inside the door, then the cautious removal of a chain. Inch by inch the door opened, until Neil stood before me. I was amazed at the transformation in him. The desert heat and sun had browned and wasted him; there was a three days' stubble of a beard upon his face, and his clothes hung loose about his wasted frame. He looked years older.

"Well, Neil, you don't seem half-glad to see me," I said, putting out my hand.

I saw his hand advance; then he glanced over my shoulder, and a cry burst from his lips. I thought he was going to slam the door in my face.

"The hawks! The hawks! Keep them out!" he shouted.

And as we stood there, the birds, huger than any other hawks I had ever seen, suddenly swooped for the door with incredible velocity. I was half inside and half outside, and in an instant the two of us were involved in a tangle of fluttering pinions.

The birds seemed to have gone mad. They swooped down upon us with the utmost fearlessness, yet it was not we who seemed to be the object of their attack. They were apparently imbued with the sole determination of getting inside the house. I saw Neil seize one of them in his hands and almost rend the head from the body. It fluttered out through the doorway, and then, as it magically recovered, soared on high and swooped down at us again.

I did my best against the evil-smelling feathered throng, but my face and hands were quickly a mass of scratches as the talons tore at me.

Then somehow we had won. The last of the winged intruders had been driven from the house, and Neil had dragged me inside and closed the door. For a few moments, the birds fluttered against it, then soared away.

At the same moment I heard one of the hounds in Dr. Coyne's sanitarium give tongue, then another and another. And I became aware that the sun had set, and darkness was fast settling about us.

I stared at Neil, who was covered with scratches, too.

"Well, we kept them out, Jim," he said. "Better come up to the bathroom and let's put some iodine on those scratches."

"Why don't you shoot those birds?" I asked him. "They must be mad."

"They—don't die, Jim. That's the trouble. I'll—tell you about it."

2

After we had washed and disinfected our scratches, Neil led the way down to the ground floor of the building. We passed through a poorly furnished living room, filled with the ugly furniture of the 1870s, fitted up with bookcases filled with books, which seemed to deal principally with Egyptology and medieval works on astrology and such subjects. Thence through another room, and so we came to a very long room at the back, which must once have been some kind of storeroom.

It was built entirely of stone, and the numerous windows were heavily shuttered, the shutters being kept in place with iron bars.

Neil switched on a cluster of electric lights in the ceiling, and I perceived that this was his museum. The room was filled with priceless trophies that he had brought back from Egypt. There were two chairs from a tomb, papyrus scrolls, a glass cabinet with various objects resting upon shelves. The room was filled with the pungent odor of spices.

I hardly noticed any of these things, however; my attention was immediately riveted upon five wooden caskets, mummy cases, placed on a dais against the wall and held in position by brackets. On the exterior of each was beautifully painted the representation of the body within. One of these was the painting of a girl, of such exquisite and noble beauty that I could hardly take my eyes away from it.

You know how closely the ancient Egyptian type approximates to certain of the finest types of today. Except that the eyes were conventionally too large, the lineaments were perfect. The little, slightly tilted nose, the small chin, the expression of breeding, of a certain wistfulness, the success of the ideal that the artist had endeavored to portray almost took away my breath.

I saw Neil looking at me and smiling slightly. For the first time he looked more like his old self than the haggard, grim-faced man whom I had met half an hour before.

"The Princess Amen-Ra," he said, watching me as I stared at the painting, "is of a very old dynasty of Egyptian kings, concerning whose date there is still some dispute. It is certain that she antedated Moses and the Children of Israel by several hundred years. Would you like to hear her story, Jim?

"After her brother's death," he went on, without waiting for my answer, "she ruled the kingdom. She lived and died unmarried. These others"—he pointed to the four other caskets—are the priests and counselors who were associated with her.

"Her reign is legendary, but it is called the Golden Age of Egypt. During her life the Nile always gave up its proper quota of fertilizing waters; the land remained at peace. Everywhere was prosperity. She was worshiped as divine.

"Only one thing troubled the priesthood. It was considered necessary that she should marry. The question was who was fit to mate with her. A foreign spouse was unthinkable, for Amen-Ra was believed to descend from the god Osiris.

"There was a young nobleman of Thebes named Menes, who had fallen in love with the princess, and his love was reciprocated. He was too powerful to be condemned or banished, yet the astrologers had predicted that such a marriage would bring down the anger of the gods upon the realm. So the priests conspired to put the young nobleman to death, together with the princess's counselors, for the sake of Egypt.

"On the night of the nuptial ceremony the conspirators broke into the palace and murdered Menes and the chief counselors who had assented to the marriage, yet not until one of the latter, by his magic arts, had caused the Nile to flood the land, and an earthquake that shook down the palace walls. The princess took her own life by poison, in despair. There seems to have been a peasant uprising, too, which completed the disaster. All this is described in that papyrus."

Neil pointed to the glass-covered scroll which stood immediately behind the casket.

"The body of Menes was never discovered," he continued. "But those who survived the disaster dug out those of the princess and her counselors, and these were carefully embalmed, without removing the brain or viscera, which was not done until a later period in Egyptian history. They were buried in the Temple of Set, and unearthed by our expedition.

"According to the Egyptian belief, after a period of some three thousand years, the Ba would return to reanimate these bodies, when the princess and her advisers would rearise from the tomb to rule the land again and restore it to its ancient glories."

"The Ba was the soul?" I asked.

"The Ba was the soul—as distinct from the Ka, the double, or astral body. There was also the winged Ish, the spirit that dwelled in the abode of the gods. But as for Menes, it is believed that his body was reduced to ashes. You see, the lovers had sworn eternal fealty, by the god Horus, a pledge that neither life nor death should separate them. And the priests were horribly afraid that Menes would return to claim his bride after three thousand years, when Egypt's ancient glories would return.

"Over the sarcophagus was inscribed a curse against anyone who should ever tamper with the tombs. The widespread legend sufficed to keep them inviolate against both desert robbers and the Moslem invaders of the country. We were the first to open them."

"But, Neil, you don't believe in that stuff about the curse, do you?" I asked him.

"Well, I didn't—when I went along with the University of Virginia expedition. But what happened? Lord Cardingham, who had largely financed the expedition, fell into an excavation and broke his neck. Burke was taken sick with a mysterious fever and died within a day. Plague, they called it—but there is no plague in Upper Egypt.

"Watrous pricked his finger with a thorn splinter and died of blood poisoning. Three of our natives died mysteriously within a week. Lewis and Holmes were taken ill and sent down to the coast. Lewis died, and Holmes was drowned when his vessel was shipwrecked off Sicily.

"By that time, I was the last left. I was supposed to be immune against the curse, because I was the physician of the party. I didn't believe—but I had seen too much to disbelieve. I determined to sift the matter to the bottom.

"I succeeded, by bribes, in persuading some of the natives to load the coffins and trophies upon a flat-bottomed boat. I managed to get them down to the coast and so to America. Dr. Coyne, with whom I had worked, and one of the leading neurologists of the world, suggested that I should have the use of this old house, which he owns, in which to carry out my experiment."

"What experiment?" I asked, looking at Neil incredulously, for his face was almost fanatical.

"First," answered Neil, "I must have it from your own lips that you are prepared to associate yourself with me, taking your chance of coming under the curse."

"I've told you I'm in to the limit," I answered. "But so far as the curse is concerned, I think it's a lot of poppycock."

Neil looked at me in a queer way, and walked to the papyrus. He began translating: " 'That Menes, the accursed one, who has been utterly destroyed by fire, may never return to any earthly habitation . . . the curse of Horus, the curse of Anubis, of Osiris, of Hapimous, of the Nile god, of Shu, of the winds, of the god Mesti the hawk-headed, rest upon him who shall violate these tombs. May he die by water, thorn, and fire. . . .' "

"Does it really say 'thorn,' Neil?" I asked, remembering that Watrous had died from a thorn splinter.

" 'May he die by pestilence and the winds and shipwreck, and by the beak and claw of Mesti. May his bowels be consumed by inward fire, and he and all his perish. May he—' But I reckon that's enough," continued Neil, looking back at me from the papyrus. His manner grew almost furtive. "How would you like to take a look at the little princess?" he asked in a low tone.

"I certainly should," I answered. "Do you mean to say . . . ?"

"Yes, I've opened them all. Of course the dampness of Pequod Island would play havoc with them. But, you see, the experiment—"

He broke off, went to the cabinet, and took out a chisel, which he inserted in the edge of the mummy casket. Evidently he had opened the casket a number of times, for the lid, which was perfectly preserved, despite the centuries that had passed, slid off, disclosing a plainer and unpainted coffin. The lid of this Neil removed in turn, and I saw before me the mummy of the young girl, swathed in the rotting linen fabric, which diffused an almost unbearable odor of natron and spices.

Only the contours were visible; the linen swathed the whole head and body like a winding sheet. Yet I could see that it had been unwound and wound repeatedly, and, I imagined, by Neil. His hands were shaking. He no longer seemed aware of my presence. Nor of the sudden fluttering of wings without the shuttered windows, and the rending of claws against the bars.

Somehow the proximity of the hawks seemed to me to be connected with what Neil was doing. I shuddered at the sound, but it was not repeated; I watched Neil begin to unwind the upper layer of linen, so that the contours of the mummy's head gradually grew plainer.

I saw tufts of dark hair appear, and I was amazed at its perfect preservation. It was the eeriest experience I had ever known, to stand there and see this figure of the long-dead Egyptian princess gradually coming to light.

Of a sudden Neil stopped in the midst of his work, looked around, and saw me. For an instant he stared at me as if he did not recognize me, as if I were some hostile intruder. And I, in turn, was astonished at the transformation that had come over him.

He looked again as he had looked at the moment of our meeting in the doorway. That lean, cadaverous form of his looked rather like that of a desert sheik than of a twentieth-century American.

"Jim—what the devil!" he began, and then seemed to recollect me. He pulled himself together with a visible effort.

"I'm all worked up over this business, Jim," he said. "Excuse me if I seem queer. I was going to show you the mummy of Amen-Ra, but I guess she'll keep."

"Now that you've gone so far, I'd like to see the rest," I answered. But he was already staring into space as if I had vanished completely from his consciousness. And mechanically his hands went on unwinding the linen shroud.

One more turn, I thought—but there were several, for the material was now as fine as silk, and perfectly preserved. Another turn, and another, and still two more; and then, just as I was beginning to wonder when the process would come to an end, the last layer fell away, and the face and torso of the Amen-Ra were revealed to me.

I stared at the face and gasped. This a mummy? This the face of a girl who had died countless centuries before? Why, she might only just have died. The skin, with its delicate olive tinge, was perfectly preserved, it even seemed slightly flushed, as if the blood pulsated underneath its peach-smooth surface. The eyes were closed, but there was the hint of a pupil beneath the white eyelid, shaded with long, black lashes.

And it seemed to me as if the ghost of a smile hovered about the mouth, a smile, a loving, mocking smile, as if the dead girl's last thoughts had been of the man to whom she had sworn by the god Horus that neither life nor death should separate them!

I looked at that face, with its beauty and high breeding, and the tragedy of the old story gripped my heart. This girl seemed so alive! It was incredible that all this had happened in the dim dawn of history.

Suddenly Neil flung himself down before the coffin. His hands clasped the sides of the wooden case. He looked into the face of the dead princess, and a sobbing moan came from his lips.

"Amen-Ra! Amen-Ra!" he cried, "I love you still, and ever I have awaited you. I have been true to the oath we swore together, and Horus, whom we trusted, will yet restore us to one another! Do you not know me? Wake from your long sleep and speak to me. Look at me, and tell me that you love me still."

And then strange sounds burst in impassioned utterance from his lips. I supposed it was ancient Egyptian that he was speaking. I moved forward and laid my hand upon his shoulder.

"Neil," I said, "you mustn't give way like this. Pull yourself together man!"

But his whole form was rigid as a rock, or, rather, like that of a man in catalepsy. And as I hesitated, uncertain what to do, once more there came that horrid rending of claws against the outside of the shuttered windows.

Of course everything was perfectly clear in my mind. Neil Farrant's mind had become unhinged by brooding over his companions' deaths. He had lived with his mummies hourly, almost, since he had smuggled them out of Egypt—and he had lived alone. Again I sought to bring him back to himself, but with equal unsuccess.

"Do you not remember Menes, Princess Amen-Ra?" he asked as he stroked the chill cheeks. "Will you not wake, only for one little instant, and remember?"

And then something happened that I knew must be imagination, but I went staggering back like a tipsy man. I could have sworn that the eyelids of the dead princess fluttered slightly, and that the faint smile about the corners of her mouth deepened just the least bit in the world. And I stood helpless while Neil kneeled there and fondled the mummy's cheek, and again I could have sworn that the eyelids fluttered.

From the sanitarium came the deep baying of one of the bloodhounds, and another and another took up the cry. I stood there, helpless, watching the living man make love to the dead woman.

3

It was the sharp ringing of the telephone in the next room that startled Neil from his spell. He leaped to his feet and stood staring from me to the mummy until his clouded brain seemed to clear.

"Well, Jim, you've seen her," he said, and I could tell from his tones that he was utterly unaware of the scene that had just been enacted. "Pretty little thing, wasn't she, and astonishingly lifelike, even yet. I've been waiting for you to come down and help me with my experiment tonight. Coyne believes in it. It explains all the mystery of the whole process of mummification—all that the explorers and Egyptologists have been trying to discover—"

But he broke off as the telephone began again to ring insistently, and moved toward the door. He was quite his normal self now.

"I guess that's Coyne," he said. "I forgot to tell you that I was to bring you over there to dinner tonight. Excuse me while I answer it."

He hurried out of the room. I was convinced that Neil recalled nothing of that wild outburst of his. He seemed like a man with a dual personality. No doubt in his alternating state he had imagined himself to be the half-mythical Menes, the princess's lover of centuries before.

Again I looked at the face of the dead princess in the light of the electric cluster. What fools one's imagination can make of one! I had been as sure as I could be sure of anything that a sort of semivitality lingered in her, that her mouth and eyelids had moved, though I had refused to believe my senses.

And my senses had tricked me; now I could see that the face, beautiful though it still was, and looking almost as natural as life, was simply the well-preserved face of a mummy. There was no trace of vitality about those waxen features.

I heard Neil on the telephone: "Yes, Coyne, Dewey's here. Got here about an hour ago. I've told him we're dining with you, and we'll be over right away. The experiment? Tonight, maybe, if you're agreeable. Yes, indeed, Jim Dewey's the right man. I trust him more than I'd trust another living soul."

I heard Neil hang the receiver up, and he came back to me.

"Yes, it's Coyne," he said. "He wants me to bring you over. He's a fine fellow, and you'll enjoy meeting him. We'll have to hurry. I must wrap up this mummy first, though. The air's too damp. I oughtn't to have unrolled the bandages, but do you know, Jim,"—he laughed—"I've taken quite a liking to the little lady. Odd a fellow falling in love with a mummy, eh?"

He kneeled down and with deft, experienced fingers rerolled the linen bandages, until nothing of the princess was visible except the contours. Then he replaced the inner and the outer shells.

"Ready, Jim?" he asked. "Let's start, then. It's only five minutes' walk over there. You go out first, and I'll see that none of those damned hawks gets in."

I stepped out of the house. High overhead, against the moon, I saw the soaring covey, but this time the hawks made no attempt to interfere with us, and in another moment Neil had joined me, closing and locking the door behind him.

"I keep this place shut tight," he said. "Those villagers have an insatiable curiosity, and they learned all about the mummies from one of the Sunday newspapers. There's a fellow named Jones who runs the ferry, who's the worst of the lot. Always prowling around here. Coyne calls him the Old Incorruptible, because he once refused an offer of five thousand dollars from the brother of one of the patients to get his brother out of the sanitarium."

We walked along side by side, striking a track that ran inland in the direction of the asylum. A storm was coming up, and great waves were pounding the beach steadily, yet the air was deathly still, oppressive and suffocating. I was wondering if Neil remembered anything of what had happened.

"We'll have to shoot off those hawks," he said. "I believe the smell of natron from the mummies affects them as catnip affects the feline tribe. I've tried to shoot them, but they're too wary."

But he had told me that the hawks wouldn't die, and I had seen him almost tear the head of one from its body, without destroying its life!

I glanced sidewise at him. He was again the Neil Farrant whom I had known, save that he was leaned and bronzed by the Egyptian suns. I determined to speak to Dr. Coyne about him, if I found the doctor approachable.

We passed beneath some fine old live oaks, of massive size, then crossed a wide and well-kept lawn. There was no fence, and no sign of the bloodhounds. In one place were the tennis nets, in another a bowling green, with no evidence even of night guards.

There were a number of smaller buildings grouped about the main one, all of them lit. The institution presented a fine well-kept, and up-to-date appearance.

We rang the bell of the front door, and a nurse in uniform opened it. She smiled at Neil.

"I believe the doctor's waiting for you," she said. "Please step inside."

In another moment we were in the presence of Dr. Coyne in a large reception room, beyond which I could see the medical office, with its cabinets of instruments, chair, and other appliances. Neil presented me, and Dr. Coyne took my hand, giving me a keen, searching look as he did so.

He was an elderly man, between sixty and seventy, as I should judge, with scrutinizing blue eyes and a deeply wrinkled face. Judgment and character were imprinted on it; a man who knew human nature in the raw, as such a man must necessarily know it.

"I'm delighted to make your acquaintance, Mr. Dewey," he said. "Farrant has often spoken to me of you, and how anxious he was to get you to collaborate with him in his work. I think you are both extremely fortunate. And now, since dinner is ready, let's go in, without formalities." He looked at my face. "I hope you didn't get those scratches trying to find the way across our island."

"No, we were attacked by some hawks," I said as he started toward the dining room.

Coyne's brow clouded. "They're pests," he answered. "I'm sorry you had an experience immediately upon your arrival. They're a sort of fish hawk peculiar to Pequod Island, and for some reason seem to have turned vicious, and to attack human beings. We've organized shooting parties, but they're too wary."

At a number of small tables in the dining room, men and women were already at dinner. Some of them rose and bowed at the doctor's entrance; others continued their meal as if unaware of his presence.

I noticed that there were more waiters than could possibly be needed. Some of these were standing against the walls, taking no part in the service, and I guessed that they were probably attendants in waiter's garb.

The doctor led the way to a small table at the farther end of the room, flanked by two enormous bow windows, through which I could see the lights of the village in the distance. The pounding of the surf was very heavy, and there was still that oppressive sense in the air.

Coyne drew me out over a very good meal. I told him about my friendship with Neil, and of the post at the Biological Institution that I had relinquished at his request in order to join him in his experiments on the island.

"Has our friend here shown you the mummy of the pretty little princess?" asked Coyne. "If not, you've missed a treat." And, as he spoke, he gave me a queer look that I could not quite interpret.

"Yes," I answered. "She must have been a beauty in her day."

"Her story is a most romantic one, according to the papyrus," said Coyne. "Farrant, you haven't told Mr. Dewey about the experiment yet?"

I glanced at Neil, who answered indifferently, "No, I haven't told him. We must try it tonight, though, Doctor. I've only been waiting for Jim's arrival."

"Well, we'll see if it can be done," replied the doctor. I could see that he was somewhat ill at ease, but could not divine the reason. Neil was fidgeting with his knife and fork; somehow it seemed to me that we were all at cross purposes.

"I suppose these people here are all convalescents?" I asked, to change the subject.

"Unfortunately no," answered the doctor in a lowered voice. "As a matter of fact, I take in general only the more or less hopeless cases. Occasionally a patient of mine recovers, but usually it is in the face of the textbook. Now that man, for instance," he went on, indicating a placid, elderly gentleman in evening clothes, whom I had noticed eating his dinner with a wooden spoon, "is liable to outbursts of homicidal frenzy. I have succeeded in convincing him that the handling of knives and forks sets up injurious galvanic currents in his system. You may notice that he is under pretty close observation by the attendants. After dinner I shall have pleasure in showing you some of my other cases, which are unable to mingle with the rest."

At this moment, a woman at a table near us dropped her knife and fork with a clatter.

"This meat is electrified, Doctor!" she cried, leaping to her feet. "It's shot through and through with gamma rays! I appeal to you, Doctor, do you permit my enemies to carry on their murderous work under your very nose?"

"Arthur, bring me Mrs. Latham's plate," said the doctor calmly to a waiter. "Please sit down and compose yourself, Mrs. Latham. Another plate for Mrs. Latham from the kitchen, please. If any such attempt has been made, madam, we shall spare no efforts to get to the bottom of the trouble."

"But they're too powerful for you!" shrilled the woman. "My enemies can use your laboratory to insert gamma rays in my food, and after all I've gone through, just because of my wretched little bit of money!"

An elderly woman in the uniform of a nurse appeared upon the scene and touched Mrs. Latham on the arm. Still expostulating, she suffered herself to be led away. With her departure, the evident signs of rising excitement on the part of the rest of the diners died down, and the meal was resumed.

"That plate shall be examined in my laboratory as soon as possible," observed Coyne, as if with the purpose of satisfying everybody. I was interested in the way the doctor had handled the incident. Soon the diners were eating and chatting pleasantly, as if there had been no interruption.

But there was something queer about the relations between the doctor and Neil. In fact, it almost seemed to me as if Coyne's attitude toward Neil, too, was a patient. I was watching it and wondering when the dinner ended. By ones and twos and little groups the patients filed out of the room. As soon as the last of them had gone, Coyne rose suddenly.

"Farrant," he said, "if you really mean to try that experiment this evening, I can be with you in an hour."

"Splendid," answered Neil. "Then I'll hurry back with Jim."

"I think it might be better for you to have everything ready when I bring Mr. Dewey with me," answered Coyne. "You'll remember I promised to show him some of those cases of mine."

Neil looked irresolute, while Coyne's manner had grown almost peremptory. "Well, just as you say. Don't disappoint me, though. You see—well, I outlined the idea to you."

"I'll come, whatever happens," answered Coyne. "You can rely upon me."

Neil left the house. The doctor watched him go. He turned to me. "Poor Farrant!" he said. "He's suffering from mental instability brought on by his experiences in Egypt and by overwork."

"You mean that he's insane?" I asked in amazed horror. Of a sudden everything seemed to be growing clear to me.

"Insanity," replied Coyne slowly, "is a mere medical term. Certainly Farrant was not brought here as a patient." The doctor paused. "But since he has been here . . . However, I think it might be better to postpone what I was going to tell you until we have visited the cases that I was speaking about. They have an intimate relationship—but there, again—"

4

He broke off oddly and conducted me out of the main building and into another opposite it, a smaller one separated by a graveled driveway. In the lobby a uniformed nurse was sitting. She rose up as we entered. Nodding to her, Coyne led the way up two flights of stairs to an upper story, which ran the whole length of the building, and had a number of doors on either side of the main corridor.

Two other nurses were seated in wicker chairs in a recess about the middle of this.

"Anything been happening, Miss Crawford?" Coyne inquired of one of them, speaking in his brusque way.

"I'm afraid old Mr. Friend is going to pass out tonight," she answered. "He's very low."

"We'll take a look at him," said Coyne, and turned to me. "Some of my oldest patients seem to be about to leave this earthly scene, and they all seem to have taken it into their heads to make their exit together."

The nurse unlocked one of the doors, and we entered. On the bed, looking as if he was in his last stupor, lay a very old man, withered and dried to almost mummylike proportions. It was odd to see how he seemed shriveling into that condition while life remained in him, as if he had been embalmed by the Egyptians thousands of years ago. It seemed impossible that life could be continuing in that withered frame. He lay perfectly still, breathing very faintly, and apparently in his last coma.

There came a fluttering of wings against the screen of the window, which I noticed was at least twice as thick and strong as an ordinary screen. For a moment one of the obscene fowls clung there with its claws, its vicious eyes staring into mine. Then, as the doctor made a threatening gesture with his hand, it disappeared silently into the night.

The doctor turned to the nurse. "If you notice any change, have Dr. Sellers administer a strong intravenous injection," he ordered. "We must keep him alive as long as possible. How about the others?"

"They're about the same as they were," the nurse replied.

She unlocked several doors successively. There were three other old men, all pretty near the end of their lives' journeys. Two of them lay stretched out on their beds in a semiconscious state, the third was seated in a chair, staring in front of him. He paid not the slightest attention to our entrance.

"This one has been with me for twenty-three years," said the doctor in a low voice. "How are you feeling tonight, Mr. Welland?" he asked, touching the old man on the shoulder.

Slowly Welland turned his head around, as if it moved by some smooth mechanism. I shuddered at the look in his eyes. Why, they were the eyes of a mummy, painted on a mummy case! The old man muttered something and then relapsed into his stupor.

"Yes, he's pretty far gone," whispered Coyne to me, and, signing to the nurse to leave the room, he led me into the little embrasure of the window.

"Before I show you my last patient, Dewey," he said, "I think we ought to come to an understanding, especially in view of the experiment that poor Farrant is planning to perform tonight. You are going to see—whether it succeeds or not—extraordinary things of whose existence I myself was for a long time skeptical. I was forced to believe in them after—after Farrant came to the island.

"He's spoken to me a lot about you, Dewey, and I don't mind admitting that I've looked up your record. Also, I'm a pretty shrewd judge of men. Our acquaintance has been short, but I believe you are peculiarly the proper person to assist in the experiment. In short, I have faith in you, Dewey, and I perceive in you that very rare thing: an open mind.

"I told you Farrant is not himself. It is a case of what is known as dual personality. Of course such cases are not rare, but they are rarer than they are supposed to be."

I didn't know what he was driving at. I looked over his shoulder, to meet the mummy eyes of old Mr. Welland, seated in his chair. Why was Coyne showing me his patients, and what had these to do with Farrant and his mummies? Somehow I believed there was a close connection; the doctor had hinted at one.

"You are familiar with the literature upon the subject?" asked Coyne.

As it happened, I was, and I told him so. He seemed delighted.

"I run this sanitarium on what might be called unorthodox lines," he said. "It has been suspected for a long time that cases of dual personality, so called, are really cases of possession."

"By—what?"

"By other entities, Dewey."

"You mean—by the dead?" I blurted out.

"By other entities, living *or* dead," Coyne answered. "There is undoubtedly another entity that is endeavoring to take possession of Neil Farrant. I think that, on occasion, it has succeeded; and it is possible that you have already noticed it."

"But—but . . ." I stammered. The suggestion that the long-dead Egyptian, Menes, was attempting to control the body of

Neil Farrant violated all the canons of common sense for me. I saw the doctor observing me with his shrewd gaze.

"Let us go and see our last patient, Dewey," was the only comment he vouchsafed, and led the way out into the hall, where the nurse was waiting for us.

"Miss Ware?" he asked.

"She's exactly the same as she's been for the past two weeks," the woman replied.

"I'll see her," said Coyne. "This," he explained to me, "is a case of what is called dementia praecox. For weeks at a time the patient will remain in the same state without apparent consciousness. Miss Rita Ware comes of a noted southern family and was at one time engaged to marry a fine young fellow, the son of a millionaire cotton-mill proprietor. She broke the engagement. Soon after, symptoms of insanity developed. She has been with me for nearly a year."

"Is there no hope for her?" I asked.

"Dementia praecox, a disease of adolescence, is generally considered incurable," replied Coyne. "In some cases, with my methods, I have accomplished a good deal. But, as I said, they are unorthodox, and I have to rely mainly on myself, though Sellers, a young fellow whom I am training—well, he's learning to apply them."

He shrugged his shoulders again. "Well," he said to the nurse, "let's take a look at Miss Ware."

The nurse led the way to a door at the end of the long corridor and unlocked it. The room within was much larger than the other rooms that I had seen. In the light of the small electric bulb that burned over the bed, I could see that it was tastefully furnished, with pictures, bright hangings, and rugs.

Seated in a large wicker armchair, her face turned away from us, was a young woman. Like the others, she gave no sign of recognizing us as we entered the room. Dr. Coyne moved around in front of her and peered into her face. He raised an arm, which, when he released it, dropped immediately back into its position.

"Come here, Dewey, please," said Coyne in an authoritative tone. "Keep your self-control. Look into her face, and—you may begin to understand."

I moved toward the chair. And at that instant the storm broke with maniacal fury. The light in the room went out, the lights that streamed through the windows of the buildings upon the lawn vanished instantly. There came a vivid lightning flash and a thunderclap.

And the storm broke. Not within a few seconds, but instantaneously. The howling of the wind seemed to rock the building. A deluge of water poured in through the open window. Simultaneously, from outside, came what sounded like the shriek of a lost soul.

For an instant, in the light of the flash, which split the heavens in twain, I saw the hideous faces and strong beaks of two of the hawks, peering in at me through the strong screen. The next, as if animated by some diabolical fury, the winged devils had torn their way through and were in the room—not two, but twenty of them.

The nurse screamed. Coyne ripped out an oath. I put up my hands instinctively to protect my eyes, but the hawks seemed to have no designs on me. One of them settled for an instant upon the head of the unconscious girl, and then the devils were in the corridor.

Coyne was cursing and shouting furiously as he ran in pursuit of them. "You fool, you fool!" he cried at the cowering nurse. "You left those doors open!" He dashed into the nearest room, and I saw the dim shapes of three of the hawks fly out within a foot of his head.

Then all the lights suddenly went on again. I was staring down at old Welland. He had dropped back in his chair, and his mummy eyes were closed. Death was on his waxen features. At the same time screams came from the rooms adjoining. "They're dead! They're all dead! The lightning must have killed them!"

A panic-stricken nurse with a white face came running toward Coyne. He simply pushed her out of the way with his two hands. "Get those hawks!" he shouted. But they were already fluttering out of all the rooms that the nurse had inadvertently forgotten to lock, winging out into the corridor through the doors, which swung to and fro violently as the gale blew through the house.

They seemed to me no longer vicious, but eager to effect their escape. And at last one of them found the open door of Rita Ware's room, and the whole flock followed it inside, and through the open window into the night.

The fury of the storm was frightful. I could hear the patients in the buildings, screaming with terror, and the shouts and running footsteps of the attendants. Flashes of forked lightning alternated with peals of thunder, and all the while the rain came down like a deluge. The nurse had fallen in a faint in the corridor. One of the others was bending over her, attempting to revive her; the third was running out of one room into another. All three of them had evidently lost their heads.

But Coyne had darted into Rita Ware's room in pursuit of the birds. Now, as the last of them winged its way outside, he lifted the girl from the floor, to which she had slipped, and, bending over her, looked into her face. A cry broke from his lips.

"Thank God they couldn't kill her, the devils!" he shouted exultantly. "She's alive, Dewey, she's alive!"

He looked up at me as I came through the doorway into the full blast of the gale. Coyne hadn't even thought of closing the window, and the water was still pouring in. I ran past Coyne, forced away the ripped screen that was hanging inside the room, and got the window down. I turned. The doctor was holding Rita Ware in his arms, as if she had been a statue.

"Look at her, Dewey!" said Coyne in a husky whisper.

I looked. I gasped. The face of the unconscious girl was, feature for feature, line for line, the same as the lovely face of the mummified princess, Amen-Ra!

5

Coyne placed her back in the chair that she had occupied. "Hold her there, Dewey," he said as footsteps came running along the corridor. "We've got to get her to Farrant's house as soon as possible. Don't stir! Just hold her so she won't slip down again."

He hurried out to meet the attendants, closing the door behind him. There followed a few quick interchanges. I gathered that some of the patients had become violent with terror.

"No, no!" cried Coyne peremptorily. "Let Sellers attend to them. He knows what to do. Then let him come here and certify some deaths. I've got more pressing business."

While he spoke, I was staring into Rita Ware's white face, trying to convince myself that the resemblance was a chance one, and failing utterly. I knew now—knew for sure that there was some subtle connection between this girl and the princess, and that Coyne had meant to tell me about it. I knew that Neil's projected experiment had some reference to the connection. Dazed, bewildered, I held the unconscious girl, and heard the footsteps of the attendants and nurses die away along the corridor.

Then Coyne was back in the room. "Well, Dewey, you've seen. You understand now," he said. "Dewey, I trust you. I've got to. And you've got to work with me, for Farrant's sake and the sake of us all. We've got to get rid of those cursed mummies. They are alive, Dewey."

"Alive?" I gasped.

"Do you think the Egyptians were fools? Those mummies have the brains and internal organs intact. It was only at a later period in Egyptian history that the priests lost the clue and eviscerated their dead. Those mummies are alive, dried up, but capable of renewed life, just as many of the lower forms of life can be dried for months and brought back to life by being placed in a suitable medium. If only Farrant had kept those hellish hawks out of his place!"

"But what are the hawks? What is their connection with this business? Surely they're just hawks that have gone mad or something," I protested.

"I've no time to tell you now, Dewey, but you've probably guessed that Rita Ware is the reincarnation of the Princess Amen-Ra.

"Don't misunderstand me or follow a wrong trail of wild hypotheses. I *know* that the soul which forms the body of a human being, after assimilating its life experience, returns to try to make a better human being, guided by the lessons of the past. The trouble is that the soul of Amen-Ra has two bodies—two living bodies, Dewey, for its former habitation has not been destroyed.

"One of them must die, either Rita Ware, or the mummy. And if it is Rita Ware who dies, we shall be confronted with the mummy of Amen-Ra, living on Earth, and capable of God knows what mischief."

"So that explains Miss Ware's mental state?" I asked.

"You've hit it, Dewey. The body was here, the soul was—but that again, I'll explain to you when I have time. I want you to promise to cooperate with me. I don't know precisely what experiment Farrant is projecting, but I fancy he has devised some way of bringing those mummies back to life.

"At the crucial moment, when the chance comes, I am going to try to put a spoke in his wheel and destroy those devils, and— bring Rita Ware back to sane and normal life."

"You mean . . ."

"No soul can occupy two bodies simultaneously, Dewey. Now

the immediate job before us is to get Miss Ware to Farrant's place. I've ordered my car brought round in front of the building. There it comes," he added as the chug of the motor became audible beneath us. "Now let's get the poor girl into it.

"And pray, if you have faith, Dewey. The old, bestial Egyptian gods may have had no reality, but they did represent points of consciousness, so to speak; and in that sense they are a dreadful reality, the embodiment of those dark powers that are always waiting to seize upon some human mechanism in order to manifest themselves.

"Come, let us get Miss Ware out to the car," he added. "I have sent the nurses away, and I want to leave before Sellers gets here."

We picked up the unconscious girl. I noticed that a strange change had come over her. Every muscle of her body, which had been limp before, had stiffened, so that she was like a person in a cataleptic trance. The flame of life was burning very low in her, if it was not extinct already. Her face had the waxen hue of death, and I could discern no signs of breathing.

Coyne's fingertips were on her pulse as he halted, holding her. "She's alive," he said, answering my thoughts. "She is alive because she is the reincarnation of Amen-Ra, and the thread of the new birth cannot be snapped. Those four old men were merely strangers whose souls were taken for the mummies."

"Souls—taken?" I cried.

"She is in no danger of death," he went on, without replying to me, "until the struggle between her body and the mummy body begins. Then we'll need to keep our heads and work together."

I shuddered. All the skepticism in me had been killed somehow, though nothing had happened that could not have been satisfactorily explained. Between us we carried Rita Ware downstairs. A small car was standing at the door, with the engine running, but there was no one in it. The uproar on the buildings had quieted down, though a woman was shrieking at a lighted window, high up on the main structure.

But the storm still lashed the island with merciless severity. It seemed worse than ever. I could hear the breakers tearing frantically at the shingle on the ocean side, and, even as we left the building, a tall tree came crashing down somewhere.

It was difficult getting Rita into the car. Her body refused to accommodate itself to our efforts in the least. It was necessary to prop her up on her feet in the rear compartment, as if she had been made of marble, and I was afraid of breaking one of her limbs.

"Don't be afraid," said Coyne as he stepped into the driver's place. "It's the living woman against the mummy, with the odds in our favor, if things turn out as I expect and hope. Only remember, we're fighting primarily to restore Miss Ware to life and sanity, and then to save Neil Farrant."

"You don't know what his experiment consists of?" I shouted above the roaring of the wind.

"I do not, but I have gathered that he has some scheme for restoring the dead princess to life, together with her attendants. And against that we must fight, Dewey.

"We are dealing with a man who is, in certain states, a cunning madman, and it will require all our ingenuity to learn his plans and thwart him."

Another tree went crashing down. The raging wind seemed as if it would pick the car up bodily and hurl it from the road. The rain was still coming down in a torrential deluge. The sound of the crashing waves was terrific. Mud splashed our sides in torrents as Coyne slowly picked his way toward Farrant's house, through a morass.

We saw the lights in it; every room was illuminated. Suddenly Coyne jammed on the brakes. "God, look at that!" he exclaimed.

A corner of the roof had been ripped away by the gale, and the slates and some of the bricks of the fallen chimney littered the track. Two big trees had been blown down, and the headlights showed them immediately in our way. Coyne and I stepped out, and instantly the deluge wet us to the skin.

But high overhead I saw the flock of hawks wheeling. They were immediately above the gap where the roof had been.

"So they got in!" muttered Coyne. "That complicates things considerably for us, Dewey."

"Shall we carry Miss Ware in?" I asked.

He grasped my arm. "Don't you understand yet?" he cried. "It's her life against that infernal mummy's, that damned vampire's. The body of the princess must be reduced to ashes. That's what I've come for, and that's what Farrant must not suspect."

We lifted Rita Ware out of the car and carried her toward the front door. I was afraid of the hellish birds, but they made no attempt to molest us. Round and round they circled, now floating upon the wind, now swooping with apparent aimlessness, till another current caught them and sent them winging upward again. And so, drenched through and through, we reached the front door.

Coyne rapped. No answer came. Somewhere inside the house we could hear Neil shouting incoherently. The doctor beat a thunderous tattoo with the old-fashioned iron knocker, and after an interval we heard Neil's footsteps within. He unbarred the door and stood staring at us in that uncomprehending way that I had noticed before. Then of a sudden he knew us.

"For God's sake hurry! We're drenched!" shouted Coyne.

He stood aside grudgingly, and we went in. He seemed to take no notice of the girl we were carrying.

"They got inside, the devils!" he shouted. "And they visited you first. I know! I'll show you! They got through the rip in the roof, and they've performed their part. The mummies are glad. They're having the time of their lives at the prospect of freedom. They're trying to get out of their caskets—Lord, I've been laughing. But they're obedient to my will!"

He laughed, clutched at the doctor's sleeve, and thrust his face into his.

"They'll have to wait awhile, even the little princess. I'm not going to let them out until I've got my experiment under way."

We two were standing in the passage, holding the body of Miss Ware, which lay between us, stiff as a log of wood. Neil looked at it.

"What's this you're bringing me?" he asked.

"One of my patients," answered Coyne, assuming that masterful manner of his that quickly seemed to dominate the other. "I'm going to perform a little experiment of my own."

Neil looked into Rita Ware's face. "Hum, pretty girl!" he laughed. "Well, they're always welcome. Maybe the little princess will like her for an attendant when she gets out. She's used to attendants, you know, and we didn't have the luck to dig up any."

I was astounded that Neil seemed to detect no resemblance between Rita Ware and the princess, though the hall was flooded with light.

"Well, let's go in," said Neil. "It won't take long, though I guess it will seem longer than it is."

He led the way through the two rooms into the museum. The lights were on, not only in the clusters overhead, but in brackets on the walls that had escaped my observation that afternoon.

The room was flooded with light, but instantly my attention was riveted upon the five caskets that stood in a row against the rear wall.

From each of four of them there came a creaking, groaning sound, followed by a tapping, as of knuckles against wood!

Neil stepped toward them. "You're lively, old fellows, and I don't blame you after all this time," he said. "But you'll have to wait your turns. Why don't you take a lesson from the princess? See how nicely she's behaving!"

He looked at the fifth casket, which stood in its place at the end of the row and, in contrast to the rest, was absolutely silent.

A faint and muffled groan broke from within one of the caskets. It chilled my blood. Neil kicked it, and there followed the same rhythmic tap-tapping that I had heard before.

Only the knuckles of a hand could have made that sound. I glanced at Coyne and saw that he was almost as overcome as myself.

With a great effort I took another step toward the caskets and listened. There was no question but that the sounds came from within them. The outer lids were on them all, and there was no visible movement. And yet I knew, beyond all possibility of doubt, that the hideous mummies were alive inside them. *And they were trying to get out!*

And all over the caskets I could see the footprints of the hawks, as if the obscene birds had been perching there!

6

For a moment, I confess, I was overcome with horror. I staggered back against the wall. Neil Farrant roared with laughter.

"I tried to convey to you in my wire that you might expect queer experiences, Jim!" he shouted. "You tell him about the hawks, Doctor."

"Dewey, it's this way," said Coyne. "The hawk was a sacred bird in ancient Egyptian mythology. Mesti, the hawk god, was venerated above all others, except Osiris and Horus. His special function was supposed to be to carry away the soul of the dead person and bring it back when the cycle of mummification ended and the dead were restored to life. Do you get me, Dewey?"

"You mean—those birds—carried the souls of those old men—into the bodies of these mummies?"

"Dewey, I'm not committing myself to a statement of my

beliefs. I am simply telling you the myth, as Farrant asked me to,'' answered the doctor.

I think I shook my head. No, it was too incredible that the hawks had transferred the souls of dying persons into those caskets. I was trying to retain my normal faculties. Yet all the while it went on, that rapping, creaking, groaning from within the caskets. Neil turned toward them.

"All right, all right," he cried. "I'll let you out. But don't be in such a hurry. Give a fellow a chance!"

He snatched up the chisel and began rapidly prying off one of the lids. He removed that of the inner case, and the pungent odor of aromatic spices at once began to fill the room again. And I cried out at what I saw. So did Coyne.

For the shapeless form of the mummy inside the case was moving within its linen wrappings. It was wriggling, undulating, like some larva, struggling against the bandages that held it.

I watched it, unable to believe the evidence of my eyes; and yet I knew they were not lying to me. The movements went on and on. At times the thing would fall into quiescence, as if exhausted by the efforts that it had made, and then the contortions would begin once more.

I was so sick with horror that many of the details of that scene escaped me. But I knew that Neil was prying off the lids of the caskets in quick succession, and that the stench of natron had become almost unbearable. And within each casket there lay, not the quiet mummy that had been there for uncounted centuries, but a writhing larva that struggled desperately to free itself from the wrappings that enclosed it, while mewing sounds came from the dead lips.

Then, last of all, Neil lifted the lids from the mummy of the princess. Sick though I was, acutely, physically sick, I moved forward to see, impelled by curiosity that could not be suppressed.

Amen-Ra's eyes were wide open!

The eyeballs were not shrunken. The iris was a deep brown, the pupils large and luminous. They were the eyes of one who saw. She saw! She was watching Neil's face, and the little smile about her lips had deepened.

The swathes of linen, which had been carelessly refolded, hung loosely about her. But she was not attempting, like the other mummies, to free herself from them; she was not stirring.

And she was not a mummy; she was a woman. The waxen look had disappeared from her skin, which had the flush of pulsating blood beneath it. The tissues beneath were those of a living person. It was a living face that I was looking at.

And it was the face of Rita Ware. There was not a particle of difference between the two faces. They might have been twins, but they were not twins; they were the same person!

Coyne leaped to the farther end of the room, picked Rita up in his arms, and laid her down beside the casket. "Farrant," he cried, "look! For God's sake, look! Can't you see that these two are the same?"

Neil glanced carelessly at Rita. "The same? How do you mean, the same?" he asked carelessly. "There is a certain superficial resemblance, but that's all. What on Earth are you driving at, Doctor?"

He stepped back to the cabinet. I saw Amen-Ra's eyes moving, following him. The unconscious, living woman and the conscious dead one lay side by side; but it was the dead one that had the flush of health on the face, deepening every instant, and the living one who looked as white as death.

Neil had taken something out of the cabinet. It was a dish of obsidian, of a dull green, and deep, shaded almost like a flower vase. Into it, from a paper, he poured a quantity of grayish powder. He set it down on a table and looked at us triumphantly.

"The secret?" asked the doctor faintly. He was badly shaken; his self-possession had almost deserted him. For the moment it was Neil who dominated our little group of three.

"The secret!" shouted Neil, and, at his words, the mummies writhed again and rapped their bony fingers against the sides of their caskets, while I leaned against the wall, too overcome to be able to utter a word. On the face of the princess was a smile of triumph, as if she understood. Perhaps Neil had somehow managed to tell her during those conversations he had had with her when he was in his alternating personality.

"I'm going to let you in on the secret now! Quickly, because there's little time to lose. The secret is what I learned from the papyri, the secret that makes the wisest of the learned Egyptologists look like children—the reason why the Egyptians embalmed the bodies of their dead.

"They weren't fools, those old Egyptians who embalmed their bodies without removing the brain and viscera. They didn't believe that the soul would ever return to the same habitation; they knew what has only been rediscovered of late—that time is an illusion; that the so-called future life and this life exist simultaneously; that every act of our physical bodies is simultaneously reproduced in the underworld by the Ba, the soul, and the Ka, the ethereal double.

"So long as the human organism remained intact, the soul would continue its active life in that underworld, until the cycle of reincarnation brought its activities to an end. Destroy the body, and the soul drowses helplessly for some three thousand years. Preserve the body, and the soul takes up the body's activities without a break or change.

"Do you think that the priests who slew Amen-Ra and her counselors escaped their vengeance when they themselves died? I tell you the drama has been going on and on, and we are to be the privileged spectators of it."

"How do you mean?" asked Coyne. He had recovered his poise to some extent and was watching Neil closely.

"This incense," answered Neil, "which I got from the tomb, hermetically sealed in a phial of glass, is the fabled drug of immortality, known to the Egyptians alone of antiquity, though the Cretans had rumors of its existence. Its fumes act upon the human organism in somewhat the same way as hashish, but infinitely more strongly. They destroy the time illusion.

"So long as it burns, we three shall be liberated from the bondage of time. We shall live in the Ba, while our inert bodies remain here. We shall be transported to ancient Egypt, because that is the idea that dominates our thoughts. We shall be spectators of the continuance of that drama that began over three thousand years ago!"

It was incredible that the mummies could have understood, and yet that knuckle rapping began again. I saw one of them, with a mighty effort, half raise itself in its casket.

"I tell you to lie down, old fellow!" yelled Neil, turning toward it. "Your time's coming. A grand time, old boy! You've been living it all these years, but you don't remember, now that you've been brought back to the flesh. Be patient!"

Neil struck a match and applied it to the powder in the bottom of the vase. Slowly a dark stain of combustion began to spread over it. Then the powder caught fire with a sudden tiny flare, and a thin wreath of smoke, with a pungent, sickly stench, began to diffuse itself through the room, quickly drowning the smell of the natron.

The powder flared up, exploding in tiny spurts. The stench

grew thicker, stifling. I was aware of a strange feeling in my head. And in a queer way the room seemed to be growing dim, enlarging into a vista of long, shadowy halls.

"Now's your time, old boys!" Neil shouted. He snatched up a pair of scissors and, stooping over the mummy at the end of the row, began quickly cutting the linen bandages. I heard grunts of satisfaction coming from the thing within. The linen folds fell back; the mummy sat up in its casket, struggling to free its lower limbs.

It was a man, about seventy years of age, his long, white hair plastered about the gaunt, skeleton face, his eyes rolling as they seemed to take in the surroundings. A skeleton clothed with skin; yet, as I looked, I seemed to see the tissues forming, the prominent bones receding.

And Neil was speaking to the monster in a strange, hissing tongue, as if explaining, while the mummy sat like a man in a bath, eyes alight with intelligence, fixed upon his.

One by one, Neil was releasing the mummies from their shrouds. Out of the caskets popped heads, faces, and shoulders of old men, of dead men returning to life.

And everything was growing misty as a dream; I seemed to see Neil, Coyne, and the mummies from far away, or as one looks at a picture book. I was no longer completely conscious of my own identity, and the fumes of the burning powder, which was still exploding in little spurts, were choking me.

Four brown, gaunt, emaciated men were sitting up in their caskets, newborn corpses, flesh and blood instead of desiccated skeletons. I saw their arms upraised, I heard their gibbers rising into shrieks.

Then, at the touch of Neil's shears, the princess rose. She took off her shroud. Wrapped in some material of white, silken sheen, that looked as if she had just put it on for the first time, she stepped lightly out of her casket, a living woman of exquisite beauty. Apparently unconscious of the presence of Rita Ware, she stood beside her, her very double. She turned toward Neil, she extended her arms toward him.

Two words in an unknown tongue came from her lips, and on her face was a smile of utter happiness.

Neil dropped the shears; he turned to her, he caught her in his arms. Their lips met. I knew he had forgotten everything but her.

I couldn't stir, but hazily I was aware that Coyne was catching at my arm.

"Dewey, this is the time!" he cried. "We must save Miss Ware and end this witchcraft. I'm going to kill her. But first . . ."

I saw him extend his hand toward the dish of incense—but with infinite slowness and uncertainly, like a palsied man; and I knew that the numbing influence of the smoke had him in its power, like myself.

"God, I can't see!" he cried, and his arm dropped to his side.

Of one thing more I was aware. With a sudden bound, the mummy in the coffin at the farther end had leaped to its feet. For an instant it stood swaying in the room, an old man wearing a robe of frayed and faded linen and a long girdle that dropped almost to his feet. Shrieks of what sounded like invective poured from his lips as he stood there with extended arms, and his head rolled and lolled grotesquely upon the neck.

Then, with a sudden bound he had reached the door, which was partly open. He collided with it, seemed to understand its usage, swung it open, and rushed, shrieking and gibbering along the hall.

Or was it Coyne? The mummy had looked like Coyne—like the doctor, thirty years older. But this was the stupefying effect of the burning incense. I could no longer think rationally. The figures of Neil and the princess, locked in each other's arms, were becoming tenuous as those of phantoms.

In its flight, the mummy had collided with one of the Egyptian chairs that were set against the wall. With infinite slowness I saw this begin to slip toward the floor. That was the last thing I knew. Utter blackness encompassed me.

7

I was myself, and yet for a moment I felt a sense of bewilderment. I was pacing a flagged courtyard, with huge cyclopean pillars on either side of it. The sun was setting, a huge, red ball, across the desert in front of me. Nearer at hand was a broad and stately river, with sloops, and lateen sails of white, amber, and buff, drawn up on either shore.

The courtyard that I paced was in front of an immense building, composed of enormous blocks of masonry, with sculptured images of the gods, of colossal size, on all sides of it. Within this building I could hear the sound of voices, which seemed to come from every part of it, and blended into a not unpleasant hum. Lights shone through apertures here and there, and the part immediately before me was brilliantly illuminated.

I was myself—I knew myself. Had I not been, for nearly six years, one of the trusted bodyguards of the Princess Amen-Ra, of Egypt? Was I not the son of a small nobleman of the country, with a score of slaves and broad acres on both sides of the sacred Nile, chosen for my position because my family had been loyal to the ruling dynasty for generations?

I knew all this as I knew anything, and yet there was a vague confusion in my mind, as if I had been dreaming. There was a curious odor in my nostrils. I had just come on duty after witnessing the embalming of a distant relative of mine, an old man who had held high honor at court.

It was the odor of the natron and spices that had affected my head, I thought as I paced the flags, my sword swinging at my side, my sandaled feet clacking monotonously on the stones. For three hours by the water clock that dripped in the courtyard I must remain on guard, since the Princess Amen-Ra was protected by her nobles, and not by the common rabble of soldiers.

Bitter and envious thoughts were stirring in my heart. This was the night on which her nuptials were to be celebrated with Menes, of Thebes, a noble who could claim no longer descent than my own, since we were both descended from the gods. She had fallen in love with him, and had sworn the Great Oath by Horus, which binds lovers together for three successive incarnations.

All Egypt was in ferment, for Amen-Ra claimed Osiris as her ancestor, and the marriage would surely end the golden age of peace that had descended on the land, when war had been forgotten and the ships brought back riches by peaceful trading with the Cretans, the Hittites, and the Atlanteans.

And I had loved the Princess Amen-Ra since first I had set eyes upon her, a lovely child, six years before. This upstart, Menes, had supplanted me, and the thought of the marriage was intolerable to me.

The sun had dipped into the desert while I was meditating. The long shadows of the pillars were merged in a universal twilight. The figure of a slave slipped past the water clock and bowed before me.

"Lord Seti," he said. "I come from the high priest, Khof. He awaits your pleasure."

"Tell him that I shall not fail him," I answered. "I shall be at his service at the appointed time."

The slave bowed again and vanished; I resumed my pacing. Presently another figure appeared between two of the pillars of the palace. It was that of a young girl, who came tripping toward me.

"Lord Seti, the princess asks your presence," she said to me.

"Who guards the courtyard if I leave my post?" I asked.

She laughed merrily. "The Exalted One has no fears, Lord Seti," she answered. "The mouthings of Khof, the high priest, are like the wind, that blows and stops, then blows again from another direction. She has her faithful followers, others beside yourself. Does the Lord Seti question the commands of the Sun-Descended One?"

"No, I come with you," I answered her. She was one of the princess's attendants, high in her favor, and I knew she looked with favor upon me. Had not my heart been aflame with love for Amen-Ra, I might have been responsive, for our families had known each other for generations, our very lands on the Nile adjoined, and she was a beautiful girl over whom many men had striven.

"It is not often, Lord Seti, that you come where I am," said the girl timidly. "But that is not to be wondered at, since the Princess Amen-Ra has bewitched you."

"What nonsense is this?" I answered roughly. "Have you no more sense than to chatter such things? Do you not know that if your words were overheard, dire would be your penalty?"

"Ah, Lord Seti," answered the girl, stopping and standing facing me in the twilight, "what care I? What is my life to me, when my love is not returned? Aye, I will speak now," she went on, her voice rising into an impassioned intonation. "I love thee, Seti, and thou hast known it for a long time, and thine infatuation for the princess is likely to involve thee in ruin.

"Now kill me with that long sword of thine," she added, making a gesture as if to bare her breast.

I was a little touched by the girl's devotion, in spite of the fires of jealousy that were burning within me. "Aye, you have spoken the truth, Liftha," I answered. "I love the princess. I have loved her since I first saw her. And who is this upstart, Menes, whom she has chosen to be her royal mate? Is his lineage longer than mine, is his wealth greater? I tell you . . ."

"Hush—hush!" whispered the girl. "If those words were heard, you would be sent to the torturer. By Osiris I adjure you not to dream impossible things. Does not the princess rely upon you and your companions to protect her against the priests? Can a man be true to his trust and harbor such thoughts as those?''

I hesitated, and again that strange confusion came upon me. I seemed for a moment to be standing in a small room in some strange land, with the princess and Menes. But Menes was attired in strange, barbarian attire, and the high priest, Khof, stood beside me, one arm outstretched toward me. He was trying to tell me something; he was threatening to kill Amen-Ra, who stood locked in her lover's embrace. And he, too, wore the same barbarian clothes.

The vision faded. Decidedly it was the result of the fumes I had inhaled at the embalming that afternoon.

''Aye, you are right, Liftha,'' I rejoined, and accompanied the girl within the palace.

Guards, consisting of my companions, nobles like myself, paced the long corridors, their swords swinging at their sides. They saluted me as we passed, and I returned their salutations. Liftha led me though a long antechamber, in which six more of the guards were posted. These men were sons of the highest nobles in the land, and yet, by favor of Amen-Ra, I had been privileged to command them.

A curtain of crimson linen hung before a doorway. From within it came the murmur of voices. The guard on duty called my name through the curtain. The benign voice of an old man answered, bidding me enter.

The curtain was raised, and I passed through alone, humbly bowing toward the dais on which Amen-Ra and Menes sat side by side. Seated on low stools in front of them were the four wise, ancient counselors of the realm, all men over seventy years of age, who had served the princess, and her brother before her, and their father and his father before that.

Amen-Ra and Menes were seated in chairs, and before them was a plain board on which was bread and salt, goblets, and a flagon of Nile water. The marriage had just been performed by one of the lesser priests, who had braved the wrath of Khof in doing so, but the royal lovers had yet to bind it by partaking of the ceremonial meal.

I bowed, and then stood up. I dared not look at the princess, but I fixed my eyes upon Menes, seated beside her like a king— Menes, who had supplanted me. Had he had wit, he must have read my mind.

But all his mind was wrapped up in the princess. The two had eyes for none except each other, and it was not until I had approached the circle of wise counselors, bowing repeatedly, in accordance with ceremonial etiquette, that Amen-Ra looked away from Menes and saw me.

She signaled me to approach her, and I kneeled before the dais.

"My lord Seti," she said. "I have sent for you because you are my friend, and I trust you as I trust no one, except my husband and these wise counselors of mine."

Of a sudden the rage in my heart gave place to coldness. It had almost been in my mind to rush upon Menes with my sword and slay him. Had the high priest Khof known that such an easy chance would come to me, he assuredly would not have laid the elaborate plans that had been staged.

I looked at Amen-Ra, and the love in my heart turned to pitiless coldness. There had been a time, while she was approaching womanhood, when I could have wooed her successfully. I knew that, and I knew that she had given me more than a passing thought before Menes appeared on the scene.

There he sat, the upstart arrayed in purple linen, at the side of Amen-Ra, regarding me with the haughty composure of a king.

"Promise me that you and your companions will guard me well this night, and forever," said the princess. "And it is our plan to advance you to a post of the highest dignity."

"You may be assured, Bride of the Sun, that I shall fulfill my duty," I replied.

She smiled. "I knew you would, Lord Seti," she replied. "And yet my astrologer tells me that there is an evil star in my horoscope. Even now he is observing it. It is at the very point of transit across Aquarius—a new and unknown star whose appearance betokens dire peril. Not till it is beyond Aquarius's fringe may Menes and I partake of the ceremonial meal together."

She turned to the oldest of the wise men and nodded to him, and he motioned to me to approach him.

"Have you news of Khof, Lord Seti?" he asked me.

"The high priest," I answered, "dares do nothing. Think you that he would lay violent hands upon one who is descended from Osiris?"

The princess heard me. "Ah, but I am all alone, except for

my lord Menes," she cried in sudden anxiety. "If the high priest excite the rabble against me . . ."

"Then, Sun-Descended, they shall die at the point of my sword, and those of my companions," I answered. "Fear not."

"It is well," she answered with new composure. "My fears are gone, Lord Seti."

She turned and smiled at Menes, and with that the last doubts in my heart vanished. At that moment the curtains behind the dais parted, and the astrologer entered. He was a man between sixty-five and seventy years of age, with scrutinizing blue eyes and a deeply wrinkled face. He bowed low before Amen-Ra, his robes, stamped with images of the sun god and the hawk god, sweeping around him.

"The evil star—hath it passed Aquarius?" asked the princess breathlessly.

"Not yet," answered the astrologer, "but even now, it is upon the fringe of the constellation. Within an hour it should be clear of it, and then, Exalted One, it will be permissible to partake of the ceremonial meal, for the peril will be overcome."

"And if it pass not?"

"If it pass not, but continue in its parabolic course, within the attraction of Aquarius, there will be peril of floods, issuing from the dominance of the watery constellation, Exalted One."

"Floods—and what besides floods?" queried the princess.

"The position of the planet Mars indicates bloodshed. There may be civil commotions, even warfare."

"Aye," answered Amen-Ra, a touch of bitterness in her tones, "but why deceive me with half-truths? Have I so many who are willing to speak the truth to me that you must needs prevaricate? What are the omens for myself and my lord Menes?"

"If, in its parabolic course, the evil star sweep within twenty-five degrees of Mars—and Jupiter, the benign guardian, be not yet arisen—there will be dangers other than those," said the astrologer reluctantly.

"Dangers?" queried the princess. She sprang to her feet. "Speak the whole truth to me!" she cried. "I adjure you, in the name of Osiris, Isis, and the child Horus, of the holy trinity whose names may not be taken in vain."

"There will be death," the astrologer whispered, and flung himself upon his face before her.

8

I paced between the statues of the gods. I glanced at the water clock. The water dripped steadily upon the flags, and the dial showed that a little more than an hour remained before my watch was ended. The palace was still ablaze with lights, but the voices within it were hushed. Not a sound could be heard without, save the monotonous lapping of the little waves of the rising Nile against his banks.

It was as if all nature waited in suspense for the passing of the evil star. And I, with my heart hot with rage and hatred—what was I but a pawn, moved by the powers of the wandering orb that had swung into the sphere of Aquarius?

Yet I pictured Amen-Ra, seated beside Menes at the board, with her wise counselors, waiting for the propitious hour to begin the repast, and my heart was touched. How lonely she was, she, the ruler of the greatest empire in the world! Again I thought of her words of faith in me, and I hesitated.

I looked up at Aquarius, swinging overhead. I could see the errant star, for, like all the Egyptian nobles, I had been taught astrology and the influence of stars and planets upon human destinies. It was just clearing the edge of the constellation; but a few degrees below it, Mars was rising, blood red, into the dark sky. And I knew that already Mars held the wandering star in his embrace.

Stooping, I removed my sandals and strode noiselessly down to the waterfront. The princess's pleasure sloop, with sails of purple linen furled, swung at her anchor. I did not turn toward her, however, but toward a smaller sloop, with sails of pure white linen. She was the swiftest vessel ever built, and she was mine. For three months skilled craftsmen had secretly labored on her, and I knew she could never be overtaken, given a start of a dozen drops from the water clock.

My chief slave, Kor, pacing the deck, stood rigid as a statue as he saw me approaching.

"Well? Is all in readiness?" I asked softly.

He moved toward me. "All is ready, my lord," he answered. "The anchor is held by no more than can be sheared away with one sweep on the ax, and the wind favors us."

"The supplies of food are below?"

"Aye, Lord Seti, sufficient to carry us to the land of Crete. All your commands have been obeyed."

"The two underslaves are aboard?"

"They wait below, Lord Seti."

"It is well," I replied. "Serve me faithfully in this matter, Kor, and you become a freeman, once we touch the shores of Crete, where I am guaranteed refuge." And I turned away with a lighter heart. I had three followers among the royal guard, young nobles pledged to my service by the Oath of Horus, and, moreover, under indebtedness to me. It should not be difficult, in the confusion, to save Amen-Ra both from the guard and from the priests of the crafty Khof.

I calculated that when the two forces met in battle, I and my three could easily carry the princess down to the sloop, and once aboard her, we would have a clear passage down the Nile and across the Middle Ocean to the land of Crete.

I turned and made my way toward the huge Temple of Serapis, which was dwarfed in dimensions only by the palace. In front of it stood the gigantic statue of the god, the corn measure upon his head, the scepter in his hand, the dog and the serpent at his feet.

The huge temple seemed in utter darkness. Nothing appeared to be stirring, save that a mongrel jackal-dog fled snarling with a mouthful of food that he had seized from the offal cast out daily by the priests. Yet, as I passed between two of the columns in front of the structure, a form leaped forward, dagger in hand, then recognized me, and fell into the same posture of stillness that my chief slave had shown.

It was the slave who had approached me an hour earlier in front of the palace.

"Greetings, my lord. The high priest Khof awaits you," said the man.

"Tell him I come," I replied, and the slave, bowing, moved away silent as a shadow.

I passed between the columns and entered the temple. The interior was so dark that only one who, like myself, had been initiated into its mysteries, could have found his way. Again a huge statue of Serapis confronted me, rising from floor to roof, the corn basket this time outstretched in the right hand, to receive the offerings of the votaries.

I passed along the aisle behind it. Now I saw the faint glimmer of a light behind the heavy curtains that veiled the entrance to the priests' room. I stopped before them for a moment. In that moment I again reviewed the plans that I had made, and I could find no flaw in them.

I had pledged my faith to Amen-Ra, and I was fulfilling it in my own way.

I raised the curtains and entered. The high priest Khof and a dozen of his attendant priests were awaiting me. He sat at the head of a small table, resplendent in his priestly garments, in the light of the small lamp that burned before him. His long white beard flowed down to his breast. His attendants were younger men, clean-shaven, after our fashion, and I could see the glint of steel in their girdles.

I bowed, and there was a moment's silence. Khof watched my face steadily. "You have been tardy, Lord Seti," he said.

"Yes, Osiris-born. The princess deigned to send for me, to have me pledge my faith to her anew."

"You pledged it?" he asked quickly.

"Aye, but not by the secret vow by which I pledge myself to your service."

"Hath the sacred meal begun?"

"Not yet, lord. She and the accursed upstart still await the word from the astrologer. And, as I passed through the courtyard, I saw that the star was still within the influence of Aquarius, with Mars riding hard to catch him. There is no escape for them, Lord Khof."

"There is no escape," he answered. "For I, who have other lore than the stars, have read what is written in the lights of my breastplate."

He glowered at me so somberly that I felt a chill of fear run up my spine. I knew that the high priest was in possession of a lore that made the prophecies of the astrologers as a child's game—a lore brought to Egypt by a wise man from India, centuries before.

"What have you read, Lord Khof?" I asked.

"I have read death and treachery," he answered, "but death to he who betrays. I have read of disasters, which, nevertheless, cannot be averted. So we must go on. Within how long the destiny of the evil star be decided?"

"In less than an hour," I answered.

"Your men—can you pledge them?"

"Sufficient of them to ensure that the plan can be carried out," I replied.

"Go back, then, to your duty. At the appointed time you will admit us to the palace. And we rely mostly upon your valor, my lord Seti."

"Aye, but what of my reward?" I asked, to make him think that my motives were other than they were. "The reward you pledged yourself to give me?"

"A roomful of silver, and the highest post in the land, under me."

"It is well. You will not find me wanting," I answered. I glanced into the faces of the younger priests. These men were fanatics, who would stop at nothing, but old Khof, crafty and guileful, had schemes of his own. These men believed that they were fulfilling the wishes of the gods in murdering Menes, but Khof knew that the gods themselves are only aspects of the One and Indivisible. It was statecraft and not fanaticism that guided him.

I bowed myself out and made my way back to my post in the courtyard before the palace. I redonned my sandals; only their monotonous click-clack broke the stillness. It was eery, that utter silence within, the thought of the princess and Menes awaiting the passing of the evil star.

And it would never pass. I looked up and saw that the star and Mars were within a few degrees of each other.

A shadow glided across the court toward me. It was the girl, Liftha. She came up to me and stood with hands crossed upon her breast, looking up into my face pleadingly.

"Well, what do you want now? Another summons from the Sun-born?" I asked roughly.

"Not so, Lord Seti. But there is evil news from within the palace."

"How so?" I asked.

"The evil star passes not. The ceremonial meal is delayed. I love thee."

I laughed. "Is that part of the evil news?" I inquired of her.

She laid her hand upon my arm. "Harken, Lord Seti. Play not with me. I am a child no longer. Pledge thyself to take me for they bride as soon as the issue of these affairs is settled, or I cannot live. Speak the truth to me and put me off no longer."

I looked at her, pleading with me there, and a sudden fury shook me. "Spoke I ever words of love to you, Liftha?"

"Never, Lord Seti, and yet love hangs not upon words, but has glances for speech, and, moreover, an unknown tongue that depends not upon the lips. It is my fate that I would know once for all."

"Know it then," I returned. "I do not love you. I love none

save Amen-Ra, and never shall. Seek some young noble among her bodyguard and forget me."

"That is thy decision?" she asked softly.

"Aye, by the trinity of Osiris, Isis, and the child Horus," I responded, speaking the oath that may not be broken.

She made a swift gesture, raising her hand to her lips. It dropped, with the tinkle of a piece of metal. I seized her by the arm.

"What folly is this?" I cried.

"'Tis nothing, Lord. Only a piece of meat set out for the jackals, filled with a potent poison. My life is ended. Be—happy—as you can. Perchance . . ."

She tottered and slipped to the stone flags. I tried to raise her, but already she was breathing her last. She died within a dozen drips of the water clock. That meat, shot through with a subtle poison known only to the priests, had been set out for the jackals that profaned the sanctuaries by stealing the votive offerings.

So the evil star had found its first victim. I looked up and saw that the star and Mars were now only a finger-breadth apart.

Then I was aware of shadows moving softly toward me among the columns, resolving themselves into the high priest and his attendants. All of them wore swords and daggers, and I could see by the bulge of their garments that they had mail beneath them.

"All is well?" asked Khof.

"All is well," I returned.

"Then lead the way," he responded.

I half drew my sword from its sheath and passed once again into the palace. The guards still paced the corridors, but the advent of the high priest merely brought them to the salute. It was only when the band was nearing the curtain of crimson that those of them who were pledged to me came quietly forward and arrayed themselves beside me.

I put out my hand and raised the crimson curtain. Nothing seemed to have changed since I had been there an hour before. The princess and Menes were still seated side by side before the board, with its untasted bread and Nile water, their counselors beneath them. Beside them stood the astrologer, his head bent upon his breast. He was saying something in a low voice, and on his face was despair.

At the raising of the curtain, Amen-Ra raised her head and looked at me. Her eyes looked straight into mine, and in that moment I think she read my heart to its uttermost depths.

She looked at me, she half rose. "What means this intrusion, my lord Seti?" she asked. "Have I sent for you, or have I—ah!"

Her glance fell upon the high priest and the body of attendants. Their swords were half out of their sheaths, and they were glaring at Menes with a fury that could not be suppressed. And what happened was so sudden that I could see it only in flashes of quick movement.

Amen-Ra turned to Menes, who had already risen to his feet and was standing there unarmed beside her. She flung her arms around his neck. The four old counselors were struggling up with cries of alarm; the guards in the antechamber were starting forward in confusion. Khof, the high priest, shouted and, swords in hands, leaped forward.

9

"Halt, Khof! Thou knowest the power reposed in me, which even thy spells are incapable of preventing?" shouted the oldest of the counselors, standing before the dais with uplifted hand. "Halt, I say, or by the gods Annbia and Mesti I shall shake down the Nile to overflow. Again I say, halt! Thou knowest."

For a moment Khof and his attendants halted. Upon the dais I could see the lovers standing, their arms about each other. There was no fear in the looks of either, but deadly scorn on the eyes of the princess as she turned her gaze upon me.

"Traitor!" she cried in a clear voice. "Traitor to your trust! Come, do your worst, but you shall pay—aye, you shall pay, or the gods exist not!"

I had hesitated, too; but now the sight of Amen-Ra in the arms of my rival proved too much for me. I sprang toward the dais. I heard the old counselor chanting the formula, used only in cases of extremity, and confided only to the hereditary wielder of the chief power beneath the throne. I paid him no attention; I leaped at Menes. Amen-Ra flung herself before him in the effort to shield him. For an instant she baffled me. Then I saw my opening, and like a snake my sword darted in and pierced him through and through.

I tore the girl away, then raised the form of the dying man in my arms and hurled it into the midst of the struggling crowd.

Yells of triumph and derision greeted my deed. By now the hall was a melee of figures, the guards fighting furiously with the invaders as they sought to rescue Amen-Ra, and then later engaging them in battle with equal ferocity, while three or four, led by Khof himself, were cutting down the counselors. And my own three men, taking no part in the fight, were trying to work their way toward me as I stood, holding the princess, who had fainted.

The eldest of the counselors, who alone survived, though horribly slashed by the priests' swords, still stood upon his feet. He was still chanting the sacred formula. He ended, with a note of ecstasy on his lips, and I saw him fall under a terrific sweep of old Khof's sword.

And then, of a sudden, the whole palace rocked. I stumbled and, still holding Amen-Ra in my arms, went rolling down among the dead and dying, who lay piled up together.

The palace was shaken to its foundations. The old, dead gods, the earliest gods of the land, long sleeping, had been stirred by the magic formula known only to the old counselor. They were moving in their hidden tombs beneath the palace and the temples; and the palace and the temples were crashing down in ruins.

The mighty columns quivered, and bowed, and fell in shapeless heaps of stone, with reverberations as if the very heavens had fallen apart. The roof collapsed above my head; the walls were riven, and the floor opened.

I felt a stunning blow upon the forehead. Everything grew black, the yells of the contending priests and guards died away. I was plunged into an abyss of blackness, silence, and unconsciousness.

Yet not for long. At this supreme moment, for which I had so long planned, I did not intend to let myself be cheated of my reward. And, with a mighty effort of will, I pulled myself up out of the depths.

All about me were huge stones fallen from the palace roof. I had escaped death by a miracle, for, by the light of the stars that shone through the opening above, I could see guards and priests lying in mangled heaps. I had escaped without even a broken limb.

Outside I heard the confused cries of a crowd, but within the palace nothing stirred or sounded. I staggered out of the hole made by the fall of a mighty stone, which had saved me. I made my way over the stones and bodies toward the dais.

And there I found her, Amen-Ra, alive, like myself, and tugging fiercely at a stone that lay across the body of my rival, Menes. And, as she tugged, she began whimpering little words and phrases of love, so that I stood and watched her, amazed at her devotion.

I spoke her name softly, but she did not hear me. I took her by the hand. "He is dead," I said. "Come with me, Amen-Ra, and let us seek safety in flight together."

She fell back, she stared at me as if she did not know me. Then it was as if a film cleared from her eyes.

"Traitor!" she cried. "You live, and he lies dead, my lover! But know this: if the gods have suffered you to live, it is only that you may suffer such torments as would move even me to pity. The curse of Thoth, the curse of Horus, of Anubis, the jackal-headed, of hawk-headed Mesti, of great Osiris himself rest upon you forever!"

She was like a coiled snake, crouched, waiting to sting me, but I sneered triumphantly. What meant the names of the gods to me, who had passed the Greater Initiation and knew that they are all aspects of the single Unity?

"I have loved you since I saw you," I replied. "Once you deigned to smile upon me, until this upstart came along. Is he of better birth than I? I love you, I say, and I speak to you no longer as servant to princess, but as man to woman, since your realm goes out in the darkness. Hark!" I added as the cries of the mob grew louder. "Even now the peasants come to drag you from your throne!

"I have a ship in readiness," I went on. "For three months my slaves have labored on her. No vessel made by man can catch her. I have wealth enough aboard her to make you a princess in some other land that I shall conquer. Come with me, and let us forget all the past in our love!"

Still she stared at me, but now her eyes seemed to soften. I mistook that look of hers; I thought that I had touched her, that she was yielding. I leaped forward and caught her by the hand again.

"I will love you as no man has ever loved a woman!" I cried. "Is it not for love of you that I have destroyed the throne of Ancient Egypt? I swear to you that I will carve you out another realm, even greater than this one. Come with me, Amen-Ra!''

Her solemn words broke in upon my frenzy; they held me as if spellbound. And there was no more hate in them. Rather they sounded like the chanting of some ancient sibyl.

"Lord Seti," she said to me, "all this was dimly foreshadowed to me by my astrologer. He could not know, since the advent of the evil star had not been predicted; nevertheless he revealed to me that someday the one I trusted most should betray me.

"Aye," she went on, "and that he, too, was a puppet of destiny, and bound to the wheel of fate. And more, Lord Seti.

"For he showed me that someday, when the cycle of reincarnation has grown complete, it is through this man that Menes, my lover, and I shall meet again, because we pledged ourselves by the oath of Horus, which cannot be broken. It is your task someday to restore what you have broken.

"Meanwhile it is my wish to rejoin my lover in the shades were Osiris rules. And for you, Lord Seti, there is one chance of redemption. Take it, and the gods will pardon you. Refuse it, and eternal punishment shall be yours, punishment so terrible that even the gods will avert their faces in pity.''

"What is this chance of redemption?" I whispered hoarsely.

She put her hands to her robe and drew out a curious dagger. It was two-bladed, and a double cutting edge, and fashioned in such a way that with the thrust, the blades separated, producing a fearful double wound that must instantly prove fatal, if delivered in the body.

"Slay me, Lord Seti," whispered the princess, moving toward me. And I saw that her eyes were alight with the longing for death. "Thus only, said the astrologer, can destiny be appeased. Slay me!" I had taken the dagger from her hand. I hesitated. I knew full well that Amen-Ra could never be mine, and yet to kill her was impossible.

"It is madness!" I cried.

"It is truth. It means eternal peace for my lover and me, and for you, release from the terrible judgment that Osiris will surely mete out to you after you die, unless you do what I have said.''

I hesitated, then thrust the dagger into my girdle. ''Never!'' I cried. ''Think you that I have done what I have done in order to lose you? Let me but have you in this life, and I am willing to face even an eternity of suffering, knowing that even eternity comes to an end sometime, and in the dim ages that are to come I shall be free once more!''

I seized her in my arms. She offered no resistance, and yet she did not faint. I bore her away. I must have gone insane with exultation. I remember shouting as I forced my way over the heaps of fallen stone, with the crushed bodies underneath. I tore at the masonry that blocked the entrance to the palace. I must have been dowered with superhuman power, for clutching the princess to me, with my hands I hurled the great masses of fallen debris to one side and the other, stones that a strong man with his arms free could hardly have lifted. Then, holding the princess, I went staggering out into the darkness.

A prowling jackal cried, and others took up the cry. Across the Nile, red flames were leaping up toward the black sky. I heard the yells of the looting mob, but I saw why they had not come near the palace. Palace and temple stood on a little slope of elevated ground, and between them and the river there stretched an expanse of water into which I went floundering, knee-deep, waist-deep.

Then, bearing up Amen-Ra, I swam fiercely to where the channel of the Nile had run, shouting the name of my chief slave, Kor. But there came no answer, and, in the darkness, it was impossible to discern where I was until I saw the tops of the timbers of the quays before me.

The Nile had already risen a dozen feet, and a great mass of water was whirling down, against which I battled with my whole strength. That waste of waters stretched away as far as I could see, red as blood in the distance, where it reflected the fires of the blazing city.

But my sloop, my pride, my hope, was no longer at her slip. Nor was the princess's sloop, with the purple sails. Nor any other. In a moment I understood. All who could escape had taken sail; Kor had betrayed me, and had himself sailed for Crete, with all my treasures aboard!

Treachery for treachery! I cried out in despair, and gathering

he limp body of Amen-Ra to me, I swam to where a platform
projected above the swirling waters. It was a wooden framework
on which the watchman had been wont to stand to shout news
of sloops or galleys approaching up- or down-stream. It had been
high above the waters, but now it was a scant two feet above the
surface, and it was only a matter of a little while before it would
be totally submerged.

I dragged Amen-Ra up with me and looked into her face. Her
eyes were open, and she was watching me with a quiet little
smile about the corners of her mouth. She looked like one who
has passed through all the wrongs and outrages of life, and fears
nothing anymore.

"Now slay me, Lord Seti, that the will of the gods may be
fulfilled," she said, "and that you may escape the penalties and
tortures of the hells."

"Never!" I cried. A fierce exultation had taken possession of
me. The love of life was rising in me; I would pursue Kor, my
treacherous slave, to the land of Crete, and regain ship and
treasures; I would carve out a new empire for Amen-Ra, or
perchance regain for her the realm of Egypt.

By the pale light of the risen moon I could see boats pushing
across the swollen stream toward the palace. I heard the shouts
of their occupants; they were slaves and peasants who, having
glutted their appetite for vengeance upon the city, were putting
out to possess themselves of the fabled treasures of the Egyptian
kings, which were supposed to lie in the crypts of both palace
and temple.

I could hear the shouting of them as I crouched on the platform, holding the limp body of Amen-Ra. Unseen behind the
projecting timbers, I watched them approaching.

But then I was aware of another figure crouching at the end
of the platform, where the shadows lay deepest. It came slowly
toward me, and I recognized, first the water-draggled garments,
and then the face of the old astrologer who had predicted the
woes that had descended on us.

A fire of rage burned in me. I snatched the double-bladed
dagger from my garments and held it aloft. I regarded the old
man as the cause of all that had miscarried. I threatened his
breast with the pointed blades.

He scrambled to his feet and came onward fearlessly. He stood
before me, and some power seemed to hold me back from delivering the fatal stroke. He looked at Amen-Ra. "Slay her!"

he whispered. "Slay her, that the will of the gods be fulfilled. Only thus may she regain her lover in the next cycle of mortal life."

"Fool," I shouted, "think you that I am willing to let her go, to lose her forever?"

He laid his hand upon my arm. "Lord Seti," he answered, "your course and hers are none otherwise than as the evil star that has swept within the scope of Mars. Soon they two part forever. So it is with you and her; in your next birth you will see her, and recognize that she is not yours. Your desire for her will pass. Slay her now, and so fulfill the gods' intentions, and the plans that were laid down before the creation of the world. Slay her, I say, and escape the punishment of the underworld, and restore her to Menes."

I heard the long howling of the jackals, driven out of the desert by the floods. I seemed to smell a pungent odor, choking, stifling me. A pit of darkness seemed to be opening before me. What devil's magic was this? The forms of Amen-Ra and the old astrologer were growing indistinct.

"Kill her!" he cried again.

I raised my arm irresolutely, but the darkness was already all about me, and I was choking in the fumes. I was falling down, down. . . . Something crashed. . . . Then my eyes were wide open, and I was in the room in Neil Farrant's house again.

10

One of the two Egyptian chairs, set against the wall, had fallen to the floor. It was the crash of its impact that had awakened me from a dream already growing dim. And the gaunt, brown form of the escaping mummy was vanishing through the doorway.

And after it, staggering, reeling, and uttering shrill, birdlike cries, the other mummies ran. But not the princess Amen-Ra; I was holding her in my arms, and in one hand I held the pair of long, sharp-edged scissors with which Neil had cut the mummies' shrouds.

I was standing nearly knee-deep in water, which was pouring steadily into the room through the open door. Outside, the rain was still pelting down, the wind raged, the storm seemed to have reached an intensity greater than anything I had ever known. The roar of the surf was even louder than the wind.

"Stop them! Stop them!" I cried confusedly as I saw the mummies disappear. I had not yet quite regained my normal consciousness—or, rather, it was still confused by the vanishing fragments of the dream.

The powder in the obsidian vase had burned itself out, but the pungent stench still filled the room. Neil Farrant was standing against the wall, apparently in a daze; close beside me was Coyne, and he, too, seemed to be trying to orient himself.

"Kill her!" he cried. "Kill her!" And then I realized that it was he who had thrust the scissors into my hand.

Kill her? The mummy? But this was a living woman whom I held in my arms, though she was wrapped in linen from the casket. Kill her? Her eyes sought Neil's and seemed unable to discern his face, for she was peering forward, as if she, too, had just come back from that infernal scene.

"Kill her! See! See!" shouted the doctor, pointing.

And then I saw the still, white form of Rita Ware upon the dais. Line for line, save for the whiter skin, the face was the duplicate of Amen-Ra's. And I remembered what Coyne had said to me, that one of the two must die.

At that moment the princess seemed to perceive Rita Ware for the first time. Suddenly, with frightful force, she disengaged herself from my arms, and snatching the scissors from my hand, she leaped at her.

It was Coyne who stopped her. The points scored red rips along his cheek. He seized the princess's hand and, with all his strength, just managed to prevent her from wreaking her hatred on the body of the living woman.

"Dewey! Dewey! The scissors! Get them! Kill her!" he cried.

The struggle that ensued was the most awful part of the whole business. I realized that Amen-Ra was no human being, but a corpse endowed with vampiric life, that the life of Rita Ware depended upon her destruction. No woman could have exercised the diabolical strength that she put forth; no, this was a thing animated by will without intelligence. Amen-Ra was the effigy of the princess of old time, and the real Amen-Ra was Rita Ware, lying as if dead upon the dais beside us.

Dimly I realized that if Amen-Ra succeeded in killing Rita Ware, we would have let loose a devil on Earth, and that Neil

Farrant's sanity, his very soul, depended upon the destruction of that vampire that had arisen from the casket.

"Menes! Menes!" she shrilled. And then some words in what must have been the old Egyptian tongue; though they awakened faint memories within me, I did not know their meaning.

But Neil heard; he awoke. He leaped toward us, no longer Neil, but again the long-dead Menes of Egypt, and in his mind, I had no doubt, he was again fighting the palace conspirators. No, fighting me. I believe he saw me as the traitor, Seti; he came leaping forward, while Coyne and I wrestled with Amen-Ra, to keep her from plunging the deadly scissors into Rita's heart.

"Hold her a moment!" I rasped at the doctor, and turned upon Neil. I had been a pretty good boxer when I was a boy, and I dealt him a blow that dazed him and sent him staggering back against the wall.

Then I turned to Amen-Ra—just in time, for she had wrenched the scissors away and turned upon Rita. I caught her hand and bent it backward till I heard a bone in the wrist snap. She spat at me like a wildcat, and the nails of her left hand scored my face. And Neil was coming back to help her.

This time it was Coyne turned upon Neil. "Kill her! For God's sake, kill her!" he cried to me, and hurled himself at Neil—a frail old doctor against a man in the prime of life, with all his muscles and sinews toughened by the desert life, and a reserve of almost superhuman strength, such as comes to one who, in a trance, draws upon the hidden storehouse of his vitality. Coyne went down under a smashing blow that stretched him full length in the water that was now more than knee-deep upon the floor.

I could never fight Neil and the princess, but fate intervened. Neil, reaching forward in the swing that knocked Coyne to the floor, tripped over the fallen chair and lay prostrate. Again I wrestled with Amen-Ra. I had her by the broken wrist, but even with the bone snapped, she was delivering frantic swings and lunges at Rita with the scissors. I flung my body in the way. The points caught in my coat—and then I succeeded in wresting the weapon out of the creature's hand.

"Menes! Menes!" she wailed, and that cry was like the echoing cry of one eternally lost.

Neil had picked himself up. He roared; he came on like a

madman; and what happened next was, by the grace of God, a matter of a split second's advantage.

I had the shears. I swung at Neil with my left hand and dealt him a stinging blow in the face that halted him. Then I turned upon Amen-Ra and plunged the deadly weapon straight into her heart.

The shears pierced through the body so hard as I struck that my fist collided with her breast. Blood spouted, ceased. For a moment Amen-Ra stood upright, pinned by the steel; and then it was as if all the devilishness went out of her face.

She was the young girl, the beauteous maiden whom I had seen in the casket, whom I remembered dimly, as if in a dream, to have seen in Egypt. A smile of heavenly sweetness flickered about her mouth. And then, before my eyes, she was dissolving into dust.

The weapon eased itself from the crumbling form. No mummy this—nothing but a little heap of dust that flaked down upon the dais. Of Amen-Ra, as I had seen her in the casket, no trace remained.

I choked with the horror of it. I flung the scissors from me and turned to await Neil's mad onset. But Neil was standing against the wall, looking about him as if he had awakened from a dream, and Coyne was rising out of the water and coming toward me.

He gasped as he looked at the heap of dust, already covered by the oncoming stream. He ran to Rita Ware and raised her out of the water, which was lapping against her face. And I saw that her eyes were open, and she was staring confusedly about her.

Coyne carried her to a couch and laid her down. She was mumbling, still half-conscious. Neil was muttering, too. Coyne turned to me.

"Thank God, Dewey!" he cried. "I knew that I could trust you not to falter. That was not Amen-Ra; this girl is Amen-Ra, reborn. So long as that vampiric double of hers had lived, three souls would have remained in hell—her own, and Farrant's, and this girl's. Thank God the spell is ended!"

Neil Farrant came staggering toward us. "Where am I?" he muttered. "Where's all this water coming from? What happened? The experiment—it didn't work? I don't seem to—remember—but I dreamed. I dreamed I was that fellow Menes, and you two were in the dream, too."

He began laughing hysterically, and then of a sudden his eyes fell upon Rita Ware. "Who is she?" he whispered hoarsely to the doctor.

"I'll tell you later, Farrant," answered Coyne. "We've got to get out of here. The water's rising steadily. We'd best get to the sanitarium while we can make it. If there's anything that's specially liable to be damaged, and we can carry it . . ." He looked doubtfully about him.

"The mummies are gone!" Neil shouted. "What happened to them?"

"Washed out of their caskets," answered Coyne tersely. "You took them out, you know."

"Well, good luck to them," cried Neil in high-pitched tones. "I'm sick of them, Coyne. That magic formula was a fake, and I feel kind of—soured on them."

He pitched forward as he spoke, but Coyne caught him and steadied him. "Take it easy, Farrant," he said. "Think you can make it? Dewey, you help me get Miss Ware away."

"Where am I, Doctor?" asked Rita faintly, and her voice was so like that of Amen-Ra that for an instant the whole picture of the dream flashed back into my mind. "I thought—they'd sent me to—your sanitarium for a rest. This isn't the sanitarium, is it?"

"No, but we're going there," replied Coyne. His lip was bleeding from Neil's blow; his clothes hung grotesquely about him, dripping water—as, indeed, did mine—and yet he was again the suave head of the institution whom I had met that night for the first time. "This gentleman and I are going to carry you," he added. "There's a high tide that has flooded us.

"No, don't try to walk. Make a seat with our hands, Dewey," he said. "You know the way?"

I assented, and together we raised the girl from the couch. The water was almost to our waists. Outside confused cries rose above the wind and the roaring of the waves. A streak of light shot into the sky.

"God, what's that?" shouted Coyne.

Neil stopped at the door. "Look out for the hawks!" he warned us.

"I guess the hawks won't trouble us anymore," the doctor answered.

Neil opened the door, and a sudden, violent gust of wind almost tore it from its hinges. In an instant the room was filled with the blast, and the water came pouring in. Carrying Rita, it was as much as we could do to wade along the central rooms and gain the front door. And as we reached it there came a violent hammering upon it.

Neil flung it open. We bent our faces to the blast. We struggled on by inches. A group of men were in a large boat at the entrance, two of them standing up with poles in their hands.

"Git in! Git in!" one of them shouted. "Didn't look for to see none of you folks alive. Why, it's you, Doctor! Don't you know your place is on fire? And them damn mummies is running wild all over the island!"

It was the ferryman, Old Incorruptible.

11

There was no need to tell us that the sanitarium was on fire, for we could see the blaze through the trees. The whole building seemed to have caught, and to be doomed. We lifted Rita Ware into the boat and struggled in after her. Coyne looked crushed.

"Reckon your folks will be saved, Doctor," said Old Incorruptible. "There's a half dozen of the boats round the place, doing their best. But I'll tell you to your face, we was coming to make an end of Mr. Farrant's mummies if that fire hadn't broke out. And we ain't going to have them things running wild over Pequod Island and scaring our womenfolks and kids."

"Nonsense! Nonsense!" answered the doctor testily. But Neil said nothing; he was bending over Rita Ware, and his face appeared transfigured.

The high tide had submerged the lower half of the island; breakers were crashing among the trees. The gale was still at its height, and even as we poled our way toward the sanitarium more trees came crashing down. But the rain was ceasing, and overhead there was a rent in the murky sky.

At the edge of the higher ground, on which the sanitarium stood, the boat grounded. We leaped out. Neil swung Rita in his arms and carried her a little way. "You stay here with Miss Ware, Farrant," said Coyne. "Come along, Dewey!"

Boats were moving all about the buildings, and I could see that the higher ground was black with figures. The fire seemed to be burning uncontrollably, in spite of the rain, and it was evidently only a matter of an hour or so before the entire group of structures would be gutted. Coyne ran, and I followed.

One of the attendants came rushing up and recognized the doctor. "We've got them all out safe," he babbled, "except the—the—the . . ."

I knew what he meant. Coyne and I ran into the thick of the crowd, which was being shepherded by the hospital staff. The attendant, who had followed us, came panting up and pointed, still babbling incoherently.

On the roof of the small building that had housed Rita Ware, four wild, half-naked forms were gathered. They were chanting and gesticulating, their arms raised to the skies.

"We can't get them!" cried a man who had joined us. "What are they? I never saw them before."

The leaping flames made the scene as bright as day. The four upon the roof, heedless of the flames that encompassed them, were leaping and dancing, and the wild chant that came from their lips was faintly audible above the roar of the wind and the pounding of the breakers.

"God, it's the doctor!" someone yelled.

And then I saw that the leader of the band was the duplicate of Coyne. Yes, Coyne in face and figure, save that he was robed in rags of linen. And I knew him; he was the astrologer of Amen-Ra's court. Back into my mind there flashed the forgotten dream, never to be effaced thereafter.

Coyne ran forward. "Nonsense!" he shouted. "I'm here! Don't you see me?"

"We've got to get them down, whoever they are," panted a little man, his face blackened with smoke, his hair scorched by the flames. "We've got all the rest out safely, but those four—I never saw them before."

"There's no chance, Sellers," answered Coyne. "It would be death to attempt it."

"But who are they? Where did they come from?" Sellers shouted.

"It's them damn mummies," yelled Old Incorruptible. "Let 'em die. We ain't going to have them frightening our women-folks and kids. Good riddance to them!"

A hoarse shout of approval came from the assembled fishermen. And all the while a wild, whirling dance went on, while the flames roared about the four, until they stood silhouetted against a wall of leaping fire.

And suddenly the end came. There came a furious uprush of fire, the whole roof collapsed, sending up a sky-high pillar of flame. Into that fiery furnace dropped the four dead-living men. One instant they stood clear against the flames—the next there was nothing but a raging holocaust.

Coyne turned to me, his face white, his body quivering. "That's the end, Dewey," he said. He turned to Sellers. "Get our folks down to the village in the boats," he ordered. "We'll have our hands full tonight."

12

I made my way back to where I had left Neil and Rita Ware. They were standing together in the same spot, and they seemed utterly absorbed in each other, so much so that neither saw me until I stood beside them.

"Well, everybody's safe," I said to Neil.

"That's good," he answered. "Jim, do you and Miss Ware know each other? She says she's met you somewhere. She thinks it was in Philadelphia."

"Well, it may have been in Philadelphia," I answered, though I had never been in that city.

"Jim, listen. You're my friend. What I'm going to say to you will sound crazy, but I'm through with the mummies and Egyptology for all time. You see, we're going to be married just as soon as . . ."

"Can we trust your friend?" asked Rita Ware, looking at me with a strange expression. "I—I've been ill, you know. A—a sort of breakdown. But I'm well now, and if you're Neil's friend. . . ."

"I hope that I shall be the friend of both of you for life," I answered. "I'm happier than I've ever been to know that this has happened."

"I know it sounds crazy," said the girl. "But, you see, we—we recognized each other the instant that we met. I don't know whether we met in this life or in some other one, but we know beyond all doubting that we just—well, we just belong."

She turned to Neil again, and I saw that both of them had forgotten me; and that was how I wanted it to be. For I knew that the Oath of Horus had brought those two souls together, three thousand years after their bodies had been sealed into their tombs. Neither water nor fire, nor my own treacherous sword, had been able to sunder them.

I turned away and went back to help in the work of rescuing the inmates. And a dead weight was lifted from my heart.

D. R. MEREDITH is the creator of two critically acclaimed crime-fiction series—one, beginning with The Sheriff and the Panhandle Murders, *featuring Sheriff Charles Matthews, the other featuring Texas Panhandle attorney John Lloyd Branson. The Branson whodunits include* Murder by Impulse, Murder by Deception, *and the forthcoming* Murder by Masquerade.

Mummy No. 50

by D. R. Meredith

"Only seventy more days, Mole!"

He danced into the little work area I had laboriously built for myself in one corner of the vast storeroom. It was quiet there in the basement of the museum—far from the sounds of running feet and shrill voices of visiting schoolchildren, far from the squeak of tennis-shoe-clad tourists walking on marble floors, and, best of all, far from the high-tenor enthusiasm of John ("Call me Jack") Adams Moore, the museum director. Many days I spent more time in the basement than I did in my office. Still, that was no excuse for him to call me Mole. The appellation lacked dignity. Besides, it called undue attention to my weak eyesight and prominent nose.

"Mole! Did you hear me?"

"Yes," I said, wincing. It was difficult not to. The director's voice was several octaves and decibels above the comfort range for one possessing my auditory sensitivity. I was continually amazed that the exhibit of Chinese pottery on the second floor did not shatter in the midst of one of his exuberant outbursts. Not that I would be distressed, in any event. As the assistant director, I resented the presence of Chinese artifacts in a museum supposedly dedicated to the culture and history of the Texas Panhandle and High Plains.

"Do you know the significance of seventy days?" asked John Adams Moore, rocking back and forth in his tiny cowboy boots and hooking his thumbs inside the armholes of his leather vest.

Men of five feet four inches should not wear Western attire, but I suppressed my distaste for the director's ludicrous appearance. I had long since discovered other, more despicable, attributes. Such as his obsession with Egyptology.

"I could hardly help knowing," I replied, continuing to polish the barrel of a 1875 .50-90 Sharps rifle, the "Big Fifty" so beloved by the buffalo hunters of the Great Plains. While not the only .50-90 Sharps rifle owned by the museum, it was the finest, in mint condition and perfect working order. I even had several hand-loaded cartridges to fit it.

"Seventy days was the period between death and burial in ancient Egypt," I continued, laying down the Sharps and turning to face him. "I believe the time was filled with a number of rituals involved in that culture's religious practices. Plus mummifying the corpse, of course."

His teeth clicked with disapproval. Have I mentioned the director's teeth? They were gleaming white and disproportionately large. The way he clicked them together reminded me of the wind-up dentures one sees at Halloween. I tried never to look at John Adams Moore's teeth.

"Mole, the embalming of the body, its preservation, was central to their religion. To the Egyptians, destruction of the corpse meant destruction of its chance for eternal life. *Die not a second time* was written on the bottom of some coffins. Their rituals were to preserve the body from harm. Most people think they were obsessed with death. Not true! They were obsessed with life, with continuing it forever!"

There was more, of course; the director was firmly in the saddle of his favorite hobbyhorse. I had heard it all before: the evisceration, the forty or more days of packing the remains in natron to mummify it, the fifteen or so days of wrapping the pitiful, dried-up flesh, the elaborate rituals and prayers accompanying each procedure. I turned back to my workbench and picked up the Sharps, hoping to discourage any further discourse on the Egyptian way of death.

He moved around to the side of my workbench and tapped my shoulder. "Mole, we're getting one. I just had a phone call from New York. I had written the director of the exhibit about

ny plans for a diorama of an *uabit per nefer*. That's a house of
egeneration to you.''

"An Egyptian funeral parlor in other words," I interrupted,
icking up one of the cartridges and rolling it between my fin-
ers before loading it in the Sharps. It was an unconscious ac-
ion, merely something to occupy my hands, a nervous habit, if
ou will.

"Now, Mole, I know you haven't been happy about this whole
ffair, but it's time to present a united front, pull together in
arness, put our best foot forward.''

Among the director's less endearing managerial traits is his
abit of using homilies that are nearly as timeworn as a mum-
nified Egyptian pharaoh. Another is to attempt to placate me
y appearing to understand the depth of my disagreement with
ringing an Egyptian exhibit to the Texas Panhandle. I had fought
he idea all the way to the board of trustees—and lost. I would
ot be so bitter if the exhibit in question had been that of King
Tut or Ramses II. But no; all that John Adams Moore, the daring of the board of trustees, could book was a pitiful display of
unerary objects, a few tarnished amulets of bronze and stone,
ome statuary, and a dilapidated mummy case. To house these
bjects, he had constructed a replica of an embalming work-
hop, and another of a tomb complete with paintings and
ieroglyphics. It was laughable, ridiculous.

"I will perform my duties as assistant director of this mu-
eum," I replied, putting the Sharps to my shoulder and sighting
own its long octagonal barrel.

He patted my shoulder. "Don't be so stiff, Mole. Your voice
ounds as if rigor mortis has set in.''

I didn't need to look at him to know those yards of white teeth
vere exposed in a smile. He fancied himself a comic. I did not
hare his opinion. "I am not stiff. I am merely girding myself
o bear the public ridicule when your precious exhibit finally
arrives.''

"Seventy days from now," the director interjected, a jovial
ote still in his voice. The man was impervious to insult.

"We have promised a cultural feast, but we can deliver the
equivalent of a prisoner's bread and water. A few scarab rings
and an ankh or two, perhaps a worn statue of some minor official, will not satisfy the public.''

"And it shouldn't, Mole," he interrupted. "That's what I
came down to your burrow to tell you. Our liaison in New York
has agreed to send us enough artifacts to furnish the embalming

workshop and the tomb.'' He drew a deep breath and clasped
his hands together. ''He's also sending us a mummy! Mummy
No. 50! Isn't that exciting?''

I lowered the gun and looked at him as he danced away a
few feet. ''Mummy No. 50,'' I repeated. ''That sounds like
a cheap Egyptian cologne. Wear Mummy No. 50 and cast a
spell over your beloved.'' I chuckled. ''Does our mummy
have a name? Did he walk the burning sands of the Nile a
a prince or a priest? Or is he perhaps a she? A princess, a
pharaoh's consort?''

He was shaking his head. ''I don't know. No one does. This
mummy has never been examined beyond being photographed
and tagged. Not all mummies are unwrapped to be poked and
prodded, you know. They begin to deteriorate when exposed to
the air, bacteria mainly, but our industrial pollution doesn't help
either. So our mummy is a mystery guest; even its name is
illegible on the coffin. But, Mole, I haven't told you the most
exciting part.'' He lowered his voice to a whisper. ''There's a
curse.''

''A curse,'' I mumbled, wishing to do a little cursing of my
own.

That toothy grin again. ''The usual adage: *cursed be he who
disturbs my rest for the spirit of the dead will fall upon him and
carry him off like a bird of prey*. A mummy *and* a curse, Mole
If I were superstitious, I would say the Great God Ra himself
had blessed us.''

With all his other sins, the man added blasphemy. Ra, in
deed. ''It does add a certain appeal to the exhibit,'' I said
cautiously.

''Appeal? It will be irresistible. The crowds will be stu-
pendous, Mole. And the donations to the museum, think of
those.''

I was. By my calculations, thanks to the cheap sensation-
alism of the exhibit, the donations should be sufficient to
increase the scope of my own exhibit of Plains Indian artifacts, the exhibit delayed for this Egyptian madness. ''You
can depend on me to do everything in my power to ensure
the success of Mummy No. 50's reign over this museum.
Long live Mummy No. 50!'' I shouted, banishing my Sharps
over my head. Not an easy gesture given the length and weight
of the gun.

''I *knew* that would be your attitude, Mole!'' he said, clapping
his hands together. ''I told the board of trustees that while you

might be disappointed, you'd understand the necessity of canceling your Indian exhibit until the next fiscal year. With the vast quantity of Egyptian artifacts, particularly the mummy, we had to increase our insurance coverage. The museum loaning us the exhibit insisted. It's ridiculous, I'll agree. Those artifacts can't buy another Mummy No. 50.''

"You canceled my exhibit?" I repeated, certain I had misunderstood.

At least he had the decency to look guilty. But not guilty enough. "Only until next year. But wait until I tell you the grand finale of our exhibit, the pièce de résistance. I only received permission for it this morning.''

And that's when I shot John Adams Moore with the 1875 .50-90 Sharps rifle.

His disappearance was a nine days' wonder, of course, and the constant presence of the police in the person of a Sergeant Oliver Hawke was distracting, but I came through unscathed. I even became a hero when I insisted that the Egyptian exhibit open as scheduled and that it be dedicated to our absent chief. I left many of the details, publicity, and printing of the brochures, to my assistant. After all, I had to take charge of the daily operation of the museum. And my nights were exhausting, particularly the last one before the exhibit's opening when I substituted the director's mummy for the authentic one.

Not that the director isn't an authentic mummy; he is. I followed the procedure as exactly as possible, including evisceration—which nicely camouflaged the fatal wound. I used the natron and resin from Moore's own diorama of an embalming workshop. I replaced those items with others of similar appearance; after all, no one would be doing a chemical analysis. As a precaution I locked the exhibition hall for security purposes—my security—and pocketed the only key.

Fortunately, I live alone on forty acres outside town, so I had no near neighbors to disturb me during the actual mummification, a loathsome process, by the way. The stench is quite incredible. The whole experiment convinced me that the Ancient Egyptians must have been born without olfactory nerves. Given the vast number of necropolises, each with its attendant embalming workshops, the entire country must have smelled like a charnel house. Certainly my smokehouse will never be suitable for curing hams again.

The wrappings caused me the only anxiety. An unexpected

inventory by an assistant curator of the museum's fashion collection turned up the absence of certain nineteenth-century linen garments. I explained the shortage away as a bookkeeping error and put the curator to work cataloguing a recent acquisition of arrowheads. Properly frayed and soaked in a weak tea solution for that aged look, a linen wedding dress makes an acceptable mummy wrapping.

Smuggling the real mummy out of the museum was more easily accomplished than I anticipated. I often took work home, so the night security guard thought nothing of seeing me wheel out a wooden crate on a dolly. I spent the rest of an exhausting night transforming the director into a clone of Mummy No. 50. I flatter myself that only a microscopic examination could determine which was which. Fortunately, the director in life was only an inch or so taller than the average ancient Egyptian. In death he shrank a little, so I did not have to resort to any unpleasant corpse mutilation to make his height tally with the older mummy.

I buried the original in a remote area of Palo Duro Canyon, by far the most unpleasant episode of the whole experience. The wind blowing around the rock formations, the rustling of nocturnal creatures, losing my flashlight, the intermittent moonlight casting eerie shadows—all that left me feeling distinctly unsettled. Not until I had smuggled the director into his sarcophagus just after dawn the next morning and had a glass of wine in my office did I stop leaping at every sound.

The exhibition was the success envisioned by the director, and the mummy its most popular attraction. Still, I greeted the last week of the exhibit with a sense of relief. The director's presence, even in his somewhat shrunken, wrapped, and blessedly silent condition, irritated me more and more, and I began avoiding the exhibit, even brusquely walking out on my assistant when he tried to introduce the subject of my predecessor's plans for a special archaeological demonstration in connection with the mummy.

I should have listened.

But never, never, even in my most fevered imaginings, had I dreamed that John Adams Moore, presently masquerading as Mummy No. 50, planned a sophisticated X-ray examination, *public invited*, of said mummy—as the grand finale he had been blathering about at the moment I shot him!

And never, never, even in my most terrifying nightmares,

id I envisage that behind the director's toothy smile, in the
nnermost recesses of his mouth, in the last molars on the
ottom, were two unmistakable, unexplainable, very modern
llings.

ROBERT BLOCH is a giant among twentieth-century writers of mystery and suspense fiction. His most famous masterpiece is of course, Psycho, *which became the classic Alfred Hitchcock film. But as "The Eyes of the Mummy" demonstrates, he also has a knack for stories of nonhuman horror.*

THE EYES OF THE MUMMY

by Robert Bloch

Egypt has always fascinated me; Egypt, land of antique and mysterious secrets. I had read of pyramids and kings; dreamed of vast, shadowy empires now dead as the empty eyes of the Sphinx. It was of Egypt that I wrote in later years, for to me its weird faiths and cults made the land an avatar of all strangeness.

Not that I believed in the grotesque legends of olden times; I did not credit the faith in anthropomorphic gods with the heads and attributes of beasts. Still, I sensed behind the myths of Bast, Anubis, Set, and Thoth the allegorical implications of forgotten truths. Tales of beast-men are known the world over, in the racial lore of all climes. The werewolf legend is universal and unchanged since the furtive hintings of Pliny's days. Therefore to me, with my interest in the supernatural, Egypt provided a key to ancient knowledge.

But I did not believe in the actual existence of such beings or creatures in the days of Egypt's glory. The most I would admit to myself was that perhaps the legends of those days had come down from much remoter times when primal earth could hold such monstrosities due to evolutionary mutations.

Then, one evening in carnival New Orleans, I encountered a fearful substantiation of my theories. At the home of the eccentric Henricus Vanning I participated in a queer ceremony over the body of a priest of Sebek, the crocodile-headed god. Weil-dan, the archaeologist, had smuggled it into this country, and we examined the mummy despite curse and warning. I was not myself at the time, and to this day I am not sure what occurred, exactly. There was a stranger present, wearing a crocodile mask, and events were precipitated in nightmare fashion. When I rushed from that house into the streets, Vanning was dead by the priest's hand—or fangs, set in the mask (if mask it was).

I cannot clarify the statement of the above facts; dare not. I told the story once, then determined to abandon writing of Egypt and its ancient ways for ever.

This resolve I have adhered to, until tonight's dreadful experience has caused me to reveal what I feel must be told.

Hence this narrative. The preliminary facts are simple; yet they all seem to imply that I am linked to some awful chain of interlocking experiences, fashioned by a grim Egyptian god of fate. It is as though the Old Ones are jealous of my prying into their ways, and are luring me onward to a final horror.

For after my New Orleans experience, after my return home with the resolution to abandon research into Egyptian mythology forever, I was again enmeshed.

Professor Weildan came to call on me. It was he who had smuggled in the mummy of Sebek's priest which I had seen in New Orleans; he had met me on that inexplicable evening when a jealous god or his emissary had seemed to walk the earth for vengeance. He knew of my interest, and had spoken to me quite seriously of the dangers involved when one pried into the past.

The gnomelike, bearded little man now came and greeted me with understanding eyes. I was reluctant to see him, I own, for his presence brought back memories of the very things I was endeavoring to forget forever. Despite my attempts to lead the conversation into more wholesome channels he insisted on speaking of our first meeting. He told me how the death of the recluse Vanning had broken up the little group of occultists that had met over the body of the mummy that evening.

But he, Weildan, had not forsaken his pursuit of the Sebek legend. That, he informed me, was the reason he had taken this trip to see me. None of his former associates would aid him now in the project he had in mind. Perhaps I might be interested.

I flatly refused to have anything more to do with Egyptology. This I told him at once.

Weildan laughed. He understood my reasons for demurring,

he said, but I must allow him to explain. This present project of his had nothing to do with sorcery, or mantic arts. It was, as he jovially explained, merely a chance to even the score with the Powers of Darkness, if I was so foolish as to term them such.

He explained. Briefly, he wanted me to go to Egypt with him, on a private expedition of our own. There would be no personal expense involved for me; he needed a young man as an assistant and did not care to trust any professional archaeologists who might cause trouble.

His studies had always been directed in recent years toward the legends of the Crocodile Cult, and he had labored steadily in an effort to learn of the secret burial places of Sebek's priests. Now, from reputable sources—a native guide in his pay abroad— he had stumbled onto a new hiding place; a subterranean tomb which held a mummy of a Sebekian votary.

He would not waste words in giving me further details; the whole point of his story was that the mummy could be reached easily, with no need of labor or excavation, and there was absolutely no danger, no silly truck about curses or vengeance. We could therefore go there alone; the two of us in utter secrecy. And our visit would be profitable. Not only could he secure the mummy without official intervention, but his source of information—on the authenticity of which he would stake his personal reputation—revealed that the mummy was interred with a hoard of sacred jewels. It was a safe, sure, secret opportunity for wealth he was offering me.

I must admit that this sounded attractive. Despite my unpleasant experience in the past, I would risk a great deal for the sake of suitable compensation. And then, too, although I was determined to eschew all dabblings in mysticism, there was a hint of the adventurous in this undertaking which allured me.

Weildan cunningly played upon my feelings; I realize that now. He talked with me for several hours and returned the next day, until at last I agreed.

We sailed in March, landed in Cairo three weeks later after a brief stopover in London. The excitement of going abroad obscures my memory of personal contact with the professor; I know that he was very unctuous and reassuring at all times, and doing his best to convince me that our little expedition was entirely harmless. He wholly overrode my scruples as to the dishonesty of tomb looting, attended to our visas, and fabricated some trumped-up tale to allow the officials to pass us through to the interior.

From Cairo we went by rail to Khartoum. It was there that Professor Weildan planned to meet his "source of information"—the native guide, who was now admittedly a spy in the archaeologist's employ.

This revelation did not bother me nearly as much as it might have if it occurred amidst more prosaic settings. The desert atmosphere seemed a fitting background for intrigue and conspiracy, and for the first time I understood the psychology of the wanderer and the adventurer.

It was thrilling to prowl through twisted streets of the Arab quarter on the evening we visited the spy's hovel. Weildan and I entered a dark, noisome courtyard and were admitted to a dim apartment by a tall, hawk-nosed Bedouin. The man greeted the professor warmly. Money changed hands. Then the Arab and my companion retired to an inner chamber. I heard the low whisper of their voices—Weildan's excited, questioning tones mingling with the guttural accented English of the native. I sat in the gloom and waited. The voices rose as though in altercation. It seemed as though Weildan were attempting to placate or reassure, while the guide's voice assumed a note of warning and hesitant fear. Anger entered as Weildan made an effort to shout down his companion.

Then I heard footsteps. The door to the inner chamber opened, and the native appeared on the threshold. His face seemed to hold a look of entreaty as he stared at me, and from his lips poured an incoherent babble, as though in his excited efforts to convey his warning to me he had relapsed into familiar Arabic speech. For warning me he was; that was unmistakable.

A second he stood there, and then Weildan's hand fell on his shoulder, wheeling him around. The door slammed shut as the Arab's voice rose high, almost to a scream. Weildan shouted something unintelligible; there was the sound of a scuffle, a muffled report, then silence.

Several minutes elapsed before the door opened and Weildan appeared, mopping his brow. His eyes avoided mine.

"Fellow kicked up a row about payments," he explained, speaking to the floor. "Got the information, though. Then he came out here to ask you for money. I had to put him out the back entrance, finally. Fired a shot to scare him off; these natives are so excitable."

I said nothing as we left the place, nor did I comment on the hurried furtiveness with which Weildan hastened our way through the black streets.

Nor did I appear to notice when he wiped his hands on his handkerchief and hastily thrust the cloth back into his pocket.

It might have embarrassed him to explain the presence of those red stains. . . .

I should have suspected then, should have abandoned the project at once. But I could not know, when Weildan proposed a ride into the desert the following morning, that our destination was to be the tomb.

It was so casually arranged. Two horses, bearing a light lunch in the saddlebags; a small tent "against the midday heat," Weildan said—and we cantered off, alone. No more fuss or preparation about it than if we were planning a picnic. Our hotel rooms were still engaged, and not a word was said to anyone.

We rode out of the gates into the calm, unrippled sands that stretched beneath a sky of bucolic blue. For an hour or so we jogged on through serene, if searing, sunlight. Weildan's manner was preoccupied; he continually scanned the monotonous horizon as though seeking some expected landmark; but there was nothing in his bearing to indicate his full intention.

We were almost upon the stones before I saw them; a great cluster of white boulders outcropping from the sandy sides of a little hillock. Their form seemed to indicate that the visible rocks formed an infinitesimal fragment of the stones concealed by the shifting sands; though there was nothing in the least unusual about their size, contour, or formation. They rested casually enough in the hillside, no differently than a dozen other small clusters we had previously passed.

Weildan said nothing beyond suggesting that we dismount, pitch the small tent, and lunch. He and I pegged in the stakes, lugged a few small, flat stones inside to serve as table and chairs; placing our pack blankets as padding for the latter.

Then, as we ate, Weildan exploded his bombshell. The rocks before our tent, he averred, concealed the entrance to the tomb. Sand and wind and desert dust had done their work well, hidden the sanctuary from interlopers. His native accomplice, led by hints and rumors, had uncovered the spot in ways he did not seem anxious to mention.

But the tomb was there. Certain manuscripts and screeds bore testimony to the fact it would be unguarded. All we need do would be to roll away the few boulders blocking the entrance and descend. Once again he earnestly emphasized the fact that there would be no danger to me.

I played the fool no longer. I questioned him closely. Why would a priest of Sebek be buried in such a lonely spot?

Because, Weildan affirmed, he and his retinue were probably fleeing south at the time of his death. Perhaps he had been expelled from his temple by a new pharaoh; then, too, the priests were magic workers and sorcerers in latter days, and often persecuted or driven out of the cities by irate citizenry. Fleeing, he had died and been interred here.

That, Weildan further explained, was the reason for the scarcity of such mummies. Ordinarily, the perverted cult of Sebek buried its priests only under the secret vaults of its city temples. These shrines had all been long destroyed. Therefore, it was only in rare circumstances like this that an expelled priest was laid away in some obscure spot where his mummy might still be found.

"But the jewels?" I persisted.

The priests were rich. A fleeing wizard would carry his wealth. And at death it would naturally be buried with him. It was a peculiarity of certain renegade sorcerous priests to be mummified with vital organs intact—they had some superstition about earthly resurrection. That was why the mummy would prove an unusual find. Probably the chamber was just a stone-walled hollow housing the mummy case; there would be no time to invoke or conjure any curses or other outlandish abracadabra such as I seemed to fear. We could enter freely, and secure the spoils. In the following of such a priest there surely were several expert temple craftsmen who would embalm the body properly; it needed skill to do a good job without removing the vital organs, and religious significance made this final operation imperative. Therefore we need not worry about finding the mummy in good condition.

Weildan was very glib. Too glib. He explained how easily we would smuggle the mummy case wrapped in our tent folds; how he would arrange to smuggle both it and the jewels out of the country with the help of a native exporting firm.

He pooh-poohed each objection that I stated; and knowing that whatever his personal character as a man might be he was still a recognized archaeologist, I was forced to concede his authority.

There was only one point which vaguely troubled me—his casual reference to some superstition concerning earthly resurrection. The burial of a mummy with organs intact sounded strange. Knowing what I did about the activities of the priests in connection with goety and sorcerous rituals, I was leery of even the faintest possibility of mishap.

Still, he persuaded me at the last, and following lunch we left the tent. We found the boulders no great hindrance. They had been placed artfully, but we discovered their appearance of being firmly embedded in rock to be deceptive. A few heavings and clearing away of minor debris enabled us to remove four great stones which formed a block before a black opening which slanted down into the earth.

We had found the tomb!

With the realization, with the sight of that gaping, gloomy pit before me, old horrors rose to mock and grin. I remembered all of the dark, perverted faith of Sebek; the minglings of myth, fable, and grimacing reality which should not be.

I thought of underground rites in temples now given to dust; of posturing worship before great idols of gold—man-shaped figures bearing the heads of crocodiles. I recalled the tales of darker parallel worships, bearing the same relationship as Satanism now does to Christianity; of priests who invoked animal-headed gods as demons rather than as benignant deities. Sebek was such a dual god, and his priests had given him blood to drink. In some temples there were vaults, and in these vaults were eidolons of the god shaped as a Golden Crocodile. The beast had hinged and barbed jaws, into which maidens were flung. Then the maw was closed, and ivory fangs rended the sacrifice so that blood might trickle down the golden throat and the god be appeased. Strange powers were conferred by these offerings, evil boons granted the priests who thus sated beastlike lusts. It was small wonder that such men were driven from their temples, and that those sanctuaries of sin had been destroyed.

Such a priest had fled here, and died. Now he rested beneath, protected by the wrath of his ancient patron. This was my thought, and it did not comfort me.

Nor was I heartened by the noxious vaporing which now poured out from the opening in the rocks. It was not the reek of decay, but the almost palpable odor of unbelievable antiquity. A musty fetor, choking and biting, welled forth and coiled in strangling gusts about our throats.

Weildan bound a handkerchief over his nose and mouth, and I followed suit.

His pocket flashlight flicked on, and he led the way. His reassuring smile was drowned in the gloom as he descended the sloping rock floor which led into the interior passageway.

I followed. Let him be the first; should there be any falling rock traps, any devices of protection to assail interlopers, he would pay the penalty for temerity, not I. Besides, I could glance back at the reassuring spot of blue limned by the rocky opening.

But not for long. The way turned, wound as it descended. Soon we walked in shadows that clustered about the faint torch-beam which alone broke the nighted dimness of the tomb.

Weildan had been correct in his surmise; the place was merely a long rocky cavern leading to a hastily burrowed inner room. It was there that we found the slabs covering the mummy case. His face shone with triumph as he turned to me and pointed excitedly.

It was easy—much too easy, I realize now. But we suspected nothing. Even I was beginning to lose my initial qualms. After all, this was proving to be a very prosaic business; the only unnerving element was the gloom—and one would encounter such in any ordinary mining shaft.

I lost all fear, finally. Weildan and I tilted the rock slabs to the floor, stared at the handsome mummy case beneath. We eased it out and stood it against the wall. Eagerly the professor bent to examine the opening in the rocks which had held the sarcophagus. It was empty.

"Strange!" he muttered. "No jewels! Must be in the case."

We laid the heavy wooden covering across the rocks. Then the professor went to work. He proceeded slowly, carefully, breaking the seals, the outer waxing. The design on the mummy case was very elaborate, inlaid with gold leaf and silver patterns which highlighted the bronze patina of the printed face. There were many minute inscriptions and hieroglyphs which the archaeologist did not attempt to begin deciphering.

"That can wait," he said. "We must see what lies within."

It was some time before he succeeded in removing the first covering. Several hours must have elapsed, so delicately and carefully did he proceed. The torch was beginning to lose its power; the battery ran low.

The second layer was a smaller replica of the first, save that its pictured face was more exact as to detail. It seemed to be an attempt to duplicate conscientiously the true features of the priest within.

"Made in the temple," Weildan explained. "It was carried on the flight."

We stooped over, studying the countenance in the failing light. Abruptly, yet simultaneously, we made a strange discovery. The pictured face was eyeless!

"Blind," I commented.

Weildan nodded, then stared more closely. "No," he said. "The priest was not blind, if this portraiture is correct. His eyes were *plucked out*!"

I stared into torn sockets which confirmed this gruesome truth. Weildan pointed excitedly to a row of hieroglyphic figures which ornamented the side of the case. They showed the priest in the throes of death upon a couch. Two slaves with pincers hovered over him.

A second scene showed the slaves tearing his eyes from his head. In a third, the slaves were depicted in the act of inserting some shining objects into the now empty sockets. The rest of the series were scenes of funeral ceremonies, with an ominous crocodile-headed figure in the background—the god Sebek.

"Extraordinary," was Weildan's comment. "Do you understand the implication of those pictures? They were made *before* the priest died. They show that he *intended* to have his eyes removed before death, and those objects inserted in their place. Why would he willingly subject himself to such torture? What are those shining things?"

"The answer must be within," I answered.

Without a word, Weildan fell to work. The second covering was removed. The torch was flickering as it died. The third covering confronted us. In almost absolute blackness the professor worked, fingers moving deftly with knife and pryer as he broke the final seals. In the yellow half-light the lid swung up, open.

We saw the mummy.

A wave of vapor rose out of the case—a terrific odor of spice and gases which penetrated the handkerchiefs bound round nose and throat. The preservative power of those gaseous emanations was evidently enormous, for the mummy was not wrapped or shrouded. A naked, shriveled brown body lay before us, in a surprising state of preservation. But this we saw for only an instant. After that, we riveted our attention elsewhere—upon the eyes, or the place where they had been.

Two great yellow disks burned up at us through the darkness. Not diamonds or sapphires or opals were they, or any known stone; their enormous size precluded any thought of inclusion in a common category. They were not cut or faceted, yet they blinded with their brightness—a fierce flashing stabbed our retinas like naked fire.

These were the jewels we sought—and they had been worth seeking. I stooped to remove them, but Weildan's voice restrained me.

"Don't," he warned. "We'll get them later, without harming the mummy."

I heard his voice as though from afar. I was not conscious of again standing erect. Instead I remained stooped over those flaming stones. I stared at them.

They seemed to be growing into two yellow moons. It fascinated me to watch them—all my senses seemed to focus on their beauty. And they in turn focused their fire on me, bathing my brain in heat that soothed and numbed without scorching pain. My head was on fire.

I could not look away, but I did not wish to. These jewels were fascinating.

Dimly came Weildan's voice. I half felt him tugging at my shoulder.

"Don't look." His voice was absurd in its excited tones. "They aren't—natural stones. Gifts of the gods—that's why the priest had them replaced for eyes as he died. They're hypnotic . . . that theory of resurrection . . ."

I half realized that I brushed the man off. But those jewels commanded my senses, compelled my surrender. Hypnotic? Of course they were—I could feel that warm yellow fire flooding my blood, pulsing at my temples, stealing toward my brain. The torch was out now, I knew, and yet the whole chamber was bathed in flashing yellow radiance from those dazzling eyes. Yellow radiance? No—a glowing red; a bright scarlet luminance in which I read a message.

The jewels were *thinking*! They had mind, or rather, a will— a will that sucked my senses away even as it flooded over me—a will that made me forget body and brain alike in an effort to lose myself in the red ecstasy of their burning beauty. I wanted to drown in the fire; it was leading me out of myself, so that I felt as though I were rushing toward the jewels—into them— into something else—

And then I was free. Free, and blind in darkness. With a start I realized that I must have fainted. At least I had fallen down, for I was now lying on my back against the stone floor of the cavern. Against stone? No—against wood.

That was strange. I could feel wood. The mummy lay in wood. I could not see. The mummy was blind.

I felt my dry, scaly, leprously peeling skin.

My mouth opened. A voice—dust-choked voice that was my own but not my own—a voice that came from death shrieked, "Good God! *I'm in the mummy's body!*"

I heard a gasp, the sound of a falling shape striking the rocky floor. Weildan.

But what was that other rustling sound? *What wore my shape?*

That damned priest, enduring torture so that his dying eyes might hold hypnotic jewels god-given for the hope of eternal resurrection; buried with easy access to the tomb! Jeweled eyes had hypnotized me, we had changed forms, and now *he walked*.

The supreme ecstasy of horror was all that saved me. I raised myself blindly on shriveled limbs, and rotting arms clawed madly at my forehead, seeking what I knew must rest there. My dead fingers tore the jewels from my eyes.

Then I fainted.

The awakening was dreadful, for I knew not what I might find. I was afraid to be conscious of myself—of my body. But warm flesh housed my soul again, and my eyes peered through yellow blackness. The mummy lay in its case, and it was hideous to note the empty eye sockets staring up, the dreadful confirmation afforded by the changed positions of its scabrous limbs.

Weildan rested where he had fallen, face empurpled in death. The shock had done it, no doubt.

Near him were the sources of the yellow luminance—the evil, flaring fire of the twin jewels.

That was what saved me; tearing those monstrous instruments of transference from my temples. Without the thought of the mummy mind behind them, they evidently did not retain their permanent power. I shuddered to think of such a transference in open air, where the mummy body would immediately crumble into decay without being able to remove the jewels. Then would the soul of the priest of Sebek indeed arise to walk the earth, and resurrection be accomplished. It was a terrible thought.

I scooped up the jewels hastily and bound them into my handkerchief. Then I left, leaving Weildan and the mummy as they lay; groping my way to the surface with the aid of illumination afforded me by matches.

It was very good to see the nighted skies of Egypt, for dusk had fallen by this time.

When I saw this *clean* dark, the full nightmare force of my recent experience in the evil blackness of that tomb struck me anew, and I shrieked wildly as I ran across the sand toward the little tent that stood before the opening.

There was whiskey in the saddle packs; I brought it out, and thanked heaven for the oil lamp I uncovered. I must have been delirious for a while, I fancy. I put a mirror up on the tent wall and stared into it for a full three minutes to reassure myself as to identity. Then I brought out the portable typewriter and set it up on the table slab.

It was only then that I realized my subconscious intention to set down the truth. For a while I debated with myself—but sleep was impossible that evening, nor did I intend to return across the desert by night. At last, some elements of composure returned.

I typed this screed.

Now, then, the tale is told. I have returned to my tent to type these lines, and tomorrow I shall leave Egypt forever behind me—leave that tomb, after sealing it again so that no one shall ever find the accursed entrance to those subterranean halls of horror.

As I write, I am grateful for the light which drives away the memory of noisome darkness and shadowed sound; grateful, too, for the mirror's reassuring image that erases the thought of that terrifying moment when the jeweled eyes of Sebek's priest stared out at me and I *changed*. Thank God I clawed them out in time!

I have a theory about those jewels—they were a definite trap. It is ghastly to think of the hypnosis of a dying brain three thousand years ago; hypnosis willing the urge to live as the suffering priest's eyes were torn out and the jewels placed in the sockets. Then the mind held but one thought—to live, and usurp flesh again. The dying thought, transmitted and held by the jewels, was retained by them through the centuries until the eyes of a discoverer would meet them. Then the thought would flash out, from the dead, rotted brain to the living jewels—the jewels that hypnotized the gazer and forced him into that terrible exchange of personality. The dead priest would assume man's form, and the man's consciousness be forced into the mummy's body.

A demoniacally clever scheme—and to think that *I* came near to being that man!

I have the jewels; must examine them. Perhaps the museum authorities at Cairo can classify them; at any rate they're valuable enough. But Weildan's dead; I must never speak of the tomb—how can I explain the matter? Those two stones are so curious that they are bound to cause comment. There is something extraordinary about them, though poor Weildan's tale of the god bestowing them is too utterly preposterous. Still, that color change is most unusual; and the life, the hypnotic glow within them!

I have just made a startling discovery. I unwrapped the gems from my handkerchief just now and looked at them. They seem to be still alive!

Their glow is unchanged—they shine as luminously here under the electric torch as they did in the darkness; as they did in the ruined sockets of that shriveled mummy. Yellow they are, and looking at them, I receive that same intuitive prescience of inner, alien life. Yellow? No—now they are reddening—coming to a point. I should not look; it's too reminiscent of that other time. But they are, they must be, hypnotic.

Deep red now, flaming furiously. Watching them I feel warmed, bathed in fire that does not burn so much as it caresses. I don't mind now; it's a pleasant sensation. No need to look away.

No need—unless . . . *Do those jewels retain their power even when they are not in the sockets of the mummy's eyes?*

I feel it again—they must—I don't want to go back into the body of the mummy—I cannot remove the stones and return to my own form now—removing them imprisoned the thought in the jewels.

I must look away. I can type, I can think—but those eyes before me, they swell and grow . . . look away.

I cannot! Redder—redder—I must fight them, keep from going under. Red thought now; I feel nothing—must fight. . . .

I can look away now. I've beaten the jewels. I'm all right.

I can look away—*but I cannot see*. I've gone blind! Blind—the jewels are gone from the sockets—*the mummy is blind.*

What has happened to me? I am sitting in the dark, typing blind. Blind, like the mummy! I feel as though something has happened; it's strange. My body seems lighter.

I know now.

I'm in the body of the mummy. I know it. The jewels—the

ought they held—*and now, what is rising to walk from that
pen tomb?*

It is walking into the world of men. It will wear my body, and
will seek blood and prey for sacrifice in its rejoicing at res-
rrection.

And I am blind. Blind—and *crumbling!*

The air—it's causing disintegration. Vital organs intact, Weil-
an said, but I cannot breathe. I can't see. Must type—warn.
Vhoever sees this must know the truth. Warn.

Body going fast. Can't rise now. Cursed Egyptian magic.
hose jewels! Someone must kill thing from the tomb.

Fingers—so hard to strike keys. Don't work properly. Air get-
ing them. Brittle. Blind fumble. Slower. Must warn. Hard to
ull carriage back.

Can't strike higher-case letters anymore. can't capitalize. fin-
ers going fast. crumbling away in air. in mummy now no air.
rumbling to bits. dust fingers going must warn against thing
nagic sebek fingers grope stumps almost gone hard to strike.

damned sebek sebek sebek mind all dust sebek sebe seb seb
eb se s sssssss s s s . . .

◉◉◉◉◉◉◉◉◉◉◉◉◉◉◉◉◉◉◉◉◉◉◉◉◉◉

ALAN ROBBINS is an award-winning writer and graphic designer. His interactive mystery novels include A Call for Murder, Murder in a Locked Box, *and* On the Trail of Blood. *Mr.
Robbins is also the creator of the* Puzzicles *mind-game series.*

UNCLE JACK EATS A MUMMY

by Alan Robbins

"He's coming here at nine tonight," he whispered, even
though there was no one in the store besides the two of us. "And
I want *you* to be here with me."

"This is insane," I said for the twelfth time. "Aren't those
grave sites guarded?"

"He bribed the guard."

"It's illegal. Doesn't that tell you something?"

"It tells me there's something there worth having."

Uncle Jack—that was my nickname for him—bit his lower lip
the way he always did and swallowed another of his aspirins.
He looked tired, but that wasn't unusual. He was only around
fifty, but a lifetime of worry left him with the face and posture
of an older man. A lifelong bachelor and hypochondriac, Uncle
Jack was a monument to anxiety. He was skinny from fear of
food poisoning, jittery from worry over household accidents,
and an insomniac from dreams of his own funeral. While I tried
to cheer him up with wisecracks or gossip, his conversation was
peppered with reports of heart attacks or automobile collisions.
He lived, as the Indians say, like a man seducing death.

"What's he got for you?" I said, breaking the uneasy silence.

"Something from the excavation at Tarahuasi." He bent his
head toward a cracked mirror and checked his tongue for spots.

"He dug it up himself?"

"And thinks it's worth a look. Relax, he knows what he's doing."

"I'm sure *he* knows," I snapped. "But do *you*?"

The *he* in question was a man named Ramón who had come into the store a few days before. He was an outsider, not from the city, and was staying at a nearby hotel. He had slick hair and rubbery lips and struck me as a bogus tango dancer from a thirties movie. One of his eyes looked slightly to left field. I didn't like that either.

He had come to the store because Uncle Jack occasionally sold Indian artifacts among his other junk. Ramón identified himself as a dealer with a special item for sale. Dealer, mind you, is a broad term covering anything from a licensed antiquarian to an outright grave robber.

It wasn't unusual. In Lima, like many cities near the Incan ruins, everyone sooner or later comes across ancient artifacts. They're practically the official knickknack of the country. Gold ear pins, flat-faced statues, lapis beads, that sort of thing. Most of the stuff is stolen anyway. But there was something about Ramón that made me uneasy. Nothing Uncle Jack would have picked up on, of course. He would have been too busy taking pills to notice a con man in a convent.

"Why don't you forget it and come to the movies with me instead?"

"I hate movies. They remind me of death."

"How do movies remind you of death?"

"I watch them frame by frame, like life slipping away."

"This is hopeless. Look, we don't know a thing about this clown," I insisted. "Why does he have to come here at night?"

"What's the difference?" he said, gargling with baking soda. "He's got something to sell."

"Suppose he tries to rob you?"

"That's why I want you to come. To protect me."

That much, at least, was convincing. He did need protection. Not from outsiders but from his own gullibility. He was so busy guarding against calamity, there was nothing left over for ordinary caution. How many times had he been ripped off by someone selling fake artifacts, or stiffed by a creditor who never returned to pay? Naturally, I agreed to come back that night.

At nine o'clock on the dot, Ramón parked his car in front of the store and walked in. He was carrying a package under his arm. It was wrapped in brown paper and tied with a cord. He seemed a little dismayed to see me standing next to my uncle at the counter.

"This is my nephew," Uncle Jack said as the other man placed the package on the counter top. "Is that it?"

Ramón untied the cord and opened the paper as he answered. "It was found in a small burial mound due south of the main tomb. The Incas often buried them at the four corners of the main pyramid to protect it."

"Then why didn't the archaeologists find it?" I asked, turning to Uncle Jack. But he was already caught in the web of the adventure and was putting on his glasses for a closer inspection.

Inside the paper was a wooden box, not much larger than a shoebox. Ramón slowly pried the lid off and slid it aside. Inside that was more paper, and within the paper, an object. Like llamas at a watering hole, the three of us tilted into the center to have a good look.

It was apparently an eroded carcass of some kind, stiff and leathery, about the size of a deflated football. It looked like something that had been buried for too long, rooty and bleak. You couldn't make out anything familiar about it, except that it probably wasn't supper. And it didn't smell like fun either. The word *dingus* came to mind, although I had no idea what it meant.

"Creeperino," I said, bypassing my college education.

"You see?" Ramón said. "It's a mummy."

"Mummy?" I said with a laugh. "It looks like a dried fish someone tried to bury."

"Look," Ramón said, ignoring my theory and pointing to the tip, "you can still see some of the teeth and hair."

Indeed, on closer inspection, there was some black thatchy material attached to the top and some teensy white slivers embedded on the surface a few inches down. But for the rest, it was hard to make head or tail of it.

"Did it shrink?" I said.

"It's a baby."

"I didn't know mummies had babies."

"When the ruler was buried, his wives were often killed along with him. If they had small babies, they were killed too, and mummified. Then they were buried at secret locations around the four corners of the tomb."

"Why secret locations?" I asked.

"There was a market for them," my uncle said.

"Still is," Ramón added with a wink.

"A market for mummy babies? What for?" I barked. "Pillows?" The whole thing was getting to me.

"Medicine," they said in unison.

I didn't say anything, but my green pallor must have hinted at a tinge of skepticism.

"Mummy has been a drug in Europe and the Far East since the Middle Ages," Ramón explained. "No decent apothecary shop would be without it. It's a powerful medicine. It's because of the minerals used in mummifying—bitumen, natron, and so on."

"Bullcrap."

"I don't think that was used."

"It's true," Uncle Jack explained. "The medicine made from these mummies is supposed to, as the Indians say, cure the disease of the clouds."

"Come again?"

"It bestows immortality," Ramón said.

I could only laugh at that one. But the others weren't joining me in the glee. They were dead serious.

"You're too young to believe in such things," Ramón said calmly, wiping his eye with a handkerchief. "That's good. That's what youth is for. Your job is to believe in fun. TV, computers, Coca-Cola. But for men of our age, belief must seek a greater reward."

"Immortality," I repeated, trying out of respect not to giggle my way through every syllable.

"Don't sound so shocked. It's nothing new," Ramón said. "Immortality's been around for thousands of years."

"As in living forever?" I asked, just to make sure we were on the same wavelength.

"Yes," Ramón said solemnly. "It's a belief held all over the world—South America, Egypt, Persia—any place where the dead were prepared for eternal life. Why shouldn't those discoveries aid the living as well. Why not?"

"Because it's totally crackbrained, that's why."

"How much do you want for it?" my uncle interjected.

"I know you're a sick man, Jacinto. That's why I came to you with it. Don't worry about the price. I'll give you a good deal."

"Who'll cook it?"

"I know an Indian who can prepare it for eating."

I heard the word, though I first must have thought it was *heating* or *beating* or anything but what it was. It took me a few seconds to interrupt.

"Wait a minute," I said, putting as much distance between myself and the ghouls as possible. "You're going to *eat* this thing? Just pour on a little hot sauce and open a beer?"

"Not like that," Ramón said. "You pulverize it and mix the powder with mineral water."

"And some rum," Uncle Jack added. "For flavoring."

"No shit!" I said, but by then I'd had it with the whole rotten mess and was storming out the door. "I hope this is a practical joke because if it isn't, and even if it *is*, it's the sickest thing I've ever heard in my life."

"Stick to your beliefs," Ramón shouted. "Go watch television."

But I was already out on the sidewalk, leaving them to conspire in the ghastly light.

I didn't visit my uncle for a whole week after that. I couldn't bear to look at him. But eventually I began to worry. I figured that he was just desperate enough to try it and get himself good and sick. So I went to the store and was surprised to find him vigorously dusting off the counter. He looked rather alert, even chipper. His gloomy color had given way to a reddish blush. Not rosy exactly, but vaguely pink. And he was standing up a little straighter, but not enough that anyone else would notice.

"You didn't really eat that thing, did you?" I finally asked when I got up the nerve.

"Sure did," he said, and flashed a smile. His teeth looked very pearly and I hadn't noticed that he had so many of them before.

"The whole mummy?" I asked, sounding like a sick TV commercial.

"It's medicine, not junk food," he insisted, taking out a plastic container with some mud at the bottom of it. "He brought it over the next day. I take a spoonful every evening. And when I wake up in the morning, I feel a thousand years younger."

I couldn't argue with him. In the first place, it was already done. Secondly, he did look a bit better. He started dressing up to go to work. Not fashionably, mind you, not spiffy, but neater. He sent his pants to the cleaners. He wore a white shirt. He even began to comb his hair with a part down the middle.

In the following week he didn't once mention a funeral, a case of cancer, a car accident, a coronary bypass, or even an infant death. The report of an earthquake on the news seemed to bore him and he changed the station to a quiz show. He threw out his aspirins and stopped peering down his throat for tumors.

By the end of the month, he had actually asked for the hand of a woman in marriage. She was thirteen years younger than Jack and had hardly ever spoken to him. She rejected him, of course, but even that didn't seem to dismay my uncle. He drank to her health and treated me to the movies.

Things seemed so good on the way to the theatre that I didn't have the heart to tell him about the news I had heard. It seems that a man sounding suspiciously like Ramón, but with a different name, had been picked up by the authorities for trying to sell a phony mummy to a local dealer. When the police went back to his hotel room, they found seven more baby mummies, all fakes, made of paper and old straw. I should have known when I saw the first one. Most babies don't have teeth.

I was about to say something to Uncle Jack, but as the picture started I turned toward him and suddenly saw the light. He was laughing at the movie, his eyes glinting, his skin twinkling from the glow of the flickering screen. I couldn't bring myself to eclipse his joy, so I sat back and said nothing. And what would have been the point anyway? Perhaps he got just what he paid for. As the Indians say, there's no great trick to immortality. As long as you live it day by day.

ABOUT THE EDITOR

A master of mystery anthologies, MARTIN H. GREENBERG has compiled over two hundred short-story collections. A noted scholar, Mr. Greenberg resides with his wife and daughter in Green Bay, Wisconsin, where he teaches at the University of Wisconsin. His last anthology for Ballantine was *Mr. President, Private Eye*. Mr. Greenberg was the 1989 recipient of the Milford Award for lifetime achievement in science-fiction editing.

From hypnotic historical fiction to the vulnerable victims of **V**ampires!!

More from Ballantine Book's best selling author...Anne Rice.

Available at your bookstore or use this coupon.

___**INTERVIEW WITH THE VAMPIRE**   33766 4.95
This vampire carries us back to the day he was inducted into the "endless life" and reveals the hypnotic, shocking, erotically charged confessions of his first two hundred years as one of the living dead.

___**THE VAMPIRE LESTAT**   31386 4.95
Best selling sequel to "Interview with the Vampire". We now follow Lestat through the ages as he searches for the origin and meaning of his own dark morality.

___**THE FEAST OF ALL SAINTS**   33453 4.95
Chronicles the lives of a people trapped in a world between black and white...for though they were descended from African slaves, they were also descended from the French and Spanish who enslaved them.

BB **BALLANTINE MAIL SALES**
Dept. TA, 201 E. 50th St., New York, N.Y. 10022

Please send me the BALLANTINE or DEL REY BOOKS I have checked above. I am enclosing $................(add 50¢ per copy to cover postage and handling). Send check or money order—no cash or C.O.D.'s please. Prices and numbers are subject to change without notice. Valid in U.S. only. All orders are subject to availability of books.

Name_____

Address_____

City_____State_____Zip Code_____

20   Allow at least 4 weeks for delivery.   TA-142